D1130075

For Doctor Rob
+ Cynthia

# YELLOWSTONE

## FINAL EXTINCTION

MICHAEL CURLEY

All the best +
happy reading

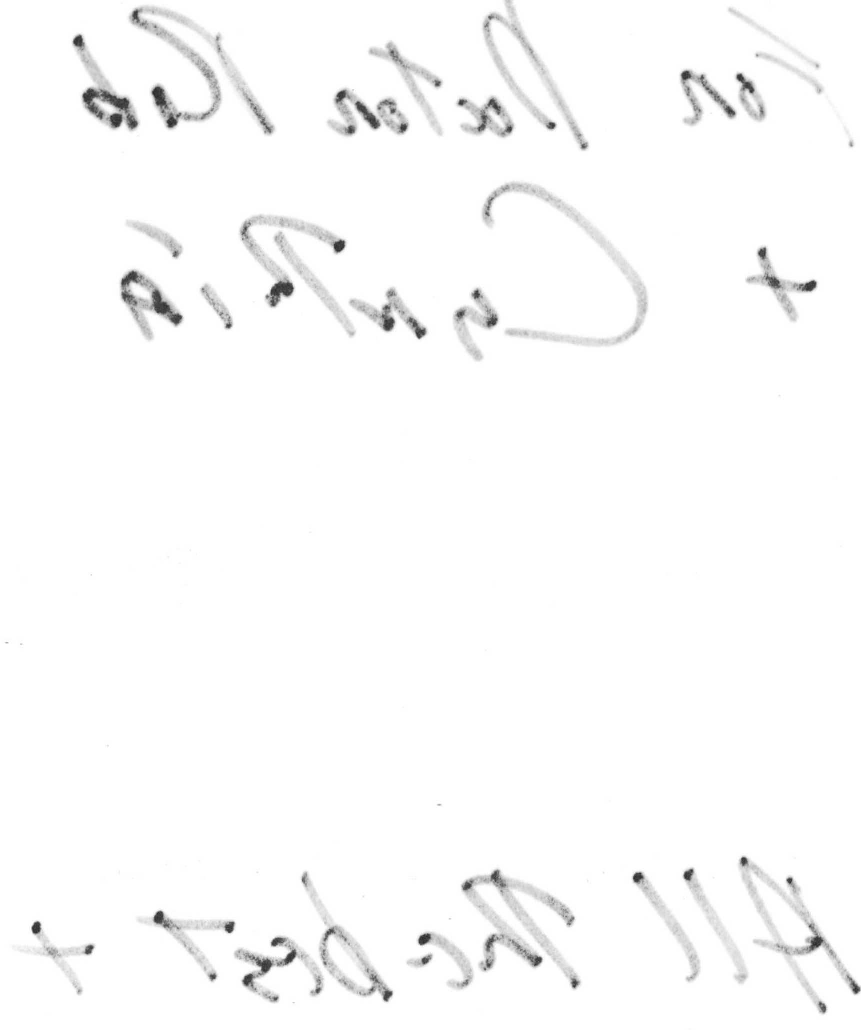

Yellowstone: Final Extinction
Michael Curley

Print ISBN: 978-0-69256-802-6
eBook ISBN: 978-1-68222-722-0

© 2015 Michael Curley. All rights reserved. No part of this publication may be reproduced, distributed, or transmitted in any form or by any means, including photocopying, recording, or other electronic or mechanical methods, without the prior written permission of the publisher, except in the case of brief quotations embodied in critical reviews and certain other noncommercial uses permitted by copyright law.

# TABLE OF CONTENTS

# ACKNOWLEDGMENTS, SPECIAL THANKS, & MORE

At 11:08pm on August 28, 2013, I pushed the "send" button to forward the text of my book, *Finance Policy for Renewable Energy and a Sustainable Environment* to the publisher. Over the preceding year, a group of tennis-playing, cocktail-drinking friends had kidded me mercilessly about writing a book like that which they said no one would ever read. They said, why not write a thriller about some environmental disaster: a book that some people might - just possibly - read? So, on the morning of August 29, I started writing *Yellowstone: Final Extinction*.

Writing this book was one of the most fun things I have ever done. Early on, I was looking for a character to be the #3 man at the FBI. My good friend and neighbor, Jim Slevin, had just the personality I was looking for. So, instead of just anonymously modeling the character on Jim, I asked him if I could use his real name. He agreed. So, the Jim Slevin you will meet in a few pages is the real thing. Much of the story of his early life is true. Jim is not, of course, the #3 man at the FBI; but he probably should be. He certainly has the character for it.

I really liked this idea of naming my characters after real people. And wherever possible modeling the characters after them. So, I kept doing it.

Back in 1993, I was working on the environmental legislation that was adopted in conjunction with the North American Free Trade Agreement with Canada and Mexico. I worked with a Congressman named Bill Richardson from New Mexico. Bill served 14 years in Congress. Then he was Secretary of Energy. Also, U.S. Ambassador to the United Nations. Finally he served as Governor of New Mexico for two terms. Over the years, we kept in loose touch. So, when I needed a President of the United

States, I thought of Bill. I asked him and he agreed. In point of fact, he really should be the President of the United States some day.

The Vice President of the United States is another man I knew. Much of his background is true. But I haven't been able to track him down to get permission to use his name. So, I made up Vice President Jeremy Mahikane. The last name, "mahikane", means "great man" in Hawaiian.

Gary Gill is very real but not the National Security Advisor to the President. David Springer is real, but not the head of the FBI. Mary Munson is real, but not the Secretary of the Interior. Jim Dickman is real, but not the Secretary of State.

Judge Fred Smalkin is not only real but is actually the retired Chief Judge of the United States District Court for Maryland. Dyan Brasington is real, but not the Deputy Attorney General, although she likes being called "General".

Barry Glassman is also very real. He is not a U.S. Senator (yet!); but he is the County Executive of Harford County Maryland.

Molly McNamara is a very real person, but not yet a 4-star Admiral or Chief of Naval Operations. In fact, at this writing, Molly is a senior – or "firstie" as they are called - at the U.S. Naval Academy. Molly is majoring in cyber warfare. I owe her. It was several of her stories about cyber warfare that led me to create the 4-star Admiral whom you will meet in a few pages, and whom I just had to name after Molly.

Cathy Garlock is real and actually owns the Bonnie Castle Resort in the 1000 Islands. Julie Chamberlain is real and is head of security at the 9:30 Club in DC, where Will Shriver and the "Adam E. Project", who are also real, have actually played. Kylie Wright is both real and a volcanologist from Vanderbilt.

Candice Teresi is a real DEA agent, but that's not her real name. Danny Arevalo is a real person, but not a DEA agent.

Both Jake Jekielek and Jim Griffin are real people; but they're not with the FBI in real life. But their personalities fit their characters to a Tee.

Jim Davis is not the head of the U.S. Geological Survey, but he is the former State Geologist both in California and New York. Hank Heasler is the Chief Geologist at Yellowstone Park, where Cheryl Jaworowski is also a geologist.

Cindy Timchal is both real and the coach of women's lacrosse at the Naval Academy. Kim Mercaldo is real, but not the lacrosse coach at Bryn Mawr.

Tom Krysil and Reese Hicks are both real, but not admirals. At least, Tommy isn't yet.

Rolly Kidder is not only real but actually served in the Brown Water Navy in Vietnam. He wrote a book about his time there called *Backtracking in Brown Water*. Phil Hall is also real and ex-Navy; but he's not the guy in the book.

Tom Young flew as a flight engineer with the Air National Guard in Iraq and Afghanistan and he's a pilot in civilian life. But he is better known as the best selling author of the Parson-Gold thriller series, including *The Mullah's Storm*, *Silent Enemy*, *Sand and Fire* and, most recently, *The Hunters*. Trish Apple is both real and a pilot, too.

Terry Arenson, or Tark, as he is called, is both real and exactly as he is in real life. And his restaurant, Tark's, is also real. And the story about the Baltimore Ravens that happened there is also true. Jackie Olup is real and in real life works both at Tark's and the Baltimore Orioles.

Larry Haislip is a great American lawyer, not a British one. But if he were a Brit, he would probably be both a Q.C. and C.M.G.

Clive Hilton is very real. He isn't – but should be – the CEO of a multi-billion dollar company.

Before he just dropped out of sight to his mega-ranch in South Africa, Roger J.B. Beach was a denizen of the City of London. Roger does, however, drive a DB9 Aston Martin Volante with Italian leather!

In Chapter 24, you will meet a group of people whom the insurance industry calls the "Freedom Squad" but who call themselves the "extraction team". Their job is to protect *Médecins Sans Frontières* volunteers working in dangerous countries. Tom Falkner is real. He's not an ex-Navy Seal. He is a classics professor.

With Brendan O'Curley, I cheated. Brendan is real. His last name is not O'Curley; it's just Curley, like mine. Brendan is my nephew. He is not a Navy Seal, but he could be.

Jerry Diaz is the godfather of the extraction team. Jerry is very real and could easily be the godfather of an extraction team.

Dr. Caroline Gorn is a real person, but she won't be a real doctor and her last name won't be Gorn until June of 2016

Here are some of the other characters in the book who are named for real people: Laura Doughty, Joyce Neve, Jennifer Schimpf, Stacey Coleman, Larry Woodard, Alberto deAlejo, Virginia Green, Michael Ruck and Katie Heffner.

Finally, you will soon read the story of Leah Abboud, a superstar athlete and scholar, who is diagnosed with terminal cancer in her third year at the Naval Academy. Leah is given six months to live. Leah is not a real person, nor is her character based on any real person. But the story is true. It happened 15 years ago. It was not a female cadet, but a male. I am pleased to report that the young man who had six months to live 15 years ago, is currently alive, well, has a family, and is pursuing a great career in the Navy.

## SPECIAL THANKS

There are many people who have contributed to the thinking that went into this book. Too many to name individually; but I have to name a few.

First are Dr. Hank Heasler, the Chief Geologist at Yellowstone Park and Dr. Cheryl Jaworowski, also a geologist at Yellowstone. They were both a great source of information about the volcano and the Park itself.

Next is Commander Tom Gamble formerly of the Naval Academy. Tom is the expert on nuclear weapons that gave me the information I needed about the bomb.

Commander Glen Quast is the expert on surface warfare at the Academy who gave me all kinds of good advice about the great chase after the bomb across the North Atlantic.

Greg Shipley was a Maryland State Trooper for 28 years. He is now the Director of Communications for the Maryland State Police. Greg gave me terrific advice on the "fusion centers" and the other law enforcement aspects of the book.

I hope you enjoy reading the book as much as I did writing it.

Yellowstone: Final Extinction

by Michael Curley

*"Some say the world will end in fire. Some say in ice."* – Robert Frost

*Scientists say that temperatures in the universe run from a hot of 1.4 x $10^{32}$ degrees, which is over 10 million-trillion-trillion degrees, to absolute zero, which is minus 460° Fahrenheit. Humans live in a tiny temperature band at the lowest end of the spectrum. The human body is 60 percent water. Most living things also have high concentrations of water. Water turns to steam at 212°. Humans would boil in their skins at this temperature. Water freezes at 32°. Living things would freeze solid at this temperature.*

# CHAPTER 1 - NICHOLAS B. DAVIS

Nicholas B. Davis woke up with a screaming headache. He didn't open his eyes. He just lay there on his back, trying to put things together. He remembered he was in the apartment of his old school friend, Richard Albion. It was Sunday. He could sleep some more. Then probably brunch with Richard. Then the train back to DC. Other than the headache, all good, he thought.

Davis rolled over to his left and touched human skin. It was smooth, not rough like Richard's. And it was cool to the touch. His eyes shot open. He lurched up on his elbow. It was a girl. A young girl. She was dead. She was on her stomach. She had Davis' Brooks Brothers belt pulled tight around her neck. She was handcuffed to the bedpost with golden handcuffs.

"Richaaaard!" Davis screamed. And kept screaming.

What seemed like ages later, Richard Albion stumbled into the room.

"Nick, what the hell......" Then he noticed the girl.

"Nick, what the hell happened?"

"I have no idea. I just woke up and found her here."

Richard went to the girl and put his hand on her neck. "Dear God, Nick, she's dead. What the hell happened?" He asked again.

"I said 'I don't know.' I just woke up and found her here."

"The marks on her neck. Looks like some pretty rough stuff. This is your belt isn't it?"

"Yeah, but I have no idea how it got around her neck."

"Well this is certainly one fine mess you've gotten into. And in my fucking flat! Get dressed." He said with disgust in his voice.

A few minutes later Davis found Richard in the kitchen.

"Here, drink this." Richard said pouring coffee.

"Do you have any ibuprofen?"

"Yeah, I'll get you some."

"I see you've retrieved your belt from around her neck." Albion said coming back into the room.

"Richard, I went through her purse. She has a New York State driver's license that says that she's 21. But what's worse is that in the lining of her purse was an Iranian passport that says that she's 15."

"Jesus Christ, Nick! 15! Not just a dead girl, but a fifteen year old minor – dead girl! She probably got the driver's license so she could work in the cafés."

"Work?"

"You *do* remember that she's a hooker, don't you?"

"No."

"Yes, she picked you up in Maxwell's Plum last night. You wanted to go there to hear our friend Larry Woodard play. You kept talking about taking her to a hotel. I managed to persuade you how unwise that would be for a man of your position. So I said you could come here. You did. You both went into the guest bedroom. And that's the last I saw of you till the morning."

"Jesus Christ, what am I going to do now?"

"I suggest that you get your sorry ass back to the capital of the free world as fast as you can."

"What about the girl?"

"You can leave her. I have some men who work the docks who are very rough characters. They'll be able to deal with the body."

"What do you mean 'deal with the body'?"

"Dispose of it. Look, Nicholas, fake ID, an underage foreigner, she's got to be an illegal. Unlikely anyone will miss her. Even less likely that they would raise a fuss even if they did miss her.

"No, get back to DC and let me handle this."

Davis finished his coffee and went back into the bedroom for his tie and jacket.

Richard walked him to the door. He turned to face Davis and looked him up and down.

"Richard, I can't tell you how abjectly sorry I am and how grateful I am for your kindness and your help."

"Nicholas, my old friend, when are you going to get over this thing with young girls. They will be your undoing. They have come between us far too often. I am tired of humoring you. This was supposed to have been our weekend. You owe me big time."

"I do." Davis acknowledged, hugging his friend. "I certainly do."

Davis turned to leave but then went quickly back into the bedroom. He took out his key and took the golden handcuffs off the dead girl. They were his - a present from staff on his 25$^{th}$ anniversary at the Federal Bureau of Investigation.

# CHAPTER 2 - MUSTAFA

As the plane cruised at 32,000 feet on the way back to Istanbul from Munich, the smiling flight attendant appeared with a glass of white wine and handed it across Mustafa al-Khalid to the woman sitting in the window seat. As the glass passed inches from Mustafa's nose, he could smell the alcohol. He shifted in irritation, thinking he really should have waited till his private jet was available; he had loaned it to the Brotherhood and had asked no questions. Although she wasn't wearing a veil, the woman next to him looked Muslim—Iranian, he thought, eying the dark arched eyebrows, the slant of her cheekbones, and the stylish designer clothes. And drinking alcohol.

It was a sensitive subject to Mustafa because his wealthy Istanbul family owned the largest brewery in the Turkey, *Antalya*, named after a biblical city on the Mediterranean coast. A major resort popular with Brits and Germans, Antalya had been visited by St. Paul and housed the bones of St. Nicholas, the West's Santa Claus. *Antalya* had also been the source of Mustafa's greatest shame. The Qu'ran says that drinking alcohol is *haram*, unlawful. As a boy, he had been sent to the exclusive Le Rosey School in Gstaad, Switzerland. From there he went on to the Ludwig Maximillian University in Munich. The Muslim kids at Le Rosey mocked him because his family sold alcohol. In Islamic law, they said, this is "*haraj*" – a sin that cries out to Allah for punishment.

At Le Rosey, life had been all about cars and money. Mustafa was not in with the in-crowd. Not even the Muslim in-crowd, which was large at Le Rosey. Many of the Persian Gulf royalty sent their children there. Mustafa was certainly wealthy enough to play in their sandbox. But he preferred his books – especially books about the Romans and the Greeks. There was much Greek about his hometown of Istanbul, and many of the great cities in Turkey had been built by the Greeks. Mustafa admired the Greeks and the Romans, not only for their military prowess in conquering the known world in their time, but also the Greeks for inventing philosophy and the Romans for inventing effective government. He learned Latin and excelled at his studies, unlike his Gulf colleagues who scraped by academically.

At the University in Munich, Mustafa majored in Classics, learned classical Greek and continued his studies in both Latin and Greek. At the University, the Muslims were poor, smart, and political. He wasn't part of them, but he stood at a distance, watched and learned. But as he grew older, he began to resent Turkey because it was secular. They didn't live by sharia law. They even used the Roman alphabet. Mustafa felt Turkey should be a religious state. When he returned to Istanbul after university, he began to take classes at the beautiful Blue Mosque. That is where he met Jasmine, who was the only girl he ever loved.

Mustafa never touched alcohol and was disgusted at Muslims who did. Still, there were billions to be made in alcohol and Mustafa didn't care if infidels, who were going to hell anyway, drank it, killed one another in car accidents, woke up with headaches, and ruined their lives.

Scowling at the Iranian woman complacently sipping her wine, Mustafa moved his hand to his jacket pocket to pull out his solid gold cigarette case filled with strong Murad Turkish-blend cigarettes. Sighing, he remembered this was a commercial flight, and he wouldn't be able to smoke until they touched down. Another reason to take his own jet.

His hand went instead to his face, rubbed the scars behind his ear and above his hairline. The plastic surgeons did an impressive job rebuilding his face, though it had taken several surgeries and hundreds of thousands of dollars. Funny, he thought, how physical damage is so much more easily repaired than emotional.

He would never forget that day—the only day that mattered—when he and his fiancée Jasmine were celebrating their engagement on his fifty meter yacht off the coast of Kusadasi. The boat was packed with members of both large families and several prominent imams, friends of Jasmine's father, who was also a revered Muslim cleric. There was a salty tang in the air, and the thin cries of seagulls wheeling above. Beneath her sequined black veil, Jasmine's dark eyes sparkled in happiness as they stood before a buffet of roasted lamb and other delicacies.

The sun was just beginning to set over Mount Karnouni on the Greek Island of Samos across the bay, when suddenly everything turned orange. At first it seemed as if the sun, reaching long golden-red arms across the silver-blue water, had grabbed the yacht in a fiery embrace. And then there was nothing.

Four days later Mustafa awoke in the hospital swathed in bandages. A relative who had missed the yacht party told him that Mustafa's yacht had been hit by a Hellfire rocket fired from a U.S. Navy Reaper drone. Jasmine was dead. Her parents were dead. Mustafa's sister, her husband, and three children were dead. The world, as he knew it, was over.

# CHAPTER 3 – SAMUEL

The Abboud family spelled their name: N-A-V-Y.

Samuel Abboud, came to America from Lebanon when he was a young boy just after the turn of the $20^{th}$ Century. His family settled in Maryland. His dad, Ishmael Abboud, was a merchant seaman and worked on ships out of Baltimore. Samuel wanted to go to sea too. As he was finishing high school, America was getting ready to enter the First World War. Samuel joined the Navy right after graduation. He was assigned to the coal-fired dreadnought battleship USS *New York* (BB-34), under the command of Captain Edward L. Beach, Sr. The *New York* was the flagship of the famous Battleship Division 9, commanded by Rear Admiral Hugh Rodman.

Battleship Division 9 consisted of four dreadnoughts plus the destroyer *Manley*. When the U.S. finally woke up to the fact that Britain was being starved into defeat, and almost two years after the Germans declared unrestricted submarine warfare and torpedoed the *S.S. Lusitania* killing almost 1,200 innocent civilians including 128 Americans, the Secretary of the Navy finally ordered Battleship Division 9 to join the Royal Navy's Grand Fleet.

The Division's Atlantic passage to Scapa Flow in the Orkney Islands off the coast of Scotland, was its most perilous episode of service. As it left Norfolk, Virginia, the fleet was buffeted by a vicious storm from the Northwest with high winds, rain, sleet and snow. As they approached the Grand Banks, the weather got even worse. Winds reached over 100mph. All four of the battleships' topmasts snapped off, crippling radio communications. The dreadnoughts *Delaware* and *Florida* and the *Manley* got separated from the *Wyoming* and the *New York*. The *Manley* used so much fuel fighting monster waves that it had to break off and put in at Queenstown, Ireland.

It was during that horrific night off the Grand Banks on the dreadnought *New York* that Samuel Abboud started making his name in the Navy. Struggling to keep its bow into the wind, the ship had taken on over 60,000 gallons of water weighing more than 250 tons in its forward compartments. The *New York* was about to founder and go down. Without any orders, Third Class Petty Officer Abboud organized a massive bailing effort with hand pumps, mechanical pumps, and even buckets. According to Captain Beach's report of that night, Samuel's initiative and quick action saved the ship and all aboard. If the bow had gone under, they could not have launched the lifeboats, even if the lifeboats loaded with sailors could have survived the wind and massive waves.

Samuel was awarded the Navy Cross for his actions off the Grand Banks on the night of November 30, 1917. What was even better was that after the Armistice, Admiral Rodman had personally arranged for Samuel's appointment to the U.S. Naval Academy.

Triumphant as Samuel's WWI service was, it was marred by the death of his father. Ishmael had been a boatswain's mate on a merchantman, the *SS O.B. Jennings*. The *Jennings* was torpedoed by a German submarine, the *U-140*, off the coast of Brittany on August 4, 1918 – just three months before the Armistice. The *Jennings* was the last American merchant ship sunk by German U-boats before World War I ended.

Samuel entered Annapolis in June of 1920. Each year he applied for Summer cruises on battleships and each Summer he was accepted. His company officers at the Academy made sure the battleship officers responsible for selecting their Summer cruise cadets knew Samuel's record. He was quite a site with a chest full of medals standing with his fellow midshipmen, none of whom had seen combat.

After the Academy, Samuel got back into active duty on battleships - this time in the Pacific. When not at sea, he was stationed either at the Navy's Surface Warfare Center near Washington, at one of the naval facilities in the Hampton Roads/Virginia Beach area, or on the West Coast closer to his sea duty. While doing a tour at the Surface Warfare Center, he courted and wed a young Lebanese girl, Sarah Shia, the younger sister of the only other Lebanese boy at Dulaney High School just north of Baltimore. They moved out to the San Diego area, when Samuel was transferred to the Coronado Naval Base. In 1940, Samuel and Sarah had their only child, whom they named after Samuel's father, Ishmael.

Samuel was back at sea on the battleship *Maryland* at Pearl Harbor on December 7, 1941. The *Maryland* sustained little damage and was back in action in early 1942. It was then that it started to hit home to Samuel just what the future of battleships would be in the navies of tomorrow. As the American forces were steaming to meet the Japanese fleet at the Battle of Midway, the *Maryland* was relegated to the backup fleet because it wasn't fast enough to keep up with the aircraft carriers.

Samuel served on two other battleships advancing in rank until on July 10, 1944 he was made captain and given command of his old ship, the *Maryland*. On that day, the ship was undergoing repairs at Pearl Harbor for damage sustained by a torpedo dropped from a Japanese Mitsubishi medium bomber. Four months later, after participating in the allied victory at the Battle of Leyte Gulf, the *Maryland* was struck again from the air. This time from one of the first *kamikaze* attacks. The attack killed 31 sailors and injured another 30. Nineteen days later, the Maryland was back at Pearl Harbor again for repairs.

Five months later, the *Maryland* was back at sea joining the Battle of Okinawa when, again, she was hit by another *kamikaze*. This attack killed 10, injured 37 and left 6 men missing. The *Maryland* steamed back to Puget Sound this time for repairs and a major overhaul. It was undergoing sea trials on August 15, 1945 when Emperor Hirohito spoke to his people for the first time on the radio and announced the surrender of Japan.

Although he loved the massive power and strength of battleships, it was not lost on him that never once – throughout the entire Second World War – was the *Maryland* hit with a shell from an enemy ship. All three times she was hit, it was from the air. And the damage was massive – forcing them back into repair docks - each time. Samuel saw the handwriting on the wall: battleships were the dinosaurs of the Navy; submarines and airpower were the future.

He stayed on with the Maryland for "Operation Magic Carpet", repatriating over 8,000 American soldiers and sailors from the Pacific. Then he and Sarah moved back from the West Coast to Washington where Samuel stayed on at various capacities at the Surface Warfare Command Center until he retired.

Even though the days of the big battle-wagons were over, senior battleship captains still had enough stick in the Navy to get their sons appointed to Annapolis. And so, after graduating from Dulaney High School near Baltimore, where his dad had gone, Ishmael Abboud headed down the road to the Naval Academy in Annapolis.

# CHAPTER 4 – THE CONVERSION

When Mustafa was in the hospital recovering from the missile attack, he was visited by an uncle of Jasmine's who lived in Saudi Arabia and who had come for the funerals. From the uncle, Mustafa learned that Jasmine's father was more than a respected imam. He was the head of the Muslim Brotherhood!

Five other members of the high council of the Brotherhood had also been on the boat. The Americans couldn't resist killing all six with one shot even if it meant killing another fifty innocent people. The Americans always crowed that only barbarians would murder the innocent.

Jasmine's uncle told Mustafa to continue his studies at the Blue Mosque. It would be good for him. He also said he wanted Mustafa to meet some of the men Jasmine's father worked with.

The men from the Brotherhood started coming. Every day. It didn't take long. Mustafa was very willing.

The imams at the Blue Mosque were impressed with Mustafa's devout faith and zeal. They humored him when he told them to refer to him as "*al-khalifa*," the deputy. When the Prophet died, the leaders of Islam, who succeeded him, took the title *al-khalifa*, or Caliph, meaning the deputy of the Prophet. Mustafa thought differently. In his mind, he was the not the deputy of the Prophet; he was the deputy of Allah, the deputy of God, himself.

The imams were certain they could persuade Mustafa to die for the faith. But – with his money – what a waste! He could finance many suicide missions by others. Indeed, Mustafa was willing to die for his faith; but, with his money and – he thought – his great mind, he felt there were better ways that he, as the Deputy of Allah, could exalt Islam.

One day, after leaving the Mosque, Mustafa sat drinking coffee at an outdoor café, when it suddenly came to him. He wasn't going to pay for someone to strap a bomb to his chest and walk into a crowded shopping mall or even fly an airplane into a building full of people. Killing even a few thousand infidels for Allah wasn't enough. He decided – then and there – that he would destroy the world!

As days went on, Mustafa realized that he must keep his plan to himself. Many of the faithful, many in the Brotherhood were willing to die for Allah. But not their families. Not their loved ones. Mustafa had no family any more. He loved no one.

There were far more infidels than there were faithful. The faithful, including Mustafa himself, would all die, yes, but they would enter the presence of Allah. And the masses of infidels would all die too - and go to jahannam - Hell - where they belonged.

# CHAPTER 5 - PLAYING THE BEER CARD

When Mustafa took over the family business he made a major decision. He would buy a brewery in another country. He would make that new company a success, too. Then he would sell *Antalya* and rid himself of the stigma of the *"haraj."*

Mustafa wanted entrée to the Russian Federation and he did not want it through Islam or his Islamic contacts. The family business would be very useful. After vodka, beer was the second most popular drink in Russia. So, Mustafa leaned on the president of his family's company, *Antalya*, the largest brewery in Turkey. He wanted to buy a major brewery in Russia: St. Petersburg, to be exact. He wanted entrée to St. Petersburg's elites – especially their military elites. Mustafa told his man that he, personally, wanted to be involved in their Russian acquisition.

Clive Hilton put up with a lot from Mustafa. As Mustafa took pleasure in telling him often, he was very well paid. He was, indeed; so he didn't mind Mustafa's goading. Mustafa knew nothing about making or selling beer. He didn't interfere with the management of the company. He just had a few pet projects that he wanted the company to be involved in. It didn't take much effort on Clive's part. He was usually only too happy to oblige. But then there was this Russian thing all of a sudden. The Turks were kin to the peoples of the 5 "stans" of the former Soviet Union: the Kazakhs, the Uzbeks, the Kyrgyz, the Tajiks and the Turkmen. Clive had plans for expanding the company into those countries. But the Turks had nothing in common with Russians. So, why Russia? Why St. Petersburg?

The biggest brewery in Russia, accounting for 38% of all beer sales in the Federation, was *Stariy Pivovar* – the "old brewer." Their headquarters and their biggest brewing plant were in St. Petersburg. The problem was that *Stariy Pivovar* was owned by the Norsk Group in Bergen, Norway.

Norsk had bought *Stariy Pivovar* for pennies a year after the collapse of the Soviet Union. With a 38% market share, they were unlikely to sell.

When Clive told Mustafa about this, he was furious. Mustafa would not take no for an answer. He demanded that Clive go to Norway and buy *Stariy Pivovar*. Clive had half a mind to quit. Mustafa was out of control. Still there was that big paycheck. There was also the possibility that once Mustafa got comfortable with Russia, he might ok Clive's plans to expand into the "stans" where their Turkish provenance would serve them well. So, Clive swallowed hard and did as Mustafa ordered. But he turned to a couple of his London School of Economics classmates for help.

Roger J. B. Beach was a Managing Director at P. Lane Donnelly & Company, a boutique investment bank in the City of London. He specialized in mergers and acquisitions. Clive called him and two days later showed up in his office at Lime and Leadenhall Streets just across from Lloyd's. Clive told Roger what Mustafa wanted. Roger confessed he knew nothing of the beer scene in either Turkey or the former Soviet Union. But when Clive outlined his own plans for expanding into the "stans" regardless of what happened with *Stariy Pivovar*, Roger said he'd learn. The prospect of doing a series of deals in Central Asia was someplace his firm was definitely interested in going.

"I don't know how you can put up with all the crap you have to take from that arsehole of a boss you have. But he and I have at least one thing in common. I drive an Aston-Martin DB9 Volante. The chaps at the factory tell me there's a bloke in Istanbul, named Mustafa, who has one too – with the same Italian cream leather interior. Can't be too many Mustafas running around Istanbul in DB9 Volantes with Italian leather interiors. So, let's see what we can do for him. If he drives my kind of car, he can't be all bad."

Clive's next stop was the chambers of Sir Lawrence Haislip, Q.C., C.M.G., on Chancery Lane off Fleet Street. Larry had done LSE before being called to the bar. While at the LSE, he had written a paper on the trade embargo with South Africa that received wide attention. Once a solicitor, he had been appointed to the commonwealth commission that negotiated the end of apartheid with President F. W. de Klerk, which led to the first free elections in South Africa's history. That election was won by Nelson Mandela and the African National Congress. No sooner had Buckingham Palace issued the letters patent making Larry a Queens' Counsel (Q.C.), than they also appointed him a Companion to the Grand Order of St. Michael and St. George (C.M.G.), making him a knight as well. He was one of the youngest solicitors ever to receive those awards.

Larry also had experience doing commercial transactions in the Russian Federation and the some of the other republics of the former Soviet Union. He said acquiring a Russian brewery wouldn't be a problem.

Roger Beach did the numbers and reported them to Clive by phone once he was back in Istanbul. *Stariy Pivovar* produced 3.5 billion liters of beer each year. They sold them for 35 rubles apiece, which was about $1 a liter. So their gross sales were about $3.5 billion on which their pre-tax earnings were close to 9%, or about $300 million. The corporate income tax rate in the Russian Federation is 20%. So, assuming *Stariy Pivovar* was a good citizen and paid its taxes, that would leave after-tax profits of about $240,000,000.

"The rest of this, I don't think you're going to like." Roger said. "The price/earnings ratio of beer stocks in growing markets like the Russian Federation is about 15:1." This means that every $1 of annual earnings would command about $15 in the price of the company's stock.

"So, my friend, you're looking at a probable price tag for *Stariy Pivovar* of about $3.5 to $4 billion."

"Bloody hell! That much?"

"I'm afraid so." Roger said, but then brightened a bit. "Now there's not much published information on a private company like *Antalya* but, that said, the population of Turkey is about half that of Russia. Furthermore, with the Islamic prohibition on alcohol, I've got to believe that Turkish beer consumption per capita is a fraction of Russia's. So, I can't imagine that *Antalya's* earnings are anywhere close to *Stariy Pivovar's*. I also don't know what other resources your man, Mustafa, can muster. But, the City has witnessed many David and Goliath matches – where the Davids have won." Roger went on. "Think your chap is up to it?"

"$4 billion is a lot of money. I don't know. Even if we mortgaged Antalya up the wazoo, we couldn't afford it. I guess I'll have a talk with Mustafa. It's not going to be pleasant. He's not going to want to hear this."

Clive thought it best not to get into a row with Mustafa at the company office. Mustafa maintained his own personal office – that the company paid for of course – out in Ortaköy near the Bosphorus Bridge to Asia. Clive called for an appointment.

Travel from the Beyoglu district to Ortaköy was never easy during the day. The traffic was always a nightmare especially on the Çiragan Caddesi that ran along the straits up to the bridge. That's where Mustafa's office was.

*Strange bird, Mustafa.* Clive mused. *Lives in a mansion overlooking the Sea of Marmara in the posh Kadiköy district on the Asian side. Works at a luxurious private office overlooking the Bosporus on the European side. His heart with his religion, in Asia. His head with his love of technology, firmly in Europe.*

"By the beard of the prophet, $3.5 billion!" Was Mustafa's reaction. Clive told Mustafa about his trip to London.

"So, we have a banker and a lawyer who know how to make these transactions. Good. Tell them to go to Norway and get a price." Mustafa said.

"But Mustafa, *Antalya* isn't worth anywhere near $3.5 billion."

"I gather that from what your Mr. Beach said. Please get on to him right away and tell him to put his findings into a report that I can show some possible investors."

"You know some possible investors?" Clive asked.

"If the price is reasonable, as your Mr. Beach says. And, if they can make a reasonable amount of money; then yes, I know several possible investors. Actually, beyond just the money, there are other reasons why they might want to invest." Mustafa was looking far away out the window when he said this – a sign that Clive shouldn't go there.

Larry Haislip took the call from Roger Beach. "Funny you should say that. Not only was I thinking the same thing, but I am looking at a painting on my wall by an early Norwegian impressionist named Per Humbla. The painting is called "Wild Geese." How appropriate!"

"Listen, my friend." Sir Lawrence went on. "I share your foreboding. I think the Norwegians would be daft to sell – even for $4 billion. But, let's look at the bright side. We have a solid company in *Antalya*, and we have an old friend like Clive in the wheelhouse. Let's see if we can't make something of all this.

"Roger, let me suggest you do one other thing. Please have your research people take a good look at the other brewing companies in St. Petersburg. I've been there. I've drunk their local beer. Most of it is swill. I suspect that, if the Norwegians won't sell, there may be another brewery in St. Petersburg that would welcome a foreign partner. Not owner, mind you, but partner. The days of the fire sales for Russian companies are long gone. Now that they have a few rubles of their own to rub together, they resent rich foreigners coming to steal their patrimony. But partners they look upon as opportunities both for new technologies and for new markets. Right up our friend Clive's alley with his vision of the "stans."

Two weeks later Clive took the call from Roger and Larry from the airport in Bergen.

"I have good news and bad news, as they say. Which do you want first?"

"I guess the bad news first." Said Clive.

"The price the Norsk guys want for *Stariy Pivovar* is $10 billion."

"Blimey! $10 billion! What happened to the $3.5 to $4 billion?"

"As Mr. Törwald, their CEO, said: they have no intention of selling. Beer consumption is growing in Russia, as is *Stariy Pivovar's* market share. Full stop. That's all the man said. No sale."

"Christ, what's the good news?"

"Mr. Törwald said they would be interested to talk to you about buying *Antalya*."

"Really? That could be interesting."

"Look before you start flogging your company, Larry and I want you to take a look at some information we've developed on another brewery in St. Petersburg. Can we come out to Istanbul and have a talk?"

"I'd rather I come to London. Once I tell Mustafa what the price is, I will need to get out of town for a few days. And, if you chaps come here, first he'll berate you and then he'll insist on getting involved, which would really muck things up. Let me ring you up tomorrow. We'll sort out the details."

As Clive expected, Mustafa was infuriated by the news. "What happened to the $3.5 billion that your British geniuses told us?"

"Those were my exact words." Clive said.

Mustafa ranted on that his investors could never make money at a $10 billion price. He was certainly right about that. Making $240 million on a $10 billion investment was a 2.4% return. They could do much better in a bank.

After Mustafa calmed down a bit, Clive broached the topic of another brewery in St. Petersburg.

"Clive," Mustafa said. "For reasons which are very much my own, I don't just want to own any Russian brewery. I want to own a business in Russia that befits my position here in Turkey. Here, we are the best. I want to be the best in St. Petersburg. I want to go there. I plan on getting an office and a flat there. I don't want to be treated as just another foreign businessman."

"Let me go to London and hear them out." Clive said. "Now I understand where you want to go. Let me see if we can find a way to get you there." Mustafa agreed.

"Clive, one more thing. Do this for me. Do it.

"After we buy our Russian brewery, I will sell *Antalya*. And when I sell Antalya, we will take the money and you can build a beer empire in Central Asia – the "stans" as you call those countries."

Next morning Clive was on the phone with Roger making plans to meet with him and Larry the following week in London.

"I am going to fax you some reading material for the plane. I'd recommend not discussing it with Mustafa until we talk in person."

* * * * *

It was Larry's plan that *Antalya* would buy the brewery that made *Severnoye* beer. *Severnoye* means "northern" in Russian. The beer was execrable. The beer was named after – and actually owned by - the Northern

Command of the Red Army. When the Soviet Union collapsed and state ownership of everything was no longer the rule, several senior generals of Northern Command bought it for pennies. Russian soldiers were paid little, including the senior officers. So this became a nice little perk for the generals. Larry told Clive that he was certain the generals would like to monetize part of their ownership. No matter what Mustafa paid, it would mean a huge profit for the generals. They would welcome a prestigious partner with some cash. And, one that actually knew how to brew good beer!

So, Larry's plan was that Mustafa would buy *Severnoye* and then Clive would begin making the best beer in Russia.

"I only know a few words of Russian." Larry said. "But once you get your new beer going, I'd change the name to *Gordost* – pride."

Clive was elated. He could barely believe it. This was exactly what Mustafa wanted.

Mustafa's company bought the Russian brewery in St. Petersburg that made *Severnoye* beer. Mustafa had no interest whatsoever in beer or Russia. But he was interested in the Russian generals and the nuclear weapons under their command. The generals welcomed Mustafa and his money, which made them millionaires. Mustafa wanted to make a grand gesture to impress his new partners. So he took Sir Lawrence Haislip's advice, which Clive had passed along, and changed the name to *Gordost* – "pride."

# CHAPTER 6 - ISHMAEL

Ishmael was in the Class of '63 at the Naval Academy. He graduated just as things were heating up in Vietnam. Ten years before, an indigenous nationalist/communist movement, the Viet Minh, under the notable leadership of Ho Chi Minh, had ousted the French from the country in the decisive battle of Dien Bien Phu. During the Second World War, the Japanese had kicked the French, the British, and the Dutch out of Southeast Asia. During the war, Ho and the Viet Minh had fought the Japanese. When the Japanese left, the French thought they'd just saunter back in. Ho and his people had other ideas. Being a French colony was not their idea of a bright future. Eight years of guerilla warfare later, their efforts bore fruit when the French were forced to abandon their former colony.

Despite his father's advice to the contrary, Ishmael chose surface warfare as his field in the Navy, following in his father's footsteps. He volunteered for the Pacific Fleet. A year after graduation, he was assigned to the USS *Maddox*, a destroyer. On 13 March 1964, his ship headed for the Pacific. They sailed the Sea of Japan and the East China Sea. Then, on 18 May, the Maddox headed south to patrol the South China Sea. It had been outfitted with a mobile van of electronic signals intelligence gathering equipment and was listening to military communications from North Vietnam in the Gulf of Tonkin when, on 2 August, it was fired upon by North Vietnamese patrol boats. President Lyndon Johnson and the American Congress used this incident to authorize the vast expansion of military activity in Vietnam. Eight years later this ended with the defeat of the United States and the unification of North and South Vietnam, but only after 58,000 American lives were lost.

Ishmael quickly realized that there wasn't much for a traditional Navy to do in this war. The North Vietnamese had no fleet. They had no armada. Just some small patrol boats for their coastal waters. They also delivered supplies to troops in the South. But, he thought there was going to be a lot of real action on the rivers and canals of South Vietnam. South of Saigon, the capital, was the vast delta of the Mekong River. This was the breadbasket of the country. The North Vietnamese and their in-country allies, the Vietcong insurgents, knew they had to control the delta to win the war. They needed to choke off commerce and troop movements. They also intended to use them to move their own troops and supplies. The U.S. Navy was ordered to stop them. This would be the "Brown Water Navy." Ishmael was one of the first to sign up.

Delighted to have a major role in the conflict, the Navy went into high gear with the extensive planning and training necessary to deploy men in such a different combat environment.

The first ordeal was a murderous week-long survival course at Whidbey Island in Puget Sound in Washington State. Next came two months of training at Mare Island near the City of Vallejo northeast of San Francisco. Mare Island is actually a peninsula, with the Napa River to its east and San Pablo Bay to the west.

To most Navy men, the initials PBR stand for Pabst Blue Ribbon beer. But to the Navy's river divisions it stood for Patrol Boat River, a small but ferocious fighting platform. PBRs were 32ft long made of fiberglass. At full speed they drew only 8-12 inches of water, making them ideal for working in Vietnam's delta region. They were powered by two 250 horsepower GM diesel engines driving two Jacuzzi pumps. PBRs were jet boats that could move at 32 knots, or 37mph. When they needed to stop, gates dropped on the pumps reversing their flow instantly. This resulted in a bone-jarring jolt, halting the PBR in about a boat-length. To reverse course, all the helmsman had to do was turn the wheel – and hang on. The PBR turned so suddenly that crews were always in danger of getting thrown from the boat.

They had twin 50 caliber machine guns in a tub mount on the bow and either another twin 50 on the stern or a 60mm mortar. They also could add a grenade launcher or a 60 caliber machine gun. PBRs were lethal weapons.

Each boat carried a crew of four: a captain, an engine man, a gunner and a seaman/gunner. PBRs traveled in pairs. The senior boat captain, the Patrol Officer, was in command.

When Ishmael finished his training, he joined River Division 535 in the IV Corps Region in the Mekong River delta south of Saigon. Ishmael was assigned to a PBR patrolling the Vinh Te canal along the Cambodian border. Vietcong and North Vietnamese troops had been crossing the border at will. Home base along the canal was a vessel called YRBM-20, for Yard Repair Berthing and Messing. This was a 250ft long unpropelled barge with a three-story building atop.

Alcohol is prohibited on all U.S. Navy vessels. And so, the men of YRBM-20 acquired a small non-U.S. Navy vessel and lashed it to the side of their barge. Since it wasn't a U.S. Navy vessel, they sold beer on it. It was the most popular part of the base. It was there that Ishmael met LTJG Rolland E. Kidder, whom all called Rolly.

Kidder came to the Navy via an unorthodox route. Son of a dairy farmer in upstate New York, Rolly graduated from Houghton College, a Christian liberal arts school and went on to the Garrett Evangelical Methodist Seminary in Evanston, Illinois, with every intention of becoming a minister of God. But after graduation, he declined the ministry.

"I dunno, Ish. Our people are in conflict with themselves over this war. I just felt I had to be here." And that was the way he explained his presence in the U.S. Navy on the Vinh Te canal on the Vietnamese-Cambodian border.

LTJG Ishmael Abboud was the senior officer (by a few months) and therefore the Patrol Officer on his pair of PBRs. Rolly was the other boat captain. They talked a lot while drinking beer and playing bridge.

"Ish, you know you're cut out for a flag officer," Rolly told him. "Your old man made it to captain. You'll go all the way to admiral. But you won't do it in the Brown Water Navy.

"Your old man was right. Submarines and airplanes – that's what the new Navy is all about. When this is over, you gotta get into planes or subs."

"I think it's too late for me, Rolly."

"Bullshit! At 25 it's too late? Bullshit! You just gotta do it. You're academy. Your old man is academy. Your old man commanded a battleship. You've got stick in this man's Navy. Go for it!"

It sunk in. When his tour in Vietnam was over, Ishmael went to the Naval Nuclear Power Training Command in Goose Creek, South Carolina, near Charleston, for 14 months of training on how to operate a nuclear reactor. Then he went to the Submarine Officers Basic Course for two months in Groton, Connecticut.

Ishmael liked the ballistic missile submarines and consistently got himself assigned to them as he moved up the ranks. By any fair measure, Ishmael had a distinguished career; but in 2002 he had a flash of genius that – he thought – just might get him his flag.

That year Ishmael was beginning a tour as the commanding officer of the SSBN *Ohio*. The "SS" is for submersible ship. The "B" is for ballistic missile. And the "N" is for nuclear. Before he went to sea, Ishmael was called into the Chief of Naval Operations, Admiral Tom Krysil's office. Ishmael knew the CNO very well. Krysil had been Ishmael's company officer at Annapolis. He was nuclear Navy and had taught Ishmael at the nuclear propulsion school in Charleston. Ishmael had also served under him in a ballistic missile sub, the *Alabama*. Ishmael expected to meet with some of Krysil's staff. He didn't expect to see the CNO himself. But he thought he'd ask to say hello.

"Is the Chief in today? We go back a long way. The Academy. Charleston. The *Alabama*. If he's in, I'd just like to stick my head in to say hello?"

"It's the Chief of Naval Operations that you have your appointment with, Commander Abboud." The Master Chief Petty Officer at the CNO's reception desk said stiffly. "Please be seated. I will call you when the Admiral will see you."

"Ish, it's great to see you again! How are the kids?"

"They're fine Admiral. How have you been?"

"What's this admiral stuff, Ish? Just cuz' they gave me a couple of stars doesn't mean anything's changed." Krysil said with a hearty laugh. "How have I been? Same old, same old. Only now instead of taking orders from senior officers I take them from the landlubber politicians across the Potomac." They both guffawed lightly.

"Ish, let me get right down to business. I'm afraid I have some bad news. I didn't want you to hear it through the chain of command. We go back a long time; I wanted you to hear it from me. The *Ohio* and three other boomers are being mothballed as part of the START II disarmament treaty. I know the Ohio is your new baby. I'm sorry. I don't trust the Russians a whit but we've got to keep our word under the treaty." Ishmael was stunned.

Ishmael needed to think. The *Ohio* was at the submarine base at Kings Bay, Georgia. Instead of flying to nearby Jacksonville, Florida, Ishmael rented a car and started to drive down from Washington. He was in no hurry. He stopped in Savannah for the night. By the park along the river, he stopped to watch a father and son fly a remote controlled model airplane. These toys are really small drones. The Navy calls them UAVs, for Unmanned Airborne Vehicles.

All of a sudden the lights went on for Ishmael. This was just what he was looking for!

UAVs could be launched from submarines. So could other things, like Tomahawk missiles. Tomahawks were cruise missiles, not ballistic missiles. Tomahawks were not covered under the START treaty. He jumped up and ran back to his room.

Ishmael realized that he couldn't say what he had to say over an unsecure phone. But he couldn't sleep either. So, he got back in his car and headed for the Pentagon. Tom would be in his office by seven; so at seven, Ishmael pulled over, called and asked to see him as soon as possible. Krysil knew Ishmael as a serious commander; so he canceled some appointments and told him to come right in.

"Tom, I know we gotta get rid of a bunch of our ballistic missiles because of the START treaty. Fine. No problem. But scrapping the four boats is a goddamn disaster. Boomers are Cold War equipment, sure. And, the Cold War's over. But instead of wasting these boats, we need to reconfigure them. We need them to fight the wars of the future – not the Cold War."

"What are you talking about?"

"I am talking about taking the Tridents off those boats and replacing them with Tomahawks – lots of Tomahawks. Cruise missiles aren't part of any START Treaty! And replacing some of the Tridents' launch chambers with silos for launching UAVs and UUVs (Unmanned Undersea Vehicles, drone submarines). That's what the Navy's going to need to fight the next war. We'll just take the B out of SSBN. They won't be ballistic missile subs any more. That'll satisfy the START II people. We'll replace the Bs with

Gs – guided missiles - Tomahawks. That's not going to violate any treaties. And we'll have plenty of room for UAVs and UUVs, too."

For a long minute Admiral Krysil looked at Ishmael. Then he said: "You know, you might be totally crazy, Ishmael Abboud. But you may be crazy like a fox. Go back to your ship. You'll hear from me about this. That, I promise."

And so, the United States Navy decommissioned four of its SSBNs and recommissioned them as SSGNs. They promoted Ishmael Abboud to the rank of captain and put him in charge of the program.

By the end of Summer in 2001, all four SSGNs had successfully been integrated into the fleet. The operation was a huge success. Captain Abboud was transferred back to the Pentagon and assigned to the Office of the Secretary of Defense. Everyone expected an admiral's flag any day.

On 10 September 2001, the White House sent the name of Captain Ishmael Abboud to the Senate for confirmation as a Rear Admiral – his first star.

The next day was 9/11.

A month later, the Senate advised the White House to withdraw the name of Captain Ishmael Abboud. They said there weren't going to be any flag officers in the U.S. Navy with Arab surnames. One of the White House staffers explained to the Pentagon that Congress was afraid the Navy'd been infiltrated by terrorists.

It was clear to Ishamel that he wasn't going to get his first star any time soon. The stigma would last for years. Ishmael was 61 years old. Better to retire. The Navy was his life. It broke his heart and his health.

# CHAPTER 7 – THE PLAN

Through the Arab Brotherhood, Mustafa found his way to a German foundation that worked with terrorist groups. It had a beguilingly misleading name: *Stiftung ErdLust*. Very difficult to translate, but something like the "earth-love foundation." Misleading for sure: the foundation specialized in researching how natural disasters could be created by humans.

As his plan evolved, Mustafa would recruit and train a small team of men who would buy a nuclear weapon and use it to set off a major natural disaster.

Mustafa organized his team, and through his connections with his new Russian partners, the generals in St. Petersburg, identified two colonels in the Northern Command who would sell them a 16-kiloton nuclear device that they had certified to the United Nations Disarmament Commission that they had disarmed and dismantled. The bomb was the same size as the one the U.S. dropped on Hiroshima. The UNDC inspector responsible for certifying the disarmament of the bomb was from India. He received one third of the purchase price - 20x his annual salary.

# CHAPTER 8 - EXTINCTION

For the last 600 million years, there have been simple animals on this planet. Over this time, there have been five great extinctions when thousands of species died out. Today, 98% of all the species that ever lived on this planet are extinct. The most famous occurred about 66 million years ago, when the dinosaurs disappeared – geologically speaking – over night. A huge asteroid crashed into the Gulf of Mexico hurling debris into the atmosphere that shrouded the earth from sunlight causing a massive temperature drop killing 75% of all species of plant and animal life on the planet. With them went the dinosaurs. But the most massive extinction so far occurred about 250 million years ago in the Permian era when 96% of all species died out. The Permian extinction, scientists believe, was caused by massive volcanic eruptions, the ash from which shrouded the earth blocking almost all sunlight and warmth. Again a massive temperature drop occurred. The animals and plants died of the cold.

# CHAPTER 9 - THE FSB

Russian counterintelligence, the Federal Security Service, or FSB by its Russian initials, watches the financial transactions of the U.N. disarmament inspectors all over the globe. The FSB feared that someone might sell an atomic device to the Chechens. But they knew that this couldn't happen without a UNDC inspector as an accomplice. So when Inspector Srinivas Prasad's bank account in Bangalore, India, received a wire transfer of $2 million from a Banka Isçilerin in Turkish Cyprus, the FSB took careful notice. They knew Prasad worked on Russian soil.

It was not difficult for the FSB to discover that the Cypriot bank had received a $6 million transfer with instructions that $4 million be deposited into two separate accounts in the bank, and that the other $2 million be wired on to Prasad's account in India. One of the accounts in the Cypriot bank was in the name of Valentin Sivaev, a colonel in the Russian Army. The other was in the name of Vsevelod Andreyev, a lieutenant-colonel. Sivaev commanded a nuclear tactical weapons regiment of the 20th Guards Army in the Western Military District headquartered near St. Petersburg. Andreyev was his executive officer. Through his contacts on the general staff, Mustafa had been able to identify the units that were decommissioning bombs and put his team onto their commanding officers. Mustafa's money talked again. Not to the generals this time, but to their subordinates who controlled the bombs.

The money had been wired by the Goldman Foundation, an organization founded and run by a wealthy bankeer named Aaron Goldman. Aaron Goldman was born Amir Hussein. Amir was recruited into the Muslim Brotherhood at the age of 15. Three years later they changed his name. Then they sent him to university and then on to the famous business school, INSEAD, in Paris for an MBA. Then they set him up in banking. Then they created the foundation and brought Amir/Aaron in to run it.

One of the major purposes of the Goldman Foundation was to launder money for terrorists. It amused the Brotherhood to have their foundation and its Director General with Jewish names.

In Jerusalem, the Shin Bet knew about the Goldman Foundation. So did the FSB. So did the FBI in the United States. But it fooled a lot of people.

Unlike the FBI, the FSB is a military service. Its officers are members of the Russian Federation's armed forces. So, a call to St. Petersburg was all that was necessary. The two colonels were arrested the next day and interrogated. But the St. Petersburg office of the FSB was not aware of the incriminating bank transfers. They were just told that the colonels were suspected of attempting to sell a nuclear device. The colonels denied everything, insisting that all nuclear devices scheduled for disarming and destruction had been disarmed and destroyed. Then they were flown to Moscow to FSB headquarters in Lubyanka Square. When presented with evidence of the bank transfers, they shut up. Under torture, they told what little they had been told by the buyers. Before they died the two colonels said that the buyers had told them that the bomb would be used on those for whom it was originally intended and that they were not going to use the bomb as just a bomb, but rather as a triggering device for a much larger explosion. During the Cold War, when the device had been built, it was intended for use against America.

# CHAPTER 10 - MICHAEL & SLEVIN

Russian and American politicians play a love-hate game on the international stage. But, when it comes to terrorism, the relationship is simple and straightforward. Whenever the FSB comes across information about terrorists targeting the U.S., they immediately inform the FBI. Likewise, when the FBI picks up any scents that Chechens are planning an attack on the Russian Federation, their first call is to the FSB.

Michael Cornell looked up from his computer screen to see the smiling face of his boss, James E. Slevin, the Executive Assistant Director of the National Security Branch of the Federal Bureau of Investigation.

"Mikey," Slevin began, knowing Cornell despised being called that name. "I have a big one for you." Slevin was holding a slim manilla folder by its edge, as if it contained human excrement. He sat down in the extra chair in Michael's cubicle.

Michael reached out to take the folder, knowing that when Slevin called him "Mikey, " it meant that there was evil afoot. "What is it?"

"You'll see. It's top secret and 'eyes only.'"

Michael quickly scanned the couple of pages in the folder. "Somebody bought an atomic warhead? In Russia?"

"Yep. You'll see. Our Russian brethren think it may be headed our way. I have no idea whether the Russians are right, or not. But this is obviously far too important to ignore."

"What do you want me to do?"

"Find out if the Rooskies are right. And, if so, stop whoever these bastards are."

“Why me?” Michael said staring down at the slim file.

“Natural disaster.” Slevin said. “The second I read ‘natural disaster’ I thought of you. You are the biggest natural disaster I know.”

“Don’t think of giving up your day job. You won’t make it in stand-up comedy.”

“Don’t be a sourpuss, Mikey. This is right up your alley. Get on it.”

“Oh, sure. Anything else this morning? I’ll put my 500 men right on it.”

“Smart ass, we will put every man and woman, in or out of uniform, in this entire country on this case, if we need to. Right now, however, we need to find out if we need to. So, get right on it and let me know what you learn.

“Michael, I don’t have to tell you what would happen if the people of the United States felt they were under nuclear attack from unknown enemies. Pandemonium! Chaos! Possibly a total breakdown of law and order! So, right now it’s just you and me. Remember. Be discreet. Top secret. Eyes only.”

“I’m going to need to talk to people. They’re gonna want to know what it’s all about. What do I tell them?”

“Weapons grade plutonium.”

“What?”

“Weapons grade plutonium. A shipment of weapons grade plutonium has been stolen and we are trying to get it back. Sound reasonable?”

“I guess it’ll have to do.”

“And, if you need back-up, reach out to Jim Griffin. He knows everyone, everywhere.”

"*The* Jim Griffin. The venerable James Griffin, who never got beyond agent grade in his hundred years with the FBI.

"Don't be a smart ass. Griff will soon celebrate his 40th anniversary here. And as far as promotions are concerned, my still-wet-behind-the-ears friend, I'll have you know that we will soon have a party celebrating both Griff's $40^{th}$ *and* his $20^{th}$ official declination of promotion."

"What?"

"Yep. Twenty times in the last 40 years, Griff has been offered a promotion and 20 times he has declined. In the last few years, we have been having a little party whenever this happens. We call them the 'Jim Griffin Memorial Promotion Declination Parties'.

"Griff says that when he graduated from law school, all he wanted to be was an FBI agent. And, as he will tell you, that is *still* all he wants to be. No supervising. No HR meetings. No paper shuffling. Just an agent. And, Michael, my boy, he is *the* best. Been everywhere. Done everything. Knows everyone. You'll love working with him."

And so, the case wound up on the desk of Michael Cornell at the FBI.

Michael had been a senior advisor to the FBI for several years. But a few months ago they had finally persuaded him to become a full agent.

Cornell had majored in Linguistics at Georgetown University while working for a moderate Republican Congressman from Utica, New York. He realized how dull linguistics was in comparison to the fascinating work he did for the Congressman. He worked on some critical amendments to Clean Water Act, which finally passed during his senior year. So, he went home to Ithaca, and went to the Law School at Cornell University, which his great, great grandfather, Ezra Cornell, had founded in 1865.

After law school, he spent time at the New York State Department of Environmental Conservation and USEPA. He finally found a specialization he liked: resiliency, the ecology of disaster. He then joined the Environmental Law Institute as a researcher in that field. Not long after, the FBI began to have concerns about environmental disasters and contacted Mike. In specific, James E. Slevin contacted Mike.

As the Executive Assistant Director of the National Security Branch, Jim Slevin was the number three man at the Bureau. He was also a legend there. Slevin came from a family of six kids in Jackson Heights, Queens, just south of LaGuardia Airport. His father was a New York City cop. Jim went to Archbishop Molloy High School. On a cop's salary, Jim's father couldn't afford to send all his kids to private colleges; so Jim relieved him of this burden by winning a baseball scholarship to Villanova. Jim was a pitcher at Molloy. A great pitcher. They called him the strikeout king. They also called him the strikeout king because in his first three years he could never seem to date the same girl twice. But in his fourth year, he got revenge by dating the prettiest girl in school, Molly Mehan, a relationship that lasted all through college winding up in marriage.

After college, Jim entered the New York City Police Department, following in his father's footsteps. In those days they didn't have too many college graduates on the force. Jim's brains, his athleticism, and his college diploma marked him for bigger things in the department.

After the police academy, the next step in the career ladder at the NYPD is an obligatory 2-year stint in a patrol car. In Jim's case it was in Hunt's Point in the South Bronx. There are over a half million people in this general area. The congressional district around Hunt's Point is the poorest one in the United States.

In community meetings there, Jim ingratiated himself to the residents. He had this self-introductory shtick that went something like this:

"I'm Jim Slevin with the NYPD. I am a FICSA. This is not to be confused with a "schicksa," which is what our Jewish friends call a non-Jewish girl. FICSA is an acronym. It stands for 'Fat Irish Cop Stealing Apples.' So all you folks with produce stands, you better put your apples away when you see my patrol car pulling up."

This corny spiel invariably left the crowd laughing. They could see he wasn't fat. They didn't know from Irish. And they doubted he'd say he stole apples, if he really did. And they felt Jim Slevin, NYPD, was a friend, not a cop to be feared, like some. Within months, it seemed like he knew every shopkeeper by name and always called out to them – with a big smile – whenever he saw them.

Jim had a knack for solving problems in the right way. Once, one of the neighborhoods near the shore of Long Island Sound was victimized by petty sneak-thieves. They stole from storefronts. They stole from produce vendors. They snatched purses.

Slowly, Jim pieced together descriptions of two boys in their late teens. The police artist produced good likenesses. There was something about the two drawings that bothered Jim. It was the police artist who said it: the boys in the two drawings were brothers.

With this piece of information, Jim started contacting all of the clergymen, school officials, and landlords in the neighborhood. It didn't take him long before he was trudging up the stairs of a four-storey walk-up where the boys lived. The boys weren't home but their mother was. She started crying immediately she saw Jim's uniform. "It's the boys, isn't it?" She said.

"What can you tell me?" Jim said gently.

The woman told Jim that her husband had worked at the fish market down on the Point. He had been hurt in a serious fall off the back of a truck. He landed on his back. He couldn't stand up straight. Walking up and down four flights of stairs left him in trembling pain. He couldn't work. She hadn't been able to find a job either. The boys stole so the family could eat.

"You tell your boys that the cops were here. That won't stop them; but it'll put the fear of God into them. Let me see what I can do."

"You mean you're not going to arrest them?"

"Not now. And not if I don't have to."

While scouring the neighborhood for the boys, Jim had visited a clergyman, who was called out of a little party in the church hall to talk to him. The pastor explained that the party was for his cleaner of 30 years who was retiring to go live with her kids in Arizona. Jim went back to see the pastor.

"Pastor, remember the day I was here your cleaner was retirng? Have you replaced her yet?'

"Not yet, Jim. What of it?"

"I have a woman who needs a job real bad. Husband hurt and can't work. Two teenage boys at home. Could you give her a try?"

"This have anything to do with all the thefts around here?" The Pastor asked.

"Not that I know of." Slevin blankly lied.

"Ok, I'll be here tomorrow. Ask her to come by."

"Will do, Pastor. Thanks."

Slevin figured that the money a church could pay a cleaner might not do it for a family of four plus some hefty medical bills. So, he came up with plan 1A.

One of the crimes that had been committed was the mugging of a delivery man for a local chicken joint called Niqui's Chiqui. What caught Slevin's attention was that they mugged him *before* he delivered the order of chicken. AND, they stole the meal in addition to the guy's money. Slevin knew it had to have been his boys.

Nevertheless, he went to see the owner of the chicken restaurant, Alberto DeAlejo.

"Alberto, that delivery guy of yours who got mugged… what happened to him."

"He quit on the spot."

"Have you replaced him?"

"Can't! Once word got out he was mugged, no one would take the job."

"I've got somebody for you. As a matter of fact, I think I have two young guys, either or both of whom would take the job. They're brothers and – from what I've learned (he said with his tongue buried in his cheek) – they work very well together.

* * * * *

"Yolanda?" Jim said calmly into the phone. "I want to come over tomorrow at 4. I'd like you to have the boys there – both of them! I am not coming to arrest them. As a matter of fact, I have some good news for all of you. So, please be sure you're all there."

Slevin looked back and forth between the two teenagers. "I know what your game has been about. I know about your dad's injury and what it's meant for your family. So here's the deal. You boys – one or both of you – have a job delivering chicken for Niqui's Chiqui." The two boys shot panicked looks back and forth, which Slevin saw clearly.

"That's exactly what I thought." Slevin said. They boys knew exactly what he meant.

"That should put some money in the family account and some chicken on the table. And, don't worry, the owner, Alberto De Alejo, knows nothing about what you and I know about the mugging.

"I told him you'd be there tomorrow afternoon. Go! And don't say a word. And……if you'll pardon my French, Yolanda," Slevin said nodding toward the boys' mother. "If you fuck this up, I'll send both of your asses to Attica for 10 years. Understand?" The boys nodded nervously.

"And, some good news for you too, Yolanda. You know the Pentacostal church just this side of the market? The pastor there is a good man. His cleaner for the church center just retired. He's looking for someone. He'd like to talk to you tomorrow as well."

And so the crime wave of petty theft in Hunt's Point came to an end.

Two years in the Bronx and a couple of minor victories like the Hunt's Point "theft ring" – all of which the NYPD's local brass noted, and Slevin was on his way to being a detective.

"Just like this goddamn outfit." Slevin's Precinct Captain said when he got promoted to detective. "Find a guy who's a people guy, and who gets the job done and, who gets along with everyone, and the brass hats immediately promote his ass outta here."

A year in the detective bureau and Slevin found himself in the Criminal Intelligence Division.

It didn't take Slevin to realize that the CID was fighting the wrong war. Sure there were drug rings. Sure there were gangs. Sure the Mafia ran hookers and gambling. Sure there was a lot of muscle in the construction industry and on the docks. But what about those who weren't out for a few bucks or a few more blocks of territory. What about those who wanted to destroy the City? What about international threats? The Berlin Wall had just come down. The Soviet Union appeared to be collapsing. But was that over? The Soviet mission to the UN was still crawling with spies. The Russians still had enough nuclear weapons to destroy the world. They were still pointed at the US. The Arab states in the Middle East hated the US for its support of Israel. There were more Jews in New York than there were in Israel. What about all this?

Every day that passed the Soviet threat seemed to recede. The Arabs had wanted revenge on the Jews since 1947. So, what was new about their empty rantings? The NYPD brass just wouldn't hear of international threats.

One of the more endearing gifts of the Irish to Western Civilization – other than parades - is stubborness. Slevin had more than his share. He thought international threats to the City were real. He was determined to convince the NYPD and the rest of the world. So he uncharacteristically immersed himself in research. Research about international threats to the City.

Slevin survived the smirks and derision of not only his colleagues at the NYPD; but he was also slighted by the FBI, the CIA, the NSA, and all three of the defense intelligence services. Even by Interpol. But even with all the condescension and all the fobbing off, Slevin thought he had put together a strong case that the City was going to be targeted by Arab terrorists. Arab terrorists, mind you, not Arab or Middle Eastern governments! What little attention the NYPD had ever paid to Arabs was paid to the UN missions of Arab states. And even that wasn't much. But nowhere on the radar screen of the New York Police Department were Arab individuals or groups – unaffiliated with any Middle Eastern government – who wanted revenge on the US for its support of Israel.

Slevin was justifiably proud of the 191 page report that he completed and sent – both to his boss, the Chief of the Criminal Intelligence Division of the New York Police Department, and to the Commissioner of Police himself. This was very uncharacteristic for James E. Slevin. He was usually a stickler for proper procedure and the chain of command. But he was sick of the cement heads in his division all the way up the chain of command. This wasn't a career thing or an ego thing. Slevin saw a real threat to the

City. He'd be damned if he'd let the fucking brass squash it. He sent it off to the Chief and the Commissioner the day before Christmas 1992.

Over the holidays Slevin mused to himself that if the brass tried to bury his report, he'd go public with it. If they tried to discipline or can him, he'd resign. He had broken his back going to Fordham Law School nights for five years. He figured he could get a job somewhere as a lawyer. Criminal law firms were always looking for ex-cops with law degrees. Anyone with inside knowledge of the "system," how it worked, and who worked it. Of course, his 191-page tome on international terrorist groups wouldn't work well on the resume he needed for a lawyer's job in the City's criminal court system. If it really came to that, he didn't need to show them.

The Chief of the Criminal Intelligence Division took one look at the cover of Slevin's 191-page report and put it on the bookcase on the other side of his office, where it joined many other unread departmental reports, some dating to the early 1970's. So, when another copy arrived on his desk with a personal note from the Commssioner saying "What the hell is this?", the Chief decided that Slevin was either going back to a patrol car in the South Bronx or out on the street.

The first step in getting rid of the bastard, the Chief knew, was a hearing in the Chief's office. Departmental lawyers, HR people, stenogrphers – all the necessary bureaucrats – convened in the Chief's office for the confrontation with Slevin.

Matters went all the Chief's way at first. The Chief gave a summary of the report. He asked Slevin who authorized him to write it. No one, of course. He ask Slevin exhaustive questions about the limited surveillance the department maintained on the UN missions of Arab states. Slevin dutifully answered. Then the Chief made a serious mistake. He asked Slevin – bearing in mind the division's efforts with the Arab states' UN missions - who in Intelligence Division shared his concerns about other Arab threats. Slevin, being a truthful man said: "No one." Case closed, thought the Chief.

"But, Chief, that's the point. We spend our time looking at the missions and we aren't looking for groups that don't work with, or for, the missions."

"But Detective Slevin, you just said no one believed in such threats."

"True, Chief, but I think the press might."

"What? What did you just say?"

"You heard me, Chief. I think the press might believe me. Don't you think? They always like a good story." Dead silence ensued. The Chief, the lawyers and the mandarins from HR all exchanged hurried and nervous looks.

Before the Chief could regain his composure, Slevin said: "If there's nothing further, Chief, I'll be back in my office." He walked calmly out.

The following week, the lawyers, the Commissioners office, the Chief, the HR people and the department's PR people all began a damage control exercise to discredit Slevin if he went public with his report. They also prepared departmental charges of insubordination against him. They all wanted Slevin out of the department.

Then February 26, 1993 happened. That was the day eight Arab terrorists set off an elaborate truck bomb in the basement of the World Trade Center. By some miracle, the bomb only killed 6 people, but it injured over a thousand.

Slevin had also sent a copy of his report to the Counterintelligence Division of the FBI. On the train north from DC in response to the World Trade Center bombing, the head of FBI counterintelligence and his whole team, actually read Slevin's report. Three weeks later the NYPD's problem with Slevin was over. They wouldn't have to fire him. They wouldn't have to fight off the press. They would never have to deal with Slevin again – so they thought. The FBI had hired James E. Slevin and ordered him to put together a team to fight terrorists and terrorist groups, like the ones who bombed the World Trade Center.

# CHAPTER 11 – LEAH & ROBERT

Other than the Navy, Ishmael Abboud hadn't had much of a life. He was in his 40s when he married Layla Mahfood, 15 years his junior. The Mahfoods were friends of the family. Layla and Ishmael had a son. Ishmael wanted to name him Samuel after his own father; but Layla's father, Robert, was dying of cancer and she prevailed on Ishmael to name their new son after him. There'll be other sons, she promised him: but there weren't.

Layla's dad fought his cancer and lived till the boy entered Kindergarten. He liked being called Bob and called the boy Bob. Layla did the same, as did a reluctant Ishmael. This proved to be a mistake.

Bob proved to be a slow learner. He was shy and he didn't do well in school. He was bullied. The older boys mocked him, yelling "bobabood, bobabood" whenever he went out on the playground. He began to hate the name Bob. He was a decent athlete, but not a star. He played baseball and soccer. He learned to sail and sailed often – not so much that he loved the sport, but rather to please his father.

Several times a year, Ishmael took Bob to Annapolis. Usually to a football game, but to other sporting events as well and just to walk the campus and see the midshipmen in their uniforms.

Five years after Bob was born, Layla gave birth to their second a child, a girl, whom they named Leah. It would be their last child. Layla's second pregnancy had been very difficult and there were complications with the birth. She never recovered. She died a month later. Ishmael was left alone to advance his career and, by the way, raise two small children - mostly long distance.

Ishmael's relatives tried to help as much as they could, but he was forced to hire four nannies so the kids could have round-the-clock care and supervision.

One time when home, one of the nannies told him how cute it was that the children did their homework together – that Bob was helping his little sister. Ishmael made it a point to watch this when the kids came home from school. He couldn't believe what he was seeing. Bob wasn't helping Leah: it was Leah, who was seven years old and in second grade, that was reading to Bob, who was 12 and in seventh grade, from Bob's seventh grade science textbook. Two years later, when Bob entered Dulaney High School, they finally realized he was dyslexic and had other learning disabilities as well.

All through Bob's high school, Ishmael kept up the drumbeat about Annapolis, about the Navy. When Bob started junior year, Ishmael went to see Bob's college counselor. The woman was very blunt: she doubted Bob could even get into a four-year college, much less the Naval Academy. Ishmael knew it was bad; but he didn't know it was that bad. Still, he tried.

Ishmael called in every favor he was owed. He finally got an audience with Vice Admiral Reese Hicks, the Superintendant of the Academy.

"Captain Abboud," Admiral Hicks said finally. "You have had a distinguished career in this service, as had your father. But the Academy just isn't going to happen for your son.

"The Navy and the Academy are totally different now from when you and your father were here. Back in the day, the Academy was run by the good old boys network in the Navy. *Manus manum lavat.* One hand washes the other. You scratch my back, Ill scratch yours. You take care of my kid; I'll take care of yours. It's not like that any more. Now, everyone watches everything and everyone. The Secretary of the Navy, every goddamn congressman and senator, and even the White House watch admissions to the Academies – all four of them – like hawks. Your son's grades, test scores, sports, extracurriculars – everything, frankly – are so far below the standards of the other applicants – that appointing him would stink of 'influence.'" The Admiral said making quotes in the air.

"Everyone would know that some other kid, who was far more qualified, was being denied appointment because of Bob. You'd hear the howls in Washington from here – 50 miles away. I'm sorry, Captain."

So, Bob wasn't going to the Academy like his father and grandfather. But Ishmael wasn't finished yet.

He gave Bob the news directly. Bob knew that, as far as his father was concerned, this was the worst possible thing that could happen. But Ishmael had barely got the words out of his mouth than he started in on Bob about enlisting.

"Your grandfather enlisted in the Navy right after he graduated from high school. The country was just about to enter the First World War. He did so well that they picked him out of the enlisted ranks and sent him to the Academy. They still do that. It's a tradition in the Navy that the politicians and the bureaucrats haven't killed yet. There are slots in the Academy that are reserved for enlisted personnel with distinguished records. One of those slots is for you.

"Bob, you can get into the Academy. It may take a couple years, like it did your grandfather. But you can do it. You just have to enlist."

And so, even though he had been accepted at Essex Community College, a two-year school, Bob packed himself off to see the Naval Recruiter.

About a year after his mother died, Bob had developed a high fever and a sore, stiff neck. Light hurt his eyes. The nanny in charge didn't know what to do. She tried contacting Ishmael; but he was at sea and it took two days. During that time, Bob's fever got higher and his neck worsened."

"For God's sake, get the doctor, woman!" Ishmael yelled when the nanny told him.

The doctor came to the house. Bob was in agony. The doctor immediately diagnosed him with a bacterial form of spinal meningitis. He gave Bob a shot of antibiotics and wrote a prescription for more. Bob's neck and the back of his head were severely swollen and red. The doctor thought there were collateral bacterial infections in the ear. The doctor had no anesthetic. There wasn't time to get any. So, with no anesthesia, the doctor punctured Bob's eardrum to relieve the pressure on his ear and spine. It was the most painful thing that ever happened to Bob. He never forgot it.

When Bob went for his enlistment physical, the doctors tested his ears. They saw that his eardrum had been punctured. That made Bob "4-F": medically unqualified for military service. Not just the Navy; *any military service.*

Bob was distraught. His father was shattered. His only son couldn't even get into the Navy at all! Bob wound up at Essex Community College. But his father would not let it go. He kept on and on about the life Bob was missing.

Two years later, Bob graduated with an associate's degree. There was only one thing he wanted when he graduated: to get away. He wanted to be far away from the Navy and his father and his family and Baltimore. There was only one thing in life that he loved: Leah. She was 15 and in high school at a prestigious private girls' school on a lacrosse scholarship. She was his best friend. If he could have taken her with him, he would have. But he knew he couldn't.

Ishmael had taken Bob to Washington several times. He liked the Rangers in the National Park Service who took care of, and provided security for, all of the national monuments. Without saying a word to his father he checked it out, liked what he saw, and signed up. After training, he was offered a post at Yellowstone National Park. He was gone. And so was "bobabood." From then on, he called himself Robert.

Leah had gone to Dulaney Middle School, as had Robert. But unlike Robert, she excelled at everything, both sports and academics.

In Maryland, lacrosse is not a sport; it's a religion. Although it is pronounced "lacrosse," it is spelled L-A-X. There are almost as many LAX stickers on the back of cars as there are Maryland license plates. The first time Leah took to the field she was six years old. Thanks to the Maryland Youth Lacrosse Association there were many opportunities to play competitively even at the age of six. Leah joined a "Tykers" league. At the old age of nine, she graduated to the "Lightnings" league. At 11, she went on to the "Midgets" league where she was spotted by Kim Mercaldo, lacrosse coach at the Bryn Mawr School, an expensive and very exclusive private girls' school.

Leah had a sixth sense about where the ball was, who the shooters were and when and how they were going to shoot. She excelled at defense. Her coaches noticed her uncanny skills and put her in the goal. Leah was left-handed and the only left-handed goalie anyone could remember. By the time she was ready to move on to the "Juniors" league, at age 13, she was a minor phenom in Maryland lacrosse circles.

Recruiting in lacrosse is a scandal. College coaches prowl the Junior and even Midget leagues looking for outstanding players. They offer college lacrosse scholarships to pre-teen kids in middle schools – just to lock in a future supply of prime talent. Kim had seen three college coaches talk to Leah's nannies, who picked her up after games. They all got the same answer: Leah's father was in the Navy at sea. No one they could talk to about Leah.

There was no such thing as high school recruiting. There were no scholarships for high school lacrosse players. But Kim made friends with

Leah's nannies to learn about Leah and the Abboud family. Mom dead. Dad under the ocean in a submarine for months at a time. Brother at Essex Community College and, by all accounts, on a fast track to nowhere. Four nannies to pay to take care of Leah and Bob. Couldn't have much money. Old Navy families were rich in tradition, but little else. Kim thought she had a case.

Because of the rabid Maryland interest in lacrosse and because of Kim's very winning record at Bryn Mawr, she was held in very high regard by both the Head of School and, more importantly, by the board of directors of the school, a few of whom had played on Kim's championship teams.

Kim spoke with the Head of School. Certainly Bryn Mawr, itself, could not offer a scholarship to Leah, of course; but what if one of the board members – out of the goodness of her heart – were willing to pay Leah's tuition? Phone calls were made. Kim made the 30-minute drive out to horse country in northern Maryland to meet with a very wealthy board member. The deal was done. In addition to Leah's lacrosse prowess, it didn't hurt the cause that she was a straight-A student. Now, all Kim had to do was convince Leah's father.

Ishmael was much more difficult to track down but even easier to convince. The Navy has a program whereby sailors under thousands of feet of ocean in submarines can talk to their families ashore. Kim tracked this program down and asked if she could speak to Captain Ishmael Abboud, commanding the *Ohio*, one of the Navy's newly rechristened SSGNs. They told her: family only. Kim first thought about lying to them. But she figured that Ishmael would blow her in. Then they'd probably sic the FBI on her as a terrorist. So, Kim went back to the nannies and finally tracked down one of Leah's aunts. Kim told the woman that Leah's full tuition would be paid for at Bryn Mawr for four years. Kim didn't say how this would happen and the aunt didn't ask. She knew Bryn Mawr's reputation and she was thrilled for Leah.

"Ishmael Abboud doesn't know the difference between Bryn Mawr and the State School for the Criminally Insane." The aunt said, mildly shocking Kim. "But you leave him to me. He'll go along."

Kim put the aunt in touch with the Navy communications people. Two weeks later she got a call from the aunt. "Ishmael agreed. Why don't you send me the papers. He'll be ashore in two weeks. I'll get him to sign."

And so Leah entered Bryn Mawr in September and began tearing up the lacrosse field and the dean's list.

Lacrosse is in the Spring, so Leah dug into the academics. She had always liked science and she found a rich seam of it at Bryn Mawr. She took physics her first year and joined the STEM Club. She took chemistry in second year and was chosen for the "Chemathon Team," where the top ten science students go to the University of Maryland for a chemistry competition against other high schools. She took biology in junior year and honors physics in senior year. At Christmas of senior year, Leah was one of only 141 high school students in the country to be named a U.S. Presidential Scholar.

Lacrosse at Bryn Mawr is a very tough sport. Practice from 3:30 to 5:30 every school day on the upper field, which is turf. Practice on Saturdays and Sundays from 9 till noon. But it has its better moments. Each spring break the varsity girls go to Hilton Head for a week for a tournament.

Bryn Mawr's sister school and archrival is the Roland Park Country School – equally expensive, equally exclusive. In Leah's four years at Bryn Mawr she gave up only two goals to Roland Park. She shut them out in her freshman year and again in her senior year. In her sophomore and junior years, she gave up one goal each to Roland Park. In Leah's first year, Bryn Mawr lost two lacrosse games, total. In her second year, they lost one. In her last two years, Bryn Mawr went undefeated. In her third year, Leah was named an all-American.

Kim talked to Leah several times about college. Even if she never set another foot on a lacrosse field, Leah could pick her college and be sure she'd never pay for any of it. All of the Presidential Scholars got snapped up by all of the major universities. But Leah said no to all these suitors. She wanted to go to the Naval Academy. She told her father nothing about this.

Kim knew the Navy coach, Cindy Timchal. Kim had played on one of Cindy's seven consecutive NCAA Division I championship teams at the University of Maryland. When Navy lured her to the Academy, the Athletic Director described her as the "finest coach in the history of the game." Kim called her old coach and invited her to watch Leah play. Cindy already knew of Leah by reputation.

"Here are Leah's stats." Kim said welcoming Cindy to the game.

"You know, Kim, if this works out, it could be a God-send. My goalie is going to be a firstie next year. I've got no real back-up. I really need a super-goalie.

"Army has just joined Division I. We're going to play them for the first time two years from now. I sure don't want to play them with a weak act in goal."

"Gotta go. I'll introduce you after the game." Kim said.

Just to gild the lily, Leah let only one goal that day in a 7-1 romp over Bryn Mawr's archrival Roland Park.

"Leah, come over here, please. I want you to meet someone.

"Leah, this is Coach Cindy Timchal of Navy."

"Oh, yes, I've seen you several times before. It's such an honor to meet you in person."

""You've seen me?"

"Yes, I've been to a couple of your games."

"Well, I hope you'll come to a couple more next year and then all of them the following year. I'm looking for a goalie."

"Oh, that's right, Brenda Fisher's going to be a firstie next year, isn't she?"

"Not only am I looking *for* a goalie; I am looking right *at* the goalie I want to replace her." Cindy said smiling.

"Me?" Said Leah, breathlessly looking back and forth at the two coaches.

"Yep. Brenda's outta here next year. And, the following year I'd like to see Leah Abboud in her place."

"Wow! I don't know what to say!"

"How about yes?"

"Oh, yes, for sure."

And so Cindy got Leah in touch with the Academy's admissions team and started the complicated process.

Many people think that because the only people who can nominate someone to the four military academies are either the President, the Vice President, or a member of Congress, these politicians nominate the kids of their biggest financial contributors. Maybe true once, but definitely not now. Being nominated doesn't necessarily mean accepted. Nowadays these politicians want to be sure that the people they nominate – the kids they go out on a limb for – will actually be accepted at the Academies. They don't want any embarrassments. They don't want to nominate turn-downs. And so they search for the brightest, and the best athletes, and the most well-rounded students to nominate.

So, how does recruiting by coaches like Cindy Timchal fit into this mix? It turns out that the Academy invented a wonderful ruse called a Letter of Assurance. This document is sent to students who have been accepted at the academy. Accepted – but not yet appointed. These letters basically say: "if you can get nominated, you are in."

The trick to this is that the Academy circulates the list of all those students who have been sent Letters of Assurance to all the members of Congress and the White House. So, the politicians know for sure that the kids on this list will get in to the Academy. They won't have to waste a nomination. And so Leah Abboud's cell phone rang. (She had been specific with the Academy about not using her home phone, since her father still didn't know.)

Leah looked at the caller-ID and didn't recognize the 202 area code number. So she let the call go to voicemail. A few minutes later she played the message back.

"Leah Abboud. This is United States Senator Barry Glassman calling with some very good news, I think. I understand that you are interested in attending the U.S. Naval Academy. I understand that you are both an excellent student and a great athlete, and that the Academy is very interested in having you come there. So, I am delighted to tell you that I would be deeply honored to nominate you to the Academy. Please call me back as soon as you can. I'd like to talk to you personally before I send the letter."

Leah called the Senator's office. When she gave her name, she was put right through to the Senator. They had a very nice chat. The Senator had gone to the University of Maryland. He followed all of the University's sports teams. Although he was in college before Cindy Timchal took over the women's lacrosse team, he said that he knew her and had met her several times, and that how pleased she was now back in Maryland, albeit at the Academy, not the University. Leah had always thought of politicians as stuffy windbags. She was delighted how warm, friendly and open Senator

Glassman was. As they rang off, the Senator said he would sign her nomination letter that afternoon.

Leah had managed to intercept the Letter of Assurance before it got to her father, but she didn't have the guts to tell a United States Senator not to send the copy of her nomination letter to her home.

"Leah, you seem to have received a personal letter from our United States Senator. Do you mind telling me what this is all about?" Ishmael Abboud said to Leah as she came in from school.

"Go ahead and open it. I have something else for you to read, too." She said rifiling through her backpack looking for the Letter of Assurance.

A few minutes later she came back into the kitchen and saw her father starring down at the two letters on the kitchen table.

"Dad, there's a game at Gilman. Some of us from school are going to go. I won't be late." She said bending over to kiss her father on the forehead. She couldn't stand to see him cry. As she ran out the back door, she started crying too.

And so, like her father and grandfather before her Leah Abboud went off to Annapolis.

* * * * *

The US Naval Academy is, of course, the premier training program in the country for Naval officers. But it is also a major university. So there's a bit of schizophrenia in some of its traditions. The President of the University is called the Superintendent of the Academy, usually a vice admiral on his last tour of duty. The Dean of Students is called the Commandant. When kids enter a regular university they are in their first – or freshman - year; and when they're in their last – or, senior year, it's their fourth year. At the Academy, this is reversed: entering students are in the fourth class; and those finishing up their four years are in the first class. Freshmen are called "plebes." Sophomores are called "youngsters." Juniors have no nickname; they're just "second classmen." Seniors at the Academy are simply called "firsties." All of the cadets are midshipmen – both men and women. The PC Nazis haven't got them to change it to something odious like "midshipperson!"

In addition to the strenuous physical training and indoctrination into the Navy, there is a relatively benign form of hazing that goes on. It's not physically threatening, but hardly fun. Plebes have to run everywhere they go. No walking. This is called "chopping." They also have to make a crisp 90-degree turn whenever they go around a corner. This is called "square cornering." Every time they encounter an upperclassman, they have to yell either "Go Navy" or "Beat Army." This is called "sounding off." And as they stand in the middle of the yard in front of their dormitory, Bancroft Hall – rain or shine - at the first formation of the day, they have to yell out the entire menu for that day. King Hall houses a massive dining room where all 4,500 midshipmen eat their three meals a day together and in unison. The food at King is not good. The middies are grateful for the two "for pay" restaurants on the campus where they can buy recognizable fast food.

Plebe year begins not in September – like a university – but in June, right after graduation from high school. During their plebe year, cadets wear the traditional sailor hats that everyone is familiar with. At the Academy these are called "Dixie cups." After 12 months at the Academy, just before they begin their second year they have a ceremony – a right of passage.

Just in front of the chapel is a grey obelisk about 20 feet tall. It is simply called "Herndon," after a 19th century merchant captain, William Lewis Herndon. It's not at all clear why "Herndon" is there at all. Herndon did not attend the Academy, or if he did, they left it off the plaque. Herndon is hardly one of the immortal names of Navy tradition like John Paul Jones.

The plaque on the obelisk describes an admittedly heroic act of a sea captain on a sinking ship. But during nineteenth century hundreds of ships must have gone down with most of their captains performing many brave acts. No one seems to know why Herndon got the honor of a memorial on the Naval academy campus.

The 4,500 midshipmen are divided up into 30 companies of 150 midshipmen each, comprised of 35-40 cadets from each the four classes. So you have plebes in the same company with firsties. Each September, the Commandant selects one of the companies to grease the Herndon monument! Yes, cover it with grease! The youngsters in the company get the honor of doing this.

Then the plebes assemble *en masse* at the monument and form a human pyramid around it – all the while trying to hold onto the greased surfaces – until they reach the top. There one of them places a "cover," which is the name Naval officers call their normal hats, on the top of the obelisk. As they gingerly deconstruct their human pyramid they all chant "Plebes no more!" They then no longer have to wear the Dixie cups that target them as plebes. They can thereinafter wear a decent "cover" like the rest of the midshipmen.

When Leah went to the Academy while at Bryn Mawr, she either went as just a spectator at the lacrosse matches or as a much welcomed guest under the wing of Coach Cindy Timchal. So she was totally unprepared for plebe summer. But she did manage to survive the strenuous physical side as well as the martial side and even the chopping and square-cornering. Everything went well until Herndon. Leah was part of the human pyramid, about two-thirds of the way up. The obelisk narrows from bottom to top. Unfortunately Leah wasn't far up enough to be able to get her arms all the way around the greasy column. So when the full weight of one of Leah's fellow women classmates – at about 30 pounds more than the 111 pounds that Leah carried – landed on her back, her grip gave out and down she went with the classmate on top of her. When Coach Timchal saw Leah hit the walkway, her whole life passed in front of her eyes.

“What’s the verdict?” Cindy Timchal asked the physician in the infirmary.

“Nothing broken. That’s for sure.” The doctor said as Cindy began to breath normally for the first time in the last two hours. “She’s very lucky. Sprained shoulder, sprained ankle, sprained wrist – but nothing that will keep her of the lacrosse field for more than a week or so. We have a very sore young woman in there.” The doctor said nodding toward the room Leah was in. “I’ve given her some pain killers. She’s asleep. I want to keep her over night just to be sure. All in all, she’s luckier than the girl that fell on top of her. That one broke two ribs and got a concussion when her head hit the pavement. Your Midshipman Abboud clearly paid attention to her PT classes. She learned to fall right. No concussion. She’ll be sore for a few days. But she’ll be back on the playing field in probably a week.”

Leah spent Monday in bed. Tuesday she managed classes. Wednesday she hobbled to the gym after lunch for “lifts.” This is what the lacrosse women call their daily weight training. Leah didn’t lift that week. She just didn’t want to be away from her teammates. So she sat with them while they did their lifts.

The lacrosse women are a tight group at Navy. They actually made up a name for their team a dozen years ago and it has stuck. They call themselves: “We All We Got.” This probably reflects the neglect they felt as more attention was paid to the women athletes in the more popular sports like swimming and diving, track and field, as well as soccer. They abbreviate “We All We Got” to an ungainly “WAWG.” They have WAWG printed on all of their practice uniforms. They even have it written on the inside of their class rings.

It didn't take Leah long to be accepted by that tight group. The year before she came, Navy went 17-1. In Leah's first year, they also went 17-1. They only lost to Duke. Duke beat them 4-1. That was the most goals Leah let in all season in any one game.

The clear high point of Leah's first year was the game against Army. West Point had been growing its women's lacrosse program with the expectation of getting into NCAA Division I. They succeed the year Leah entered Annapolis. So, Leah's team in her first year was the first women's lacrosse team - ever - at Navy to face their arch-rivals. Navy beat Army 2-0. Leah shut them out!

Varsity athletes at Navy are given the privilege of wearing their letter sweaters every Friday. These sweaters feature a large gold "N" on a field of – what else? – Navy blue. Teams that have beaten Army have a gold star on their sweaters right next to the "N." So, as Leah limped down to the gym on the Friday after her Herndon fall, she proudly wore her letter sweater, which – thanks largely to Leah -the Navy lacrosse women could now wear with the gold star.

In Leah's youngster year, Navy went undefeated. But in her third year a cloud came over Leahs' playing. She was beginning to have severe headaches.

Leah had decided she wanted to become a Navy pilot after graduation. Her company officer was a pilot. The company officer told her that the worst thing that could happen to a Navy pilot – other than being shot down or crashing – was to be grounded by a flight surgeon. Leah didn't want to wash out of aviation before she even started. She didn't want any doctor interfering with her lacrosse either. She didn't say anything to her coach either. But her lacrosse suffered. It wasn't a disaster but Navy lost three games that season. And Leah let in more goals than she had in her first two years combined.

She managed to hide her headaches through her summer cruise after third year. But when she went home on leave she told her father. Much to his credit, Ishmael sent Leah straight off to Johns Hopkins Hospital for an examination.

The news was bad – very, very bad. Leah was diagnosed with a stage 4 glioblastoma multiformae, a very rare form of brain cancer. It was so rare that there were no accepted protocols to treat it. The cancer was so far advanced that the only known treatment was some experimental work being done at the Duke University Medical Center.

The Navy is very good to its sailors. It covers all kinds of illnesses and injuries, in or out of the line of duty: *but it doesn't cover experimental treatments!*

After years of paying for nannies 24/7 and later paying for his own growing drinking problem, there was absolutely no $100,000 that Ishmael could come up with for the experimental treatment that Duke would charge them.

The Hopkins doctors told Leah she had six months to live.

## CHAPTER 12 - THE BOMB

"Griff, my friend?"

"Whenever you call me your friend, I know you want something."

"Not your life and property, Agent Griffin, just some friendly advice."

"Like what?"

"Like where in the hell can I go to get a crash course on atomic bombs."

"Do you really mean bombs, like Hiroshima and Nagasaki, or nuclear weapons?"

"I guess I mean nuclear weapons."

"I have no real clue. Never been asked that one before. Got to be hundreds of nuclear weapons experts within 10 miles of where we're standing. But damned if I could even guess where to find them. But, where I think I'd start, ya know, is Annapolis."

"Annapolis? You mean the Naval Academy?"

"Yeah, the Navy's got submarines and God-knows-what-else loaded with nuclear weapons. They gotta teach their young officers something about shooting them off, don't they?"

"You'd think. Know anybody there?"

"Yeah, I do. I go to a lot of football games there. I've gotten to know some of the people there pretty well. Let me make a few calls. I'll get right back to you."

* * * * *

“The guy to talk to at the Academy is CMDR Tom Gamble. He teaches nuclear weapons, among other things. He’s waiting to see us. I’ve got us a car. Let’s go.”

“Us?”

“These are my friends. Are you coming or not, sunny boy?”

“Yes, Agent Griffin.”

* * * * *

“Griff, did you talk to Commander Gamble?”

“Yeah.”

“What did you tell him?”

“That we wanted a 90-minute course on nuclear weapons.”

“Did he ask why?”

“Yeah, he said: ‘What’s this all about?’”

“So?”

“So I told him what Clinton said about gays in the military: don’t ask, so you can’t tell.”

“That’s not exactly the way I remember it.”

“This is government work, young man. Close enough.”

“Griff, I see you are a man of the Yogi Berra school of spoken English.”

“And proud of it, sunny boy. Fuck you.” He said smiling ear to ear.

* * * * *

As they entered the Main Gate, the security officer asked to see photo ID. The driver fumbled for his. Griff and Michael showed their FBI credentials, at which the guard gasped lightly, and motioned their car through. It was just another 200 yards to the front of the Visitors Center. There Commander Gamble had sent one of his students to guide Griff and Michael to his office underground below the Nimitz Building.

* * * * *

"So, Agents, where do you want me to begin?"

"Commander Gamble, my entire knowledge of nuclear weapons consists of seeing mushroom clouds on video clips."

"That's about the extent of mine, too." Griff chimed in.

"Ooooo-K. So, we'll do nuclear weapons 101. No problem."

"Well, over a hundred years ago, now, Albert Einstein figured out that that mass and energy were related by an equation that we all know of as $E = mc^2$. The '$c^2$' here is the secret relationship between mass and energy. The point here is that if you can add some '$c^2$' to a piece of 'm,' you get a whole lot of 'E.'" So, back in the 30's, a bunch of scientists led by Robert Oppenheimer figured out how to create some $c^2$ and turned this benign equation into a weapon of mass destruction, only two of which have ever been used in war – by us against the Japanese in World War II.

"What makes an atomic explosion different from a normal, if you will, explosion?" Griff asked.

"Good question. Most explosions are chemical reactions, just violent ones. When you pour vinegar on baking soda, you get a chemical reaction – a pretty strong one. When the firing pin of your sidearm compresses the gunpowder in the back of a cartridge, it sets off a chemical reaction so strong that it can hurl a piece of lead a couple thousand yards at about three times the speed of sound.

"Chemicals like gunpowder and TNT are large molecules. They are held together by a binding force. When that force is affected by pressure or by a chemical reaction, energy is given off. Quite a lot of energy is given off. With conventional weapons, this all happens at the molecular level. With nuclear weapons, it happens at the atomic level. And, here's what makes this difference so important. The energy in a nuclear reaction is *75 million times* greater than in a comparable molecular reaction. One pound of Uranium-235 has the same explosive force as 16 million pounds of TNT."

"How do nuclear weapons actually work? How are they detonated?" Michael asked.

"U-235 is an unstable element. It has too many neutrons in its nucleus. These extra neutrons bang into other nearby U-235 atoms. Normally, nothing happens. When nothing happens, it is because the U-235 is at a subcritical mass. But when you get too much U-235 in one place, then you have a supercritical mass and the rogue neutrons start tearing the U-235 atoms apart. As I said, U-235 is inherently unstable. It wants to be torn apart. It wants to be torn apart into lighter, more stable elements. That's what nuclear fission is. When this happens – when errant neutrons start tearing the U-235 atoms apart, the process gives off massive amounts of energy. That's what a nuclear explosion is.

"So how do we get this U-235 to explode? We take two subcritical masses and smash them together to form a supercritical mass. Then we duck."

Griff and Michael laughed.

"A tactical nuclear weapon is one that explodes with a force of between 15 and 100 kilotons of TNT. Anything over 100 kilotons is classified as a strategic nuclear weapon.

"Commander, we're interested in weapons in the 15 kiloton range." Michael said.

"You don't have to call me Commander. You're not in the Navy. Tom is fine."

"Good. I'm Mike and this old fart goes by Griff." Tom and Michael laughed as Griff gave them both the finger.

"I sorta thought you might be interested in a weapon in that range. Our friends, the Russians, have a 16-kiloton tactical nuclear weapon that's in wide use. But they're slowly disappearing because of disarmament. That, by the way, is the size of the bomb we dropped on Hiroshima

"Well, here's how these things work. In a device that size, there is about 140 pounds of U-235. One hundred forty pounds of U-235 is a supercritical mass. So, the material is separated into two components, both of which, obviously, would have to be subcritical.

"One of the components – what we call the 'bullet' – weighs about 55 pounds. The other, called the 'target,' weighs about 85 pounds. Think of the 'target' as a large doughnut sitting at the end of a tube the diameter of the doughnut hole. Then think of the 'bullet' sitting *in* the tube at the other end. The bullet is exactly the size of the doughnut hole. Behind the bullet is a wad of conventional high explosives. Those conventional explosives are the trigger. When you want to detonate the device, you first detonate the conventional explosives. This sends the nuclear bullet shooting down the tube. Once the bullet reaches the nuclear doughnut, there's supercritical mass. The neutrons start tearing the U-235 atoms apart at 99% of the speed of light. The energy this process gives off is heat – about 2 million degrees of heat. X-rays coming from the nuclear reaction heat the nearby air up to over 14,000 degrees instantly. This heat causes the air to expand violently. The pressure of this instantaneous, massive air expansion is what the blast wave is. That, and the heat are what kills most people in the first few seconds of a blast.

"To give you some perspective, the moving air mass travels at about 1,000 miles per hour. That's a 1,000-mile an hour wind, gentlemen! If a 200-pound human encountered wind of this speed, his body would accelerate from 0 to 682 miles per hour in one second! Quite a jolt, wouldn't you say? As one of my old chief petty officers would say, if you get hit by one of these blast waves, the first thing you should do is go to the nearest phone and cancel your plans for the weekend."

They all laughed at this gallows humor.

"There is another destructive element of these weapons. They produce a very large, very powerful Electro-Magnetic Pulse, or EMP. This magnetic pulse fries all unprotected electronic gear. We have a wonderfully euphemistic acronym for this effect: TREE. It stands for Transient Radioactive Effects on Electronics. It fries absolutely everything. Your cellphones. Your computers. Your lights. Anything that runs on electricity. It even fries the power plants so they can't even make electricity.

"Tom, tell us more about how much damage a 16-kiloton warhead could do."

"Well, as I said, that was the size of the bomb we dropped on Hiroshima. As I recall, that bomb had a barometric trigger that detonated at about 2,000 feet over the city. The blast flattened a four-and-a-half square mile area. Vaporized 80,000 people. Then there's always the residual radiation sickness that kills thousands more."

"What about cities like Los Angeles or Chicago? What if a 16-kiloton warhead were set off over either of those cities?" Michael asked.

"Maybe a million people would be vaporized. Certainly many hundreds of thousands.

"How mobile are they? How big are they?"

"The bomb we dropped on Hiroshima, the one they called 'Little Boy,' was 10 feet long, had a diameter of 28 inches and weighed close to 10,000 pounds."

"So, something you could actually put in the back of a big van."

"Oh, that was 1945. They are a lot smaller now and a lot lighter. So, today, maybe 3 feet. Maybe 200-300 pounds. Something you could definitely put in the back of a van, even a small one. The only dimension that doesn't change is the diameter. You remember I called the 'target' part of the bomb a fat doughnut? Well, that part – at a weight of 85 pounds - has to be about 28 inches in order to have the right configuration to achieve supercritical mass.

"Shit." Michael said softly.

"Amen." Said Griff quietly too.

"Griff, here, said not to ask what you guys want this information for. So, I am not going to ask. But, good luck and God speed!"

# CHAPTER 13 - RICHARD

Before Nicholas Davis even boarded his train at Penn Station, Ahmad el-Rabbani appeared at the door of Richard Albion's apartment.

"My men will be here in minutes." He said. "Where do you know that man from?"

"You mean Davis? We went to the Bruton School together in Britain. When Davis was a boy, his father was in the foreign service and worked at the US Embassy in London.

"Your men did a good job, Ahmad. Most convincing. Davis believed the whole thing. And the drugs will be out of his system before his train gets in. So, even if he goes directly to a doctor – which he is much too scared to do – they will find nothing.

"What are you going to do with the body? I trust your men aren't going to carry her out past my doorman in a body bag?

"Mr. Albion," el-Rabbani said with an air of condescension. "My men are professionals. They will come up the service elevator with a small packing crate, just big enough for the whore's body."

"Ahmad, have you ever heard the saying *de mortuis nil nisi bonum* – never speak ill of the dead."

"Richard, you can keep your clever sayings. The girl was a whore. An Iranian pig of a whore. A Muslim girl who drank, wore indecent clothes and had sex with infidels for money. She didn't deserve to live. I should never have agreed to bring her to America. But pigs like her have their uses – as we both have just seen.

“Yes. We have indeed.

“You know, Ahmad, Davis almost left his handcuffs here. When he was just at the door leaving, he went back to get them. Pity. I wanted to present them to him when I go to Washington to collect my debt.

“What will you with the body, Ahmad?”

“My men will make certain there is no means of identifying her. Then they will take her body tonight to the lower West Side. There is a bike path there along the Hudson. Just north of Pier 40, there is a bridge over the bike path called the Bow Notch Bridge. They will dump the whore’s body there.

“As soon as they do so, they will call 911 from an untraceable phone. They will report the body, as if they were riding on the trail and just came across it. Then they will wait, out of sight, until the police arrive.”

“Do you think there will be a problem with the time of death?”

“No, the Medical Examiner will tell them something like 18-24 hours. The police will not be surprised. Who would dump a body in broad daylight?”

“Thank you Ahmed. You have done your usual thorough job.”

“And now it is time for you to do a thorough job too.” Ahmed said…. and he added only in his mind ‘*louti*’ – old faggot!.

“Not for a few weeks. I need for Davis to begin to get over this. I need him to begin to forget.”

“Do not wait too long, Richard Albion. We cannot afford to wait for you to complete your part of the plan.”

# CHAPTER 14 - ATLANTIC PASSAGE

A week after the call to the FBI, Srinivas Prasad, returned to Russia to continue his work for the UN Disarmament Commission. As soon as his plane reached its gate at Sheremyetyevo Airport, the cabin crew chief announced that everyone should remain seated. No one should attempt to deplane. When the cabin door opened, two agents of the FSB appeared and went directly to seat 13A.

"Your identification papers?"

A trembling Prasad produced his diplomatic passport and his UNDC identification card.

"Come with us." As they yanked him from his seat and led the terrified bureaucrat off the plane into an unmarked car on the runway.

The FSB could not interrogate an employee of an international agency with the same gusto and the same physical persuasion methods that they had used on their two colonels, who were Russian nationals; so they tortured Prasad mentally. First, being taken to the Lubyanka, the old KGB headquarters, from which few prisoners ever emerged alive, was horrific enough! Next, they showed him the bank transfer documents to all three accounts. Next they showed him photos of the two Russian colonels who had been tortured to death. Then they lied to him saying that his diplomatic immunity did not extend to political crimes involving nuclear weapons. They told him they would charge him under Russian Law. The bank records and the dying statements of the two colonels were enough to convict. The penalty was either death or life imprisonment on the Novaya Zemlya above the Arctic circle.

Then they told Prasad that they had reversed transferred the $2 million out of his Bangalore account. They said they were going to transfer out all remaining funds in Prasad's account – which amounted to his life savings. Finally, they threatened his family. Prasad told his interrogators everything he knew.

Other than corroborating the statements of the two dead colonels, Prasad told his interrogators two crucial pieces of information: first, that the colonels had trained the buyers on how to assemble and disassemble the device; second, that the buyers had required that the bomb be disassembled for shipment.

This was bad news for Michael Cornell who got the news within hours. It meant that the device could be smuggled into the U.S. in more than one innocent looking guise and that it would be reassembled somewhere on U.S. soil.

The colonels' men had driven the two bomb components up through Karelia and the western end of the Kola Peninsula to the small wharf on the west side of the City of Polyarny on Kola Bay. Polyarny is about 650 miles north of St. Petersburg and about 30 miles north of Murmansk. It took the colonels' men almost 15 hours to make the drive. Polyarny was an ideal port of departure. It was a closed city. No one would notice a military vehicle making a delivery to the harbor.

One of the terrorists, a man named Jamal, went with them. The colonels knew that Jamal had gone with their men. But what they didn't know was that Jamal did not return with their men. When they arrived at Polyarny, Jamal had handed each of the soldiers an envelope with 100,000 Rubles, about $3,500, which was far more than a year's pay for each of them. The two soldiers had not told the colonels for 2 reasons. First, Polyarny was a closed city. Foreigners, like Jamal, were not allowed there. They would be in very big trouble for bringing an outsider there and even bigger trouble for leaving him there. The second reason was that they figured the colonels would assume that Jamal paid them off and demand the money for themselves – or, worse, - report the soldiers for leaving a foreigner in a closed city. So, when they returned, the soldiers simply reported that all had gone according to plan and that they had taken Jamal to St. Petersburg on the way back.

The colonels thought nothing more of it. So, when they were tortured by the FSB, they said that a terrorist had accompanied their men to Polyarny but had returned to St. Petersburg with them. The FSB thought nothing more of it either. Just some prudent terrorists making sure the colonels didn't double-cross them and that their bomb got to its proper destination.

The bomb components had been picked up in Polyarny by a small freighter. The captain was surprised to find Jamal there in a closed city. The captain and his crew were extensively vetted by the GRU or Chief Intelligence Department, which was the military intelligence service and the largest intelligence agency in Russia. Even so, they were not allowed to disembark from their ship within Polyarny.

The captain was even more surprised when Jamal handed him a letter and said in badly accented Russian: "*Otkrito*" – grammatically incorrect, but meaning to open it. The letter indicated that Jamal would be the captain's passenger on the voyage. The letter also instructed the captain to inform Jamal when they were passing seventy degrees north latitude and ten degrees east longitude (70° N, 10° E), which was off the northwest coast of Norway still 3°+ above the Arctic Circle. There the captain would be given another letter. Finally, the letter ordered the captain to maintain radio silence until otherwise instructed.

The captain was neither surprised nor annoyed. He was being very well paid for delivering the two crates. And receiving new orders at sea – which is obviously what Jamal would hand him – was nothing new either. He had been plying the Arctic Coast of the Russian Federation since just after the breakup of the Soviet Union. Most of his voyages involved changes in destination after the ship had set sail.

In this case, 70° N, 10° E was just exactly where a ship would have to change course depending on its destination. If it were actually going to Cyprus, anywhere in the Mediterranean, or Africa, 70° N, 10° E would be the exact place where he would turn due south into the North Sea, then the English Channel, and then out into the North Atlantic. On the other hand, if the ship's real destination were in the Western Hemisphere, then 70° N, 10° E would be the exact place where the ship would turn southwest towards the Faroe Islands or Iceland.

Jamal turned out to be a model passenger. He had a sleeping bag and a mess kit. He slept and took his meals in the cargo compartment with the two bomb crates. He never left that compartment.

Three days later, when the ship reached 70° N, 10° E, the captain called for Jamal as instructed. And, as expected, Jamal showed up with a second letter.

This letter instructed the captain to sail directly to Rotterdam and told him exactly where to dock.

* * * * *

The FSB also told the FBI that the harbormaster in Polyarny had reported that a small freighter named the *Kalupsó* had picked up cargo in Polyarny and had said that its destination was Cyprus.

Michael Cornell kept looking at the message that said: Cyprus. Cyprus! Why would any terrorists targeting the U.S. send an atomic bomb to Cyprus?

He queried the FSB to see if they knew anything. He got back a cryptic reply: "Many ships leave our northern ports for Cyprus. Few ever reach there."

Would they be kind enough to explain what this means?

The FSB replied – again cryptically - that the shippers of goods from Russia often changed the destinations of those cargoes once they were at sea.

Many ships left Russia, they finally explained, loaded with goods bound for Cyprus and then got diverted. The nominal buyers of these goods were Cypriot companies. These companies in Cyprus, however, turned out to be owned by the managers of the plants in the Russian Federation that manufactured the goods. In mid-ocean the ships would receive radio messages to divert to Canada, Mexico, Brazil, or sometimes Africa where the real buyers of the goods were. The Russian manufacturing company would sell to the manager-owned company in Cyprus for X dollars. The manager-owned company in Cyprus would then sell to the real purchaser for 2X dollars, or sometimes as much as 4X or 5X the dollars. Russian workers were generally underpaid. So were the executives of Russian companies. These "sales" to Cyprus were one small way for the managers to get even with the owners of their companies. This was a neat little Russian take on capitalism.

Oh? Did the FSB know if this happened to the *Kalupsó*?

The FSB said they would check with their communications department, which was the remains of the Federal Agency for Government Communications and Information with the unfortunate Russian acronym FAPSI. This was the old 16$^{th}$ Directorate (electronic intelligence) of the KGB that was absorbed into the FSB in 2003. The structure of FAPSI was modeled after the U.S. National Security Agency.

Michael mused on the name of the ship bringing the bomb to the U.S: the *Kalupsó*. In English, it would be called the *Calypso*, like Captain Jacques Cousteau's famous vessel. In Greek mythology, Calypso was a divine nymph, who seduced Odysseus and kept him for 7 years on her island. *Kalupsó* was the Greek verb "to conceal." In the case of Odysseus, Michael imagined that it meant that Calypso concealed the knowledge of how to escape and get home. The opposite of concealing was *apokalupsó*, which is where the word "apocalypse" comes from, which, of course, means revelation. In English, the meaning of "apocalypse" has evolved to mean the end of the world, which comes from its being the last book of the Roman Catholic bible, where it purports to describe the end of the world. How fitting, Michael thought.

* * * * *

*They put the bomb on a boat north of Murmansk. Is that crazy? Tom Gamble said it would take more than 10 days for a small steamer to make it from Murmansk to the East Coast. If they're smart enough to get an atomic bomb, would they risk it bobbing around the North Atlantic for 10 days? That doesn't seem so smart. Why didn't they just put it on a plane? They certainly have an airport at Murmansk. There's a large airport in St. Petersburg. There are lots of military installations in that part of Russia. Some of them must have airfields. It just doesn't make sense. And, most important, how can we be sure it's really coming here? What if the USA story the terrorists gave the Russians is just a ruse to throw us off? What if they're really going to detonate it in Jerusalem? Or, if it IS really on a ship heading to the US, where's it going to dock or land or whatever you call it?* Thinking these thoughts was how Michael entertained himself over dinner alone at Clyde's in Georgetown.

Forty-five minutes later, walking down M Street to his tiny apartment, Michael placed a call to CMDR Gamble.

"Tom, it's Michael Cornell. Sorry to bother you again." He said to Tom's voicemail. "Does the Navy have any resources that could help me track down that steamer that I asked you about? Please give me a call when you can. Thanks very much."

Michael climbed the stairs to his apartment over the celebrated "Dixie Liquor" store at 3429 M Street. His apartment was expensive. Washington itself is expensive. Georgetown is one of its priciest precincts. Living there among his old college haunts was one of the few luxuries he allowed himself. The apartment was on the third floor and had just one bedroom, which was all he needed (and could afford). The pride of the place was a small shaded deck in the back. It was protected by trees from the gawks of his neighbors up the steep slope on Prospect Street. Unless there was a blizzard or a deluge, this is where Michael Cornell spent most of his home time.

Georgetown University was only two blocks away. Most of the good nightlife was on M Street. Consequently, more than one Happy Hoya had tumbled down the almost vertical decline of 35th Street, owing his life to the limbering effects of an over indulgence in alcohol.

Michael didn't hear from CMDR Gamble that evening. At about six the next morning, he boarded the 38B bus for Farragut Square. He had a car, but he kept it off the street in a garage on K Street under the expressway. He drove as little as possible in the mayhem of DC streets. At Farragut Square, he hopped the subway to Metro Center. Somewhere underground on the subway the call from Tom Gamble came in but didn't get to Michael's phone till he was coming up the escalator at the 12th Street exit from the metro. By then, CMDR Gambles's message was on voicemail.

"Mike, got your message. I do know a guy who might be able to help you. When I say this I mean that he might just know the answer to what you're asking. I have no idea whether he does or not. But even if he does, he might not tell you anything. His name is Phil Hall. He's a commander like me. He's in Naval Intelligence. And," There was a pause. "He's assigned to NSA. So, you see what I mean about maybe he's not talking." Tom gave Michael CMDR Hall's contact information and ended with: "Good luck."

* * * * *

"CMDR Hall, this is Agent Michael Cornell of the Federal Bureau of Investigation."

"Yes, what's this about, Agent Cornell?"

"I got your number from CMDR Tom Gamble at the Academy. He has been helping us with a serious problem that he said you might be able to help us with as well. We have a ship that left the north coast of Russia that we think is carrying a very dangerous cargo. We don't know where it is going. But wherever it's going there's going to be major trouble when it gets there. We need to find that ship. Can you help us?"

"I'm not sure I can help you. And I'm not sure I can, if I can… If you know what I mean."

"Sir, I think that wherever we need to go with security clearances, we can get there. It's *that* important."

"Ok, Agent Cornell. I take it this matter is highly classified."

"Top secret. Eyes only, sir."

"Ok, Agent Cornell. I'm at Fort Meade. We will need to talk in a SCIF. I'll reserve us one at the main building. What time can you get here?"

"I can be there by 11."

"That's fine. You'll have ID of course. You'll have to leave your phone and any other electronic devices at the guardhouse. I'll phone over there to let them know you're coming."

"Great. Thank you. See you at 11."

* * * * *

"Mike, what's your thinking on this?" FBI Assistant Director Jim Slevin asked.

"Jim, there's just too much we don't know. And there's a lot that just doesn't add up. Why a ship? Why not a plane? Why tell the Russians that the bomb would be used on us? What if they're really going to blow up Jerusalem? I need some answers. I hate this flailing around in the dark. I gotta start making some sense out of this stuff from the Russians."

"Ok, ok, I hear ya. What do you want to do?" Slevin said.

"I need to let this CMDR Hall in on our little secret. With his Naval Intelligence *and* NSA backgrounds he's never going to go for our 'enriched plutonium' bullshit. I need him to find the goddamn ship that the Russians loaded the bomb on. We've got to find that ship whether it's coming here or going to Israel or anywhere else. These bastards aren't going to just sit on the damn bomb once they put it ashore. So, it's either our major-major problem or it's going to be someone else's major-major problem, in which case we need to warn them."

"I never thought about it going somewhere else." Slevin mused. "Yeah, Jerusalem's a big possibility. And wouldn't it be something if the terrorists who bought the bomb sold it to the Chechens. It could be heading right back to Russian soil as we speak.

"Ok, enough of my craziness. You have your authorization to tell CMDR Hall that we're dealing with a nuclear warhead. Gook luck with him."

"Oh, by the way, Jim; do you know what a skiff is?"

"Of course."

"What is it?"

"Are you nuts? It's a small boat."

"CMDR Hall said we had to meet in a skiff. What does that mean?"

"Oh!" Slevin laughed. "Mike, that's not a s-k-i-f-f. That's a Sensitive Compartmented Information Facility, S-C-I-F."

"A what?"

"A Sensitive Compartmented Information Facility. It's what you might call 'an electronic safe room.' It's a room where no one can electronically eavesdrop on you, more or less. You know those conference rooms with no windows on the first floor? The ones in the middle of the floor? Those are all SCIFs. This office is not officially designated a SCIF, but it is one. They didn't tell you about SCIF's at Quantico?"

"Must have slept through that one."

"I guess you did sleep through it. Now, get outta here. And keep me posted."

*Sensitive Compartmented Information Facility!* Michael mused as he took the elevator to the garage. *Dear God, save us from military-speak!*

* * * * *

Michael took I-95 up to Route 32 to Fort Meade. He drove up to the main gate. There the guards asked his name and his business there. He showed them his ID and turned over his cellphone. The guard said, "Look this way, please." And took his picture. A moment later, they produced a badge with both his name and picture on it. They pointed to the main building and showed him where to park.

The security man at the front desk asked his name, checked his badge and looked at his ID. "CMDR Hall is on his way. You are in SCIF-4. Second door on the left down the hall."

"Agent Cornell?" A tall brown-haired commander's uniform with a good build said as he came through the door.

"Commander, nice to meet you and nice of you to see me."

"Same here. What can I do for you?"

"We have at least two unidentified Arab men who bribed two colonels of the Tactical Nuclear Weapons Division of the 20th Guards Army in St. Petersburg, along with a UN disarmament inspector, and got themselves a 16-kiloton nuclear warhead, which they put on a small ship in Polyarny four days ago. That's all we know."

"I take it you want us to find this ship."

"Exactly."

"Can we talk to these colonels?"

"They died during interrogation by the FSB." Michael said with a perfectly straight face.

"Not surprised. Do you know where in the Polyarny inlet they set sail from and a more precise time of departure?"

"The FSB just said the wharf in the City of Polyarny."

"No background on why or what their target might be.""

"No. The bomb might be destined for New York, Jerusalem or even Disneyland, for all we know. There *is* one thing about the time of departure, for what it's worth. The 20th Guards are stationed in St. Petersburg. There's a good highway, the M-18, between St. Petersburg and Murmansk, which is about 1400 kilometers; and then another 30-40kms of pretty good military roads up to Polyarny. So, I figured it took about 15 hours to get the bomb up there."

"Wait! Two Russian Army colonels drove a 16-kiloton warhead 1500 kms up to a ship in Polyarny?"

"Well, not the colonels, themselves; they got some enlisted men to drive. But, Commander, isn't the whole thing totally crazy? Why didn't they put it on a plane – either in St. Petersburg - or Murmansk even – if they really had their hearts set on a drive? If it were on a plane, they'd be wherever they were going by now, instead of banging around out in the Atlantic. That's what's driving me nuts Commander. If these guys are smart enough to get these two dearly departed Russian bastards to sell them an atomic bomb, how could they be so stupid as to put the bomb on a little boat and let it bob around in the North Atlantic for over a week?"

"I have no idea why they'd put it on a ship, Agent Cornell. But the enlisted men who drove it? Did they die during interrogation too?"

"I don't think so. We don't actually know."

"Could you find out? It would be important to find out when that ship left Polyarny. We can probably take it from there, but it would be important to find out – within an hour or so – when the ship left Russia."

"I'll get back to the FSB and see if they can tell us. They've been pretty cooperative so far."

"They damn well ought to be cooperative with the help we've given *them* over the past few years. Ok, so let me know what they say. But I won't wait for them. We'll start looking right now."

"Thank you so much, Commander. I really appreciate your help. As you can see, we are really lost."

"Not a problem. We'll do everything we can to help."

"Thanks again." And as he walked to the door, Michael said very non-chalantly. "Do you mind my asking how you look for a ship like this?"

"Yeah, I do mind your asking." As he turned to look, Michael saw a big smile on the Commander's face.

* * * * *

Michael got back to headquarters at 1:30pm and had the message off to Moscow within an hour. He looked at his watch. 2:30pm on the East Coast was 10:30pm in Moscow. He wouldn't hear back tonight. He figured they'd get on it first thing in the morning. The soldiers were in St. Petersburg, so the FSB guys would have to get word to their people up there. Then they'd have to round up the soldiers and question them. Michael put a specific request in his message that the FSB not murder the enlisted men. He wasn't as blunt as he wanted to be; but he hoped he made it clear that they might want to talk to those men again. Michael hoped the FSB be able to get back to him in the morning.

He got his wish. The FSB worked quickly. Their message was on his desk when he got in at 6:30 next morning. The enlisted men not only told the exact time they loaded the bomb on the ship; but they also volunteered, for the first time, that one of the terrorists got on the ship as well. Nobody had thought to ask. This was valuable information that Michael passed on to CMDR Hall immediately.

* * * * *

That evening, as he just got back to his apartment, his phone rang. It was CMDR Hall. "Agent Cornell, I think I have some good news for you. Your ship is not headed for North America."

"It's not! Incredible. That's terrific. Where the hell is it going?"

"Not sure. There's a spot off the coast of Norway just above the Arctic Circle where ships coming out of the Barents Sea from the north coast of Russia either turn west towards the North Atlantic and the Western Hemisphere or due south towards the North Sea and either the Baltic Sea or the English Channel. Your friends turned South."

"Any chance they might have guessed you were watching them and turned South just to put us off the scent."

"It's possible they could have guessed. But *very* unlikely. That would have been a real long shot. And they certainly didn't know anything about what we are up to up there. Even the Russian Navy doesn't know much. No way a bunch of terrorists – or what - could have found out.

"So, it's heading toward Northern Europe, huh?"

"Yeah, from the west coast of Norway south into the North Sea. Once it gets to the bottom of the North Sea, the ship would either turn east toward Sweden and the Kattegat and eventually the Baltic, or it would turn southwest toward the English Channel. Then, maybe, out into the Atlantic."

"Again, any way they might go into the English Channel then out the back end into the Atlantic then across to New York?"

"Sure, it's always possible. But, that would add several more days to their travel time. Turning southwest from the north coast of Norway towards New York is a hypotenuse. Going down to the English Channel and then across would be like taking the other two legs of a right triangle. It's a lot further. And it's like you say: why bob around in the North Atlantic more than you have to?"

"Okay, well this is very good news. I'm going to pass it on right now. Thanks very much."

* * * * *

"That's great news Michael." Jim Slevin said. "Come tell me the details first thing in the morning. But right now, I'm going to send a note out to Jim Dickman at his home and then, if Jim agrees, I am going to call Ezer Allon. Ezer's the Mossad guy at the Israeli Embassy. Great news for us may spell very bad news for Israel. If there's any chance they're taking that bomb to Israel, they gotta know right now. But before I call any foreign embassy, I am going to let our distinguished Secretary of State, Mr. Dickman, know what I am up to."

"Jim! Jeezus! The Secretary of State! Isn't this getting out of control?"

"Michael, my friend, if this were a threat to us, I go directly to the White House. If it is a threat to any other country, we pass it to our liaison at State. But if it is a direct threat to any close ally – especially Israel, for which Mr. Dickman has a soft spot in his heart – I am authorized to go directly to the Secretary himself.

"Mikey, you are paranoid about titles. Jim Dickman is a good man. He'll definitely want to do the right thing.

"So, you're going to call him right now?"

"No. No calls, Mikey. This is a SCIF issue. Any discussions occur in SCIFs. Any other communications are in writing. After they are read, they are either put in a top-secret file or they are burned and a record of who burned it, where, and what time, is put into the top-secret file.

"So, I am going to write up what you told me. Tell the Secretary that I want to call Ezer Allon and that I would like to brief Ezer first thing in the morning. Mr. Dickman will read my note, check a yes or no box, and give the document back to the agent who brings it to him.

"By the way, are you coming in at your usual hour tomorrow?"

"Yeah. I'll be in by 6:30."

"Good, I'll tell Ezer to come as early as he can. He'll want to know everything we know."

# CHAPTER 15 - VBSS

"Agent Cornell, I have some more news for you. Your ship entered the Mediterranean Sea a few minutes ago." Commander Hall said over the phone.

"Really? Any idea of its exact location? Or where it might be headed?"

"Yes, I do. We need to talk in a SCIF."

"Want me to come out to Ft. Meade again?"

"No, we need to meet at the Pentagon. Because of the possible involvement of one or more of our close allies, the matter has shot up the chain of command. I understand your agency has alerted the Israelis. So have we. We'll talk more when you get here. Are you familiar with the Pentagon?"

"Nope. Never been there."

"Come around to the North side, the one facing the Potomac. Your name will be at security. We will be in room 2E510. The guards will call up, and we'll send a seaman to escort you."

"Ok. When? Now?"

"Yes."

"Ok."

* * * * *

CMDR Hall extended his hand. "Good to see you again, Agent Cornell. "Men," he said to the two chief petty officers behind him. "This is Agent Cornell of the FBI. Agent Cornell, Chief Doonan and Chief Eldridge."

"Likewise." Michael said to CMDR Hall, and then, nodding to the two chiefs with a smile. "Gentlemen, nice to meet you.

"Commander, when you said this matter has shot up the chain of command, you clearly weren't kidding. The Chief of Naval Operations?"

"Admiral McNamara, besides being CNO, is the genius who invented the system you are about to see and which you will never speak about again. Clear?"

"Clear. One thing. This conference room is quite austere. I mean for an admiral, especially a woman admiral?"

"If you're thinking pink curtains, stow it. Some poor bastard made the mistake of saying that to her. He's now packing for a three-year tour in Antarctica."

"No. Not pink curtains. I was thinking more like mahogany and leather instead of plastic and naugahyde."

"Oh. This is her working conference room. She's got another – ceremonial – one with the leather and the brass and the crystal and all."

CMDR Hall stepped aside giving Michael a view of the electronic wall map behind him. On it was a flashing red dot almost exactly between Gibraltar and Ceuta at the eastern end of the strait. Above it was a flashing blue dot closer to Gibraltar.

"Let me brief you on what you're seeing and going to hear about," CMDR Hall said, "before the CNO comes in."

"The Chief of Naval Operations, herself, is going to join us?"

"This is her baby. Like I said, she invented all of this. Have a seat." The Commander said gesturing to the chairs across the conference table from the electronic map.

"This electronic intelligence system is called the "Auditor." It's very new. It's totally operational but not fully deployed. It is based on a theory that Admiral McNamara published which says – in the simplest terms – that no two things are alike. She calls it "The Principle of Singularity."

"'Singularity' has picked up other - sort of fringe, scientific - meanings in the last couple years, but they have nothing to do with the Admiral's theory. She actually published it in a Naval journal while she was at the Academy. Ten years later, when the brass finally realized how important it was, they quietly went around collecting up as many copies of that journal as they could find and burned them. The entire subject is now classified. At least as classified as anything can be that has already been published." The Commander said with a shrug.

"As far as ships are concerned, this Principle of Singularity has two facets. First, no two ships sound alike. This means that if you made a recording of the sound each ship makes as it moves through the water, that record would be unique. Hence, you could identify that ship the next time you heard it. You wouldn't know what ship it was, of course, but you would know that it was the same ship that you heard before.

"The second facet is visual. No two ships look alike. You and I might look at two destroyers or two submarines and think that they look like each other. And they do, of course, to us; but not to a computer with hyper-dense optical resolution. A computer can tell the two destroyers, or two submarines, apart.

"So, what's the Auditor system? It is two pieces of equipment. First is a listening device, which we can drop from an airplane. It's not a sonar buoy that sits on the surface and pings for ships. Our Auditor sinks right to the bottom of the sea. It sits there on the bottom quietly listening for noises that it recognizes as ships' screws. Once it hears a ship, it records what we call its audio signature. Then a few seconds later, it transmits that ship's audio signature to a satellite hovering above in geosynchronous orbit. The satellite is the second piece of equipment. The Auditor also transmits the ship's exact position, its speed and its bearing. The satellite then takes a picture of the ship and records it. Once this is all done, we can identify that exact ship wherever it may be. Hours later, hundreds of miles from any Auditor, in the middle of the ocean, we can spot that ship from space and know – for sure – that it's the same one.

"So, Agent Cornell, you remember my telling you about that spot off the northwest coast of Norway where ships either turn towards Europe or towards the Western Hemisphere? That location is at exactly seventy degrees north latitude and ten degrees east longitude (70° N, 10° E), about 3° above the Arctic Circle. We call it 70/10. We have an Auditor there, permanently. Anything going north into the Arctic Ocean, we don't see. But anything coming south out of the Barents Sea from the north coast of Russia - toward Europe or the West - Auditor will have a record of.

"Needless to say." The Commander said gesturing to the wall map. "We also have an Auditor in the Straits of Gibraltar. If you drew a straight line between Tarifa and Ksar es Seghir, the Auditor would be right there in the middle about 2500 feet down on the sea floor.

"The red dot on the map shows the exact position of the Kalupsó.

"What's the blue dot above it?"

"That, Agent Cornell, is a British destroyer, the HMS *Dartmouth*. The *Dartmouth* is keeping an eye on our target."

"Target?"

"Yes, in a few hours, the *Dartmouth* will be joined by elements of Task Force 68 of our Sixth Fleet."

"And then what?"

"A VBSS."

"Excuse me? A what?"

"VBSS: Visit, Board, Search & Seizure."

"We're going to board the Kalupsó. Task Force 68 is the Navy Expeditionary Combat Force. It has FAST teams, which are "Fleet Anti-terrorism Security Teams." These are guys from the Marine Corps Security Force Company Europe. They're good at boarding vessels. They even have an ordinance disposal team. But that's not going to help them much with a nuclear warhead."

"It'll be a few hours, you say?"

"Yeah. Nobody wants to spook the Kalupsó anywhere near Gibraltar. Hell to pay if the bastards set of the bomb in the straits."

"Of course. The Russians told us specifically that the buyers wanted the warhead disassembled for the voyage. The crew of the Kalupsó wouldn't know squat about re-assembling it; but the terrorist on board just might."

Just then the door to the right of the electronic map opened and a very attractive, early-forty-something, with short blonde curly hair, dressed in an four-star admiral's uniform blew into the conference room.

"You must be Agent Cornell." The Admiral said. Michael thought he caught her giving him a quick look up-and-down.

"Yes, pleased to meet you, Admiral."

"So, where are we Commander?" She said.

"I'd say about three hours away. That'll put the ship about 50 miles from the straits. Far enough away to be safe."

"The Brits and TF-68 all in place and doing the right things?"

"Yes, m'am. It looks like we're in good shape."

“Ok. Keep me posted. The White House wants to keep the Israelis right on board. I’ll call over there now and let them know we’re three hours away from VBSS.

“Nice to meet you.” The Admiral said to Michael, holding out her hand and smiling.

“Nice to meet you, too, Admiral.” Michael said looking her straight in the eye.

“Commander, there’s no point my staying here watching the dots move across the map. Would it be possible, though, for you all to let me know what happens out there?” Michael said gesturing to the map.

“One of us can give you a call. No problem.” CMDR Hall said. The two chiefs nodded.

“Great. Thank you very much. See you.” And then turning to the two chiefs. “Gentlemen, thank you very much. See you as well.”

* * * * *

Just as he was about to leave for lunch with Jim Griffin, Michael’s phone rang. It was CMDR Hall’s number. Michael looked at his watch. It was 12:30 in DC. That meant 6:30pm in the western Med.

His heart began to race. The Marines had boarded the Kalupsó. No bomb.

# CHAPTER 16 – ADMIRAL MCNAMARA

Michael's cell phone rang. He thought he recognized the prefix as a Pentagon number; so he answered it.

"Agent Cornell, this is Master Chief Petty Officer Montoya in the Chief of Naval Operations Office. Can you come over here to see the Admiral, asap?"

"Yes, I can, chief. I'll be right over."

* * * * *

"You look startled, Agent Cornell." Admiral McNamara said as Michael walked through the door to her little conference room.

"I didn't expect to see you, Admiral. I thought I'd be seeing CMDR Hall and the chiefs."

"They're not here. I wanted to talk to you.

"After that disturbing news from the Med, I went back to do some checking to try and find out what happened to your bomb."

"Oh, God bless you, Admiral. That's exactly what I was hoping you – or your men – would say." Michael said through a big sigh. "God are we lost!"

"Admirals don't get blessed very often, Agent Cornell. Thank you for saying that." She said with some color rising in her throat.

"Anyway, the Auditor was designed for the really nasty parts of the world: the Straits of Malacca, Straits of Hormuz, Straits of Tiran, etc., etc. But as CMDR Hall told you, we also have them in some relatively innocuous places like 70/10 and, as you saw, the Straits of Gibraltar. What he didn't tell you is that we have one in the Pas de Calais at the eastern end of the English Channel. If you drew a line between Calais and Dover – right in the middle of that line, on the sea floor – is one of our Auditors.

"In addition to the interface between the Auditor, itself, and its satellite, there is a third machine involved. That is a computer that collects and stores the data; but, more importantly, correlates it.

"I went back and took a look at what the Auditor system knows about your ship.

"You know where 70/10 is located. And you now know where our Pas de Calais Auditor is located. From 70/10 to the Pas de Calais is 1380 miles. Both Auditors clocked your ship moving at 10 knots, or 11.5 miles per hour, which is about 275 miles a day. That means the Kalupsó should have reached the Pas de Calais in exactly 5 days, give or take an hour or two. It fact, it took her an extra 18 hours to get there. That means, Agent Cornell, that your little bomb-carrying ship put in someplace for 18 hours – plenty of time to offload or transfer the warhead - between 70/10 and the Pas de Calais."

"Really?" Michael said clearly astonished.

"Yep. The distance between the Pas de Calais and Gibraltar is just 200 miles further. So, that's about 5 ¾ days or five days plus 18 hours. And that's exactly what the Kalupsó did on that leg of her trip – almost to the minute. So, somewhere between 70/10 and the Pas de Calais is where your ship put in and dumped the bomb, for sure."

"Really?" Michael repeated his eyes agape. "Do you have any idea where it might have put in?"

"We are checking and we're doing more searching, as we speak; but my guess is Rotterdam."

"Why, may I ask, Admiral, do you think Rotterdam?"

“It’s the fifth largest port in the world. Seems to me a little ship like the Kalupsó, carrying an atomic bomb, would, above all else, like to get lost in a crowd. The crowd would be in Rotterdam.”

“You think a crowd, Admiral? I was thinking they might just sneak into a tiny little town along the Dutch or German coasts.”

“They could do that, Agent Cornell. But they’d be taking a huge chance. Any strange ship in a small port would be noticed. No matter how small, if there’s a port, there’s a harbormaster. No sea captain would ever attempt to land his ship without clearance from the harbormaster. The smaller the port, the stranger the ship, the more people would be curious. The harbormaster would, in any event, log the ship in. There’d be a record of its coming and going, where it came from, and where it was bound for as well as its cargo – even if the captain lied about the cargo.

“When I said, a second ago, that we were checking; that is precisely some of the checking we are doing. Only we have asked Interpol to do the checking to avoid raising eyebrows, if possible. They are querying every single port on the North Sea coast of Germany, Holland and the few French ports east of Calais like Dunkirk. They are also checking with the local equivalents of our Coast Guard. If your ship put in at a little port, we’ll find it.

“More likely, I think, though, is Rotterdam. There they’d be lost in the crowd. There the cargo manifest would simply be faxed to the harbormaster’s office. If one of the clerks there saw something suspicious, he’d flag it for further inquiry. If not, it’d go in a file and get forgotten.

“There would be a record, however. And that’s what we’re getting right now compliments of our friends at Interpol. In the next hour or so, we will know exactly when the Kalupsó arrived, where it docked, what’s on its cargo manifest, where it’s bound for, and what time it left.

“Would they lie about their destination?”

"Very unlikely. Take the US for example. We require every inbound ship to file a customs declaration stating the name of the ship, its planned port of entry, its ETA and its cargo. Once a ship lands in the US, our customs people take the manifest, board the ship, inspect it, and check to see if everything is in good order. The ship's inspection includes dogs sniffing for drugs and explosives as well as Geiger counters that are very sensitive. An inspector once told me that his Geiger counter once detected a souvenir World War II compass that a ship's officer had in his stateroom. In those days, compass dials were painted with radium. So, the Geiger counter picked up probably a few grams of 50-year old radium paint through a wall in the officers' quarters! No, Agent Cornell, they are not going to lie about their destination and they are not going to lie about their cargo – if they're planning to enter a US port or get anywhere near the US shoreline. Getting the bomb into the US is going to be a lot more complicated than just putting it on a different ship in Rotterdam.

"The one thing I think we can be sure of is that the bomb will be on a ship that passes over my Auditor in the Pas de Calais. We have already calculated when the Kalupsó left Rotterdam. So we are going over all of the Auditor's records to see what ships went west through the Pas de Calais within an hour – either way – of the Kalupsó's departure. Then we'll expand the search to two hours. And so on. So, Agent Cornell, we'll find the ship for sure; but will we recognize it? Fortunately the Rotterdam harbormaster's records are electronic and available. We will look at every ship that left Rotterdam around the departure time of Kalupsó and we will identify its destination and its supposed cargo. We will know each ship's speed and bearing and be able to calculate its ETA at its destination. We will also pass this information on to our brethren at CMDR Hall's office at NSA and ask them to listen to each ship's communications. It's not a sure thing. But I think we'll come up with something."

"Thank you very much, Admiral. I hope to God you're right."

"Me too, Agent Cornell. Me too."

"What happens now, Admiral?"

"I've ordered CMDR Hall to coordinate all of the information gathering. And I have told all elements of Naval Intelligence and the Atlantic fleet to report to the Commander on this matter. I have also put through a formal request to NSA for their help. My Auditor can find your ship but NSA's ears can listen to what it's saying, which is what you need to know. I've asked CMDR Hall to keep in close touch with you and your people.

"As for what's going to happen. Once we get the list of ships leaving Rotterdam within our time envelope, we will identify each one. Then we will break them down by destination and report our findings to you. Then your people and my people need to talk about which ships are our likely targets. Once we agree on the targets, we'll have my satellites watch their position to see if they stay on course and then we'll have the boys and girls at NSA listen to them to see who they're talking to and who is giving them orders. So, CMDR Hall will get onto you as soon as we've got something for you."

"Will you stay involved?"

"I certainly intend to. But I do have a day job…."

"Yes, you certainly do, Admiral!"

"But, Agent Cornell, if you feel lost… call."

"Thank you very much, Admiral."

"May I ask you something about your baby, the Auditor?" Michael said as he started for the door.

"Maybe." The Admiral said with a nice smile.

“Nothing secret. I just wanted to ask how you came up with the name ‘Auditor’? It sounds so un-military.”

The admiral laughed. “That’s exactly why I chose it. Agent Cornell, do you know what an “MRE” is? It’s a food kit. A box lunch, if you will. A box full of food that a soldier can eat in the field. Got that?” She said smiling. “So you know what MRE stands for? Get this: ‘Meal Ready to Eat.’ Can you believe that? It’s called a ‘Meal Ready to Eat!’ Can you imagine what pack of monkeys came up with that!” She and Michael both laughed.

“The one I just learned the other day was SCIF.”

“Absolutely. That’s another one.” The admiral said continuing to giggle. “By the way, we’re in a SCIF right now. That’s why the room’s so dull. So the sound waves don’t get nervous. SCIF! Military thing-namers all deserve Nobel prizes in cement-headedness!

“You know, I have given explicit orders to every command in this service that no one is to name anything – any thing, any device, any process, any system, any anything - without my written approval.”

“’Roger that,’ as I think they say, Admiral, and bravo!” Michael said smiling as he started again for the door.

“You know, Agent Cornell, you’re a good man. Most of the men I have to deal with every day have their eyeballs floating in testosterone. You said you were lost. The men I deal with would never say they were lost if they were totally fogbound, which many of them are much of the time. And when I was telling you about the Auditor, you had this look of wonder on your face. None of my men would let their guard down like that.”

Turning around and looking her straight in the eye, Michael said, “Admiral, you are a good man too. A *very* good man.” Then he winked at her and turned to the door.

Color started rising in her neck and face. Then she said as Michael walked out, “You know, that’s the first time I’ve ever been winked at in uniform.”

Over his shoulder he said, “I hope not the last.”

# CHAPTER 17 - LOST

This time Michael was ushered to a different SCIF at NSA headquarters at Ft. Meade. This one had an electronic map of the North Atlantic Ocean on the wall. CMDR Hall was there to meet him along with the same two chiefs, Doonan and Eldridge whom he had met in Admiral McNamara's office.

"I thought we'd walk you through an overview of what we're doing in the North Atlantic to find your ship."

"That would be great." Michael said.

"Chief Doonan." CMDR Hall said gesturing to the chief.

"Yes, sir." Chief Doonan said moving to the map.

Using a laser-pointer, the chief gestured toward the coast of Holland.

"Rotterdam, Agent Cornell, is the fifth busiest port in the world. It berths over a hundred vessels a day on average. The day the Kalupsó left Rotterdam there were 119 ships that left the port in the 12 hours before and the 12 hours after she left.

"About 75% of the Port of Rotterdam's trade goes to Asia or the Western Hemisphere, with the vast majority of that coming to the US. Of the 119 ships that we were initially interested in, seven went to the Med. They're already there. Naval Intelligence, MI6 on the British side and Shin Bet on the Israeli side are following up with each of those ships.

"There are 56 ships that are coming this way, more or less. When I say 'this way' I mean between Canada and the Panama Canal. We tracked all of them, as you know, going through the English Channel. The port of Brest in France reported in that all of them passed out into the North Atlantic on schedule. As of an hour ago, all 56 ships are behaving themselves. They are all on course, all in the appropriate shipping lanes, all keeping their speed up, all GPS-ing regularly, all using their radar, and all making routine radio calls, etc., etc."

"So, what are we looking for, chief?" Michael asked.

"One of these guys going off the reservation. One of the ships deviating from her reported course. Maybe one of them sending or receiving coded messages. So far, *nada*.

"So whadda we do?" Michael asked.

"We keep on them." CMDR Hall cut in. "Something will tell us who we're looking for. One of the ships will get re-routed to another port. One of them may get instructions about dropping off their cargo – messages that will contain words and phrases we'll pick up on. I just wanted you to come out here to get a feel for what we're doing. All of the red lights on the map are the ships we're watching – all 56 of them. And we'll keep watching them until something breaks."

"Ok." Michael said. "And you can still keep me posted?"

"Absolutely. We'll call the minute we get a break. Thanks for coming."

"Thank you guys!" Michael said leaving.

* * * * *

The traffic was brutal getting back in on I-95 from Fort Meade. It took an hour and a half. *In the last four hours I have learned that nothing has happened.* Michael shook his head as he headed up the elevator from the FBI garage. He put his coat down on the chair opposite his desk in his cubicle and looked for paper messages. He went to the kitchen and got himself an uncharacteristic late afternoon cup of coffee. The real stuff, not decaf. He looked at his messages there in the kitchen. Nothing about the bomb. Just routine Bureau stuff. It could wait.

Then he walked over to the south side of the building facing the Potomac River and Virginia. He found an empty conference room and just went over to the windows and looked out. He could see the top of the Pentagon across the river. It looked like an alien spacecraft, he thought. He took out his phone and dialed.

"Office of the Chief of Naval Operations, Master Chief Petty Officer Montoya speaking, sir!"

"Chief Montoya. It's Agent Cornell from the FBI. May I assume the Admiral is busy?

"Yes, sir. She's in a meeting."

"Would you give her a message for me?"

"Yes, sir. Of course, sir."

"Would you tell her that I'm lost?"

"Say again, sir? You want me to tell the Admiral that you are lost?" Chief Montoya asked pronouncing those words very carefully.

"Yes, Chief. The Admiral will know what I mean." Michael said reassuringly. "She'll understand. So, you'll give her that message as soon as she's free?"

"That's a roger, sir. I'll tell her that you're lost as soon as she gets out of her meeting.

"Thanks very much, Chief Montoya. I appreciate it."

"Not at all, Agent Cornell."

* * * * *

Thirty minutes later Michael's phone rang.

"Cornell."

"Agent Cornell, it's Chief Montoya in the CNO's office.

"Yes, Chief, thank you for calling."

"The Admiral said to come over."

"Come over?"

"Yes, she said to come as soon as you can and told me to clear her schedule when you can make it."

"Great. I can get there in 30 minutes."

"That's a roger, Agent Cornell. I'll have your ID waiting at the North Gate."

* * * * *

"I assume this isn't a social call but I thought I'd show you my real office before we adjourn to the SCIF. I assume our SCIF matter is why you're here, no?

"Yes, Admiral. Actually, I was actually going to invite you down to my office. You'd like it. My office is about the size of your desk." She laughed.

"Very cool. Very Navy." Michael said surveying the scene.

"Most assholes come in here looking for chintz curtains."

"Not this asshole. You're definitely not a chintz-curtain girl in my book."

Admiral McNamara laughed. "I didn't mean you."

“Not to worry. Wouldn’t be the first time I’ve been called that. And I’ve been called worse.”

“You know, Agent Cornell, that you break all the rules.”

“What’s that, Admiral?”

“Cops never have a sense of humor.” She said with a nice smile.

“Oh, well, I guess I could say I’m not a real cop…… but then Chief Montoya would have to throw me out of here for trying to impersonate one.” She laughed again.

“Ok, so off to the SCIF we go. You have a bomb to find and I have a Navy to run.

“So, why are you lost?” The Admiral said quietly, closing the door to the SCIF.

“Admiral, I know you didn’t make your rank driving carriers and subs – much less tramp steamers; but what would you do if you were carrying an atomic bomb across the Atlantic Ocean and had pretty good reason to think the U.S. Navy was looking for you?”

The Admiral starred at the map on the wall for a long second and then said slowly: “I’d go dark and get out of the shipping channels.”

“I’m sorry. I don’t understand. What does that mean?”

“Going dark means turning off all of your electronic communication devices. Everything: radar, radio, GPS – anything that can send a signal, even cellphones.

“The shipping lanes are nothing more than a series of compass bearings. But in reality, they function as well-traveled highways on the oceans. They were devised in the 19th Century to keep ships from running into each other. Between any 2 major ports there are two shipping lanes, one inbound and one outbound for the respective ports. If you're steaming between, say, Southampton and New York, you need to stay on certain compass headings going out and another set coming back.

"Well, I guess this is starting to make some sense."

"You had a briefing at Ft. Meade with CMDR Hall's people, no?"

"Yeah. They said a lot of stuff that I didn't get. They just didn't say it the way you did. They didn't put all of this in the context of looking for a ship that had gone dark and left the shipping lanes. It was just a bunch of facts. Left me feeling that they were looking for the proverbial needle in a haystack – where the haystack was about 25 million square miles of ocean.

"I guess I should have asked them more questions instead of coming here to bother you with them."

"Don't feel that way. Don't feel stupid. Your questions are the right ones. And I certainly don't mind your calling me. I told you you could and I meant that.

"Let me give you a little more context about this search that were doing. If you go dark, the only way someone can find you is visually. And when you get out of the shipping lanes so they can't find you visually either.

"CMDR Hall has all of our resources monitoring those 56 ships crossing the Atlantic from Rotterdam. We know where each is supposed to land. If they are smart - and they certainly seem to be - they will know we are looking for them and that we'll be waiting for them when they put in to port. So, they will do something to make themselves invisible to us. First, go dark, so we can't find them electronically. Then get out of the shipping lanes so we can't find them visually either.

"And it's not just one out of 56. Some of those 56 ships belong to well established and highly reputable shipping companies. They cross the Atlantic a dozen times a year, often going back and forth between the same two ports. It would be a cold day in hell that those companies would ever get tricked into carrying a bomb on one of their vessels. And, an even colder day in hell for them to agree to do it if they knew about it.

"No, it's not just a one in 56 needle-in-a-haystack game that were playing with your bad guys. Every hour those ships are at sea, CMDR Hall's men are winnowing that list down smaller.

"Believe me, Agent Cornell, one of the ships on CMDR Hall's list will try to disappear. When they do, CMDR Hall's team will be on them in minutes. Then their last known location becomes the middle of a target and we start drawing rings around that target every hour based on the speed that ship can make. Meanwhile our North Atlantic Fleet will bear down on that area along with every aircraft we can muster.

"Ships like the one we are looking for make only about 10 knots an hour. That's the radius of a circle. Square it and multiply by *pi*. That's the only place the ship could possibly be. In one hour, that's about 310 possible miles. If you assume they aren't going to turn around and go back to Rotterdam, you can cut that area in half. I can assure you, Agent Cornell, that the U.S. Navy can search that big a territory with no problem whatsoever.

"*We will find those bastards!*

"I know it may be cold comfort for me to say so, Agent Cornell, but 'have faith.' We will find them."

Michael nodded started to leave.

As the Admiral opened the door for him, she said: "Let me ask you something, Agent Cornell, was the reason you came here 100% that you didn't understand CMDR Hall's search procedures, or was it, maybe, 95% that you didn't understand our search procedures and, maybe, 5% that you wanted to see Admiral McNamara again?"

Michael stood outside the door facing the Admiral with a very stupid look on his face.

"It was my turn this time to make *you* blush, Agent Cornell." She said with a bright smile as she closed the door.

# CHAPTER 18 – PASSAGE TO CANADA

Before he dealt with Slevin, Michael realized he needed to talk to Commander Hall. As he was getting up to head to a SCIF, his cellphone rang. It was the Commander.

"How soon can you get to a SCIF? Major developments here."

"Two minutes. I'll call you on the secure line."

* * * * *

"Agent Cornell, I think we may have the break we're waiting for: one of the ships that we're keying in on just went dark."

"Oh, thank God! Which one? Where's it heading?"

"It's called the *Valhalla*. Freighter. Liberian registry. German owners, we think. Chartered. We don't know by whom. Carrying – according to its manifest when it left Rotterdam – fertilizer. Bound for Newport News, so they told the Dutch.

"The *Valhalla*. The *Valhalla* and the *Kalypsó*. Interesting choice of names. Fertilizer from Europe to Newport News?" Michael thought out loud. "They need European fertilizer in Virginia?"

"No idea."

"What now Commander?"

"The CNO has ordered our nearest aircraft aloft to find her. I don't know how many and I don't know from where. But you've met the CNO. You know how into this she is. I'm sure she's put everything we've got within striking distance into the search. They'll head just west of her last known location. The *Valhalla* is in the shipping lane for Newport News."

"The shipping lane? She's in the shipping lane?" Michael asked remembering what the CNO had said about getting out of the shipping lanes.

"Yes, heading straight for Newport News and right into the arms of our Atlantic fleet."

"Ok, thanks. Can you keep me posted?"

"Will do."

Michael went to the Elephant & Castle at 12th & Pennsylvania for a Thai Salad and one – he thought to himself – beer. But at least it was an ESB – Extra Special Bitter – a good British beer. Then back to his place in Georgetown.

"Any luck with the *Valhalla*?" Michael asked, calling Commander Hall before he went to bed.

"I was afraid it was you who was calling. The *Valhalla* isn't where she's supposed to be." *That's just what I thought.* Michael thought to himself.

"We can't search the ocean for a dark ship at night if we have no clue where she is. We'll pick the search back up at first light. We'll have planes everywhere she could possibly be – based on her speed - before dawn."

"Do you mind if I come out first thing in the morning?"

"No. Not at all. I'm going to get some sleep. Dawn in the area we're looking at in the North Atlantic is about 3:30am Eastern time. I've asked LT Marcia Womack to come in at 3:30 to man our desk. There'll be a couple petty officers here with her too. What time do you want to get here so I can tell LT Womack to clear you with security?"

"I should be there by 6:30. Would you ask her to call me at 6 so I can put her number into my phone?"

"Roger that. And I'll probably get in a couple hours later unless something breaks. I've told LT Womack to call me if we get a break."

"Ok. See you tomorrow then."

* * * * *

"LT Womack?" Michael said into his phone as he was getting into his car.

"Yes, Agent Cornell. I have some good news for you. One of our F-18's spotted the *Valhalla* about 10 minutes ago. We're sending an Orion in right now for a closer look. They're also readying a VBSS team from the Marines on the Eisenhower. The CNO, herself, has given the CO of the Eisenhower Strike Group command of this operation."

"That's good news, indeed, Lieutenant. I'll see you in about 30 minutes. Can you get the guards to let me in?"

"You're all set, sir. And, Commander Hall said you know the drill at the gate."

"That I do. See you soon."

* * * * *

"Nice to meet you, Lieutenant." Michael said to the attractive black woman officer in her late twenties extending her hand. "Is this a SCIF?" He said extending his arm toward several banks of computer consoles.

"This whole office is secure, sir."

"So we can talk freely about our little problem?" Michael said smiling.

"Exactly, Agent Cornell." LT Womack said smiling back.

"Lieutenant, let me ask you something. Where I work, at the FBI, everyone from the maintenance and cafeteria folks to my boss call me Mike or Michael. I've noticed that nobody here does this. CMDR Hall calls me, Agent Cornell. He calls his chiefs, chief. And, they, of course, call him sir, always.

"That's the way we have to do things here.....sir." She said.

"Even when there's no one else around? I've been in an office alone with CMDR Hall, and he still calls me Agent Cornell."

"You weren't alone, sir."

"Whaddya mean, Lieutenant?

"Everything is recorded here, sir, 24/7." LT Womack said pointing to the ceiling. "It's for security."

"So, you mean that if I ran into CMDR Hall – or you – at a bar in Georgetown, you'd still call me Agent Cornell?"

"Yes, I'm afraid so. It's not that we're trying to be unfriendly. It's just the training."

"Ok. I won't badger you any more, Lieutenant." Michael said elongating the word lieutenant, but smiling at the same time. LT Womack smiled back.

"I almost forgot to tell you, there's more good news. One of the Eisenhower's Orions did a flyover of the *Valhalla*. She's hot."

"Come again, Lieutenant?"

"The *Valhalla* is radioactive.

"Whoa! Outstanding! We may actually be getting somewhere."

"There's one thing, though, that's very curious about her."

"What's that?"

"Before the Orion got there, she'd changed course."

"Really? To what new heading?"

"Due South."

"Really? Can you show me on the map?" Michael said referring to the electronic wall map above the computer consoles.

"She was right about here." The lieutenant said pointing to a location due east of Newport News and right at the border of two different colors on the map.

"What's the different colors mean here."

"Oh, that's the Air Defense Zone. Two hundred miles out from the coast."

"So, what happened here?"

"It looks like the *Valhalla* approached the ADZ and turned south.

"What happens when a ship enters the Air Defense Zone."

"They have to identify themselves. They have to let us know who they are."

"So, if the *Valhalla* crossed over into the Air Defense Zone, then it couldn't have stayed dark?

"That's right. They would have to turn on their radios and transponders and identify themselves to the Coast Guard."

"And if they don't?"

"The Coast Guard pulls the fire alarm. They notify us and all or their own assets both at sea and in the air. Someone is ordered to go out to look the intruder over. Meanwhile, they start their prep for interdicting and VBSS-ing her."

"So, the intruder has to either go "un-dark" or face an unamused US Navy and Coast Guard."

"Exactly, sir."

"And the *Valhalla* chose not to have to do that by hugging the edge of the Air Defense Zone."

"I suppose you could say that, sir."

"Does the *Valhalla* know she's been spotted by some interested warships?"

"I'd guess so, sir. The *Valhalla* knows she's dark. So, she probably realized that was why the F-18 buzzed her. The Orion, too. Hang on, sir. There's a message coming in.

"The Orion that's shadowing her reported she just changed course again."

"West into the Air Defense Zone?"

"No, due east."

"East? Back, towards Europe? What do you make of that?"

"I don't know. Her captain probably knows we're going to board her. But he can't get away. He can't outrun an F-18. He's gotta know that."

"That seems so strange. I would have assumed that our bad guys would have lied to the captain and the ship owners about the nature of the cargo. That said, the captain must have smelled a rat when he was told to go dark and get out of the shipping lanes. So why, all of a sudden, this squirrely behavior? They've obviously been caught. Why not turn the lights back on and 'fess up? It's like he's trying to stall us. I don't like this. What would you do if you were the captain of the *Valhalla*, Lieutenant?"

"I think I'd do like you said. Cut the engines. Turn the lights back on and face the music."

"How long to interdiction, Lieutenant?"

LT Womack checked her screens. "The Marines haven't taken off from the Eisenhower yet. Probably still briefing them on what to expect. I'll bet none of those boys has come face to face with a live nuke before. I'd say we've got at least an hour, sir, with the distances out there between the two ships. The *Valhall*a doesn't know it but she's heading straight for the Marines."

"Lieutenant, what's all this other stuff here with the computers?"

"Background. Names and background info on all of the ships we were looking at. Weather. Sea lane configurations. That sort of thing.

"Could I look at the info we have on all of the ships? I mean all 119 that left Rotterdam within a day of the Kalupsó?"

"Yes, sir, they're all there. Here, let me set it up for you."

Just then Chief Petty Officer Raymond Doonan walked in, saluted the Lieutenant and greeted Michael formally.

"Better than that," LT Womack said, "I'll have Chief Doonan set it up and show you what we've got. You can do that in the next room. Same consoles, but you and the Chief can have some peace and quiet.

"Sure thing, Lieutenant. Agent Cornell, what can I show you?"

"Well, let's start with the 119 ships on our list. Who are they all?"

"I'm sorry, sir, I don't follow you."

“I want to see whatever information you have on these ships, Chief. I’m supposed to be a detective. Please humor me.” Michael said smiling.

“No problem, sir. Where do you want to start?”

“Well, you’ve been tracking the 56 ships that are headed this way for the last few days, right?”

“Right.”

“So what about the other 63 ships? Where are they supposed to be going?”

“Let’s see. I think you know that 7 are in the Med in the good hands of our people there as well as the Brits and the Israelis. They’re all headed for ports in France and Italy. One going to Split in Croatia.

“Forty-five are headed to Asia. They’re in the Med too heading for Suez. The Israelis have a special watch on them. But they’re all regular shippers – mostly Japanese - and big companies. Not the type to take a bribe to carry a bomb.

“That leaves us with 11, 6 of which are headed for South America – and are all behaving themselves. The remaining five are going somewhere in Northern Europe.”

“The ones heading for Northern Europe. How are they doing?”

“We don’t know, sir.”

“Can we find out?” A reluctant look on the chief’s face. “Please, Chief, bear with me. I’m not as nuts as I look.”

“Ok, sir. I’ll have to contact NATO. They’d be watching them.”

“More news.” LT Womack said sticking her head in the door. “The Marines are in the air. Also, the *Valhalla* changed course twice. Once due north. Then northeast. She’s now in the shipping lane – Newport News/

Hampton Roads to Portsmouth. But she's in the wrong lane. She's in the westbound lane. She's heading right into oncoming traffic.

"She wants to be seen. I don't get this at all. I don't like it. Chief Doonan, can we continue."

"Yes sir. Four out of the five are accounted for and have already landed without incident. The unaccounted for ship was a small passenger vessel heading due north for Trondheim, Norway. She checked in with Stavanger as she was passing. And then, nothing."

"Nothing? What does that mean?"

"It means that nobody's heard from her since."

"And no one gives a shit? A passenger vessel goes missing and no one cares? Didn't any of the people waiting on the pier at Trondheim wonder where their Uncle Olaf was?"

"Actually, it probably did get there. There's just no report. Let me check, sir." Said Chief Doonan flushing.

"Also, Chief, how big is she? What is her name? How fast is she? You say she's a passenger vessel. That means no cargo at all?"

"Just a second, sir." Chief Doonan said, now clearly flustered.

"Chief, does one of these other computers have access to Google and other civilian type programs?"

"Yes, sir. The one on the far right."

Michael sat down and pulled up a map of Norway. Stavanger was about on the same degree of latitude as the top of Scotland. Looks like about 450 miles north of Rotterdam. "Anything, Chief?"

"Well, got a name. Got a picture. Not much info on the ship itself. Looks like your usual passenger shuttle. Island-to-island type of thing. All over the Caribbean. Wherever they have lots of inhabited islands, like the Baltic too. Its home port is Tumba, Sweden. It can carry some freight, but not much."

"How much?"

"Luggage type freight. You know the passengers' luggage."

"How much space would you say, Chief. As big as this desk?"

"Oh, no. More than that. Big enough for three or four desks that size. The name I can't pronounce. The last two words are something like "av gudarna."

"Av gudarna?" Of the gods. Can you spell me the first name, Chief?"

"B-e-d-r-a-g-a-r-e." As the Chief spelled, Michael typed it into the translate program of the desktop.

"Bedragare av gudarna. Deceiver of the gods." Michael said aloud. "Well, I'll be damned."

"Agent Cornell. I'm going to get some coffee. Want one?"

"Love one, Chief. Black with sugar, please."

Michael sat looking at the map of the North Sea and the Norwegian Sea.

"I hear you're giving my Chief a hard time." CMDR Hall said coming through the door with a smile.

"Just teaching the young man a little detective work, Commander." Michael said returning the smile.

"Yeah, but I gotta ask you something. You're ragging his ass about a ship that went north from Rotterdam. North. In other words, it is going back on the same course it came in on. If your friends took the trouble of taking the bomb all the way south to Rotterdam, why, in God's name, would they backtrack and take it north again?"

"I don't know Commander. But, you know something. The bomb came out of Russia on a ship called Kalupsó. Calypso is a goddess. Now we're chasing a ship of the U.S. coast called *Valhalla*. Valhalla is where Viking warriors go who die in combat. Now the Chief and I are looking for a ship called the *Bedragare av gudarna*, which means, 'deceiver of the gods.'"

"Agent Cornell are you really suggesting that just because these three foreign ships share some colorful literary name origins, that they are all somehow involved in a conspiracy to set off a bomb in the United States of America?"

Realizing what a total airhead he sounded like, Michael retreated by saying: "No, just an odd coincidence.

"Do you know what 'deceiver of the gods' refers to, Commander? It's the name of an album by the Viking death metal group, Amon Amarth. You know where Amon Amarth is out of?"

"Nope."

"Tumba, Sweden. Same place as the ship. Know what 'amon amarth' means? Ever read *The Lord of the Rings*? It's the name for Mount Doom in one of the elvish languages."

"Is this what they teach you at Quantico?"

"Every day. They make us memorize this shit." They both laughed.

Chief Doonan reappeared with the coffee and CMDR Hall left saying over his shoulder: "Don't wear my Chief out with your crap. He's got real work to do."

"Just one more question, Chief? How fast can the ''Gudarna' go?"

"Probably 25 to 30 knots. I'll look it up and see if the owner says.

"Yep. They say it can go 28 knots, and I believe it."

*Okay*, Michael thought. *That's about 33 miles per hour, or about three times faster than the 'Valhalla'.* Michael went back to the computer and its map programs.

It's about 3,300 miles from where the '*Gudarna*' went dark off the coast of Norway and the coast of North America. For a ship that fast, that's four days and change. If the '*Gudarna*' had crossed the Atlantic with the bomb, it would have been here yesterday. Yesterday!

"Chief, can you run a check on the '*Gudarna*' especially their owners? Sort of interested why a ship with such a name would be so off course?"

"Ok, sir." Chief Doonan said with a modest amount of frustration in his voice.

"Agent Cornell, the Marines are in place and beginning the VBSS." LT Womack said from the doorway.

Michael sat for a while and thought. A day and a half from Rotterdam would have taken the '*Gudarna*' to the spot across from Stavanger where they went dark. Three more days from Stavanger would have got them to the U.S. coast. That would have been two days ago.

Another two days and they could have landed anywhere on the North Atlantic coast of the U.S. That would be today!

"Marines have boarded the *Valhalla*." LT Womack said from the other room.

Michael kept looking at the computer maps, this time of the north-east coast of North America. *Yesterday!* He thought. *Where could they have gone*?

"Agent Cornell, it turns out the '*Gudarna*' owners have a little history smuggling dope. Not a big thing, as you know, in Sweden. And, otherwise their record is clean. No significant complaints from passengers. No other trouble."

* * * * *

The Camp Islands comprise 11 tiny spots of land in the North Atlantic just off the southeastern coast of Newfoundland. They are uninhabited. They are about 20 miles due northwest of Bell Isle that lies right in the middle of the Great Lakes-Northern Europe shipping channel of the Gulf of St Lawrence. Belle Isle has the distinction of being the northernmost peak of the Appalachian Mountains that stretch southwest from there to Alabama. It was named in 1534 by French explorer, Jacques Cartier.

The Camp Islands are about 7,000 feet from east to west. There are two relatively large islands separated by a channel running north/south. Below the channel is the third largest of the Camp Islands. The area between these three islands is a well-protected bay.

* * * * *

"Oh fuck/shit!" Came the simultaneous voices of CMDR Hall, LT Womack, and Chief Eldridge who had joined them.

"What?" Michael yelled.

"No goddamn bomb again!" CMDR Hall said. "Just a load of hazardous nuclear waste that these bastards are trying to smuggle to some rural dump, where they've bribed the locals to look the other way while they bury this stuff….. and probably poison their goddamn grandchildren. Shit!"

"Commander, can you get word to the Marines to search that waste – or, better, get the crew to search it - to make sure there's not a bomb hiding at the bottom of that crap."

"I'm pretty sure they will have thought of that, but I'll remind them."

"Chief Doonan, is there a way we can query the Coast Guard or even the Canadian Coast Guard?"

"What did you have in mind, sir?" Chief Doonan said casting a glance at Commander Hall, which Michael saw but ignored.

"I'd just like to know if the Coast Guard or the Canadian Coast Guard have noticed anything – and I mean anything – out of the ordinary?"

Chief Doonan glanced at Commander Hall who nodded.

"Ok, sir. Will do."

Michael retreated to the back room and to the civilian computer console where he sat there looking at maps of the northeast coast of North America.

"Sir?" Chief Doonan said about 10 minutes later. "Neither the U.S. nor the Canadian Coast Guards report anything unfamiliar in the last 24 hours."

"Chief, I didn't just mean today. I meant since we've been doing this search. Like, at least, the last four days."

"You want to know if the U.S. Coast Guard and the Canadian Coast Guard have noticed anything suspicious in the *last four days*?"

"Yes, Chief Doonan. The last four days."

"I'll see what I can do, sir."

* * * * *

"Agent Cornell, the CNO would like to talk to you."

"Admiral McNamara? What's this about?"

"I told you she's been watching this like a hawk. Right now, she's a very unhappy admiral and she'd like to talk to you."

At least there was a headset so that Michael didn't have to talk to Admiral McNamara on a speakerphone in front of all of her people.

"Agent Cornell, when my people are doing their goddamn best to find your fucking bomb floating somewhere in the Atlantic, would you mind telling me why you are ragging their asses about some fucking little passenger boat ferrying people around the Baltic that's gone missing? And some horseshit about all of the vessels we're searching for have some spooky names related to the Norse gods, or something?"

"Admiral, the name of the ship is the *Bedregare av Gudarna*, the deceiver of the Gods. It is owned by a bunch of Swedish stoners. It does 28 knots. That's three times faster than the – borrowing your phrase – fucking *Valhalla* or *Kalupsó*. Although it is a – quote – passenger ship – unquote, its baggage compartment is big enough for about three or four 16-kiloton nuclear warheads. And it has, apparently, disappeared off the face of the earth."

"So, you're telling me that this stinking little island-hopping passenger boat, crossed the 3,000 mile North Atlantic…..with….a...fucking….. nuclear…..warhead…..in

…..its……." A long pause.

"Well, of course that's what happened!" The Admiral said slowly. "We're looking west; they're going north. We're looking at 10-knot freighters; they're doing 28-knot passenger boats. They're crossing the Atlantic in five days; we're looking at 10.

"Sorry for being such a shit, Agent Cornell, put CMDR Hall back on, will you?"

"Sure, Admiral, nice talking to you too." Michael said handing the receiver to CMDR Hall.

"Ok, Agent Cornell." CMDR Hall said putting down the receiver. "You got your wish. We're going to check out every ship that tried to land in Canada or the U.S. in the last five full days."

Michael retreated back to the other room where he could be alone and away from the withering glances of the Navy staff. He sat again looking at the map of North America deciding what to do when they found how the bomb reached North America.

A half an hour later, CMDR Hall said: "Agent Cornell, we may have something. About a week ago, a coastal steamer out of Charleston set out for St. Catherines, Ontario, with a load of farm machinery. But instead of going directly into the Gulf of St. Lawrence through the wide southern channel east of Nova Scotia, it apparently went about 500 miles off its scheduled route - out of its way north - and met up with another vessel just north of a place called Belle Isle, which lies right in the middle of the shipping lane between the Gulf of St. Lawrence and Northern Europe. They met at some uninhabited islands off the southeast coast of Labrador called the Camp Islands. The Canadian version of NSA is going back to find out what the two ships said to each other."

Another 10 minutes passed. CMDR Hall returned. "The ship that the Charleston freighter met had apparently been dark. It only identified itself in code that only the Charleston ship would recognize. But we asked the Canadians to wash the signal from the dark boat against the Europeans' records. The dark boat was the '*Gudarna*."

"And the two ships met when?"

"Three days ago."

"Shit." Michael said looking at the calculations he had made. "They're already in the Great Lakes. I gotta call this one in. I hope to hell it's not too late."

As he was dialing Jim Griffin's number at the Bureau, he asked CMDR Hall what the name of the Charleston steamer was.

"I was just going to tell you that. It's the *Elysian Fields*."

When he heard that, he didn't even look at CMDR Hall.

"Griff. Got a priority one. Our package is on a ship out of Charleston called the *Elysian Fields*. It should be in St. Catherines, Ontario right now. Will you get on to the brethren at the Royal Canadian Mounted Police and ask them to seize the vessel and detain their crew? Will you tell Slevin? I'm on my way in from Ft. Meade right now."

"CMDR Hall, LT Womack, Chief Doonan, It's been great doing business with you. Thanks very much for everything. I'm outta here."

"Agent Cornell, we've got a call in to the CNO. Don't you want to speak with her?"

"Can't afford the time. But please tell her something for me. Tell her that I'm not lost any more. She'll know what that means."

* * * * *

When he retrieved his cellphone from the security gate, Michael noticed there was a voicemail message only seconds before. He thought he knew what it would be about. It was Admiral McNamara.

"Agent Cornell , I just wanted to apologize. Apologize for two things. First, that we didn't help you. Second, for being a pompous ass and mouthing off at you like I did. And last, please keep me in the loop. I want to know what happens."

Michael pushed the "call back" button but the call went to voicemail.

"Admiral, no need to apologize. Your people were great. They were terrific. Really terrific. I asked them to find ships, and they found them. It wasn't your people who fucked up. It was the goddamn FBI agent they were working with who fucked up. It was your guys' job was to find ships – which they did, perfectly. My job was to determine which ship to look for, which I didn't bother doing until it was almost too late. Your team gets an 'A' for ship-finding. Agent Cornell gets a 'D' for detective work. Really, I shoulda gone over those lists days ago. Anyway, I hope to God we're not too late.

"I got your message about keeping you in the loop, which I certainly will do. But let me ask you, is your wish to stay in the loop 100% because you are worried about your country; or is it 95% concern about your country, and 5% because you want to talk to Agent Cornell again?

"Don't bother trying to hide your face. I am talking on a super-duper special FBI phone that let's me watch people blush at the other end of the call, even though I've already hung up.

"Back to you soon."

# CHAPTER 19 - THE BONNIE CASTLE

Kingston, Ontario is at the head of the Thousand Islands in the St. Lawrence River that flows from Lake Ontario, the easternmost of the Great Lakes, up past Montreal and Quebec City into the Gulf of St. Lawrence and then on to the Atlantic Ocean. The term "Thousand Islands" is a misnomer. There are some 1,864 recognized islands in an archipelago that spans 50 miles of river between Ontario and New York. Some of the islands are in the U.S. Some in Canada. It is a perfect place for smuggling. 1,864 places to hide!

Kingston is a good-sized city of about 125,000 but doesn't have a big commercial port. There are only a couple of wharfs just south of the Wolfe Island Ferry Terminal on the Cataraqui River that joins the St. Lawrence there.

The radioactive parts of the bomb were unloaded at Kingston as agricultural equipment and moved 17 miles down the St. Lawrence to Gananoque, a town of about 5,000 permanent residents located where the Gananoque River joins the St. Lawrence.

Because the Thousand Islands were a hub for smuggling, the River often swarmed with Canadian Border Service Agents, Ontario Provincial Police and the RCMP, as well as their American counterparts from the U.S. Coast Guard, Homeland Security, sometimes the New York State Police, but always the Drug Enforcement Administration (DEA). That is because the major commodity smuggled through Kingston wasn't nuclear weapons, but drugs. The Jefferson County Sheriff's Department, was the eighth law enforcement agency in the scrum. They knew the River the best and they coordinated all of the eight agencies' patrolling and other drug enforcement efforts there.

But despite the impressive array of manpower and focus, the eight agencies – collectively – had had little success in stanching the flow of drugs crossing the River.

So, because they were looking for drug smugglers the various police agencies in Kingston took no notice of a small freighter with U.S. markings offloading agricultural machinery. They were looking for other quarry.

Once the RCMP office in Kingston got the word from the office in St. Catherine's, they got right to work. They went over all the traffic to and from the port. They talked to witnesses. They checked the harbormaster's and all of the shippers' paperwork. And they looked at all the surveillance video from the many CCTVs that covered the Kingston waterfront.

They wound up focusing on a small rented flatbed truck. It had left the port and turned right on Ontario Street heading north toward the Lasalle Causeway. The Causeway was highway #2 that hugged the coast all the way down the St. Lawrence.

The driver had used false ID to rent the truck and paid in cash. But from the mileage records and elapsed time, they deduced that the truck had gone no further than Gananoque.

Since the principal commodity smuggled in the Thousand Islands is drugs coming into the U.S., the DEA maintains a close relationship with the RCMP. The DEA didn't have an office on the border, but they had what they call a post-of-duty. The Special Agent-in-Charge was Candice Teresi. Candice was 32. Very young to be an agent-in-charge of anything. But she was that good. The head of the New York office realized that if Candice weren't up there, he'd need to have 4-5 more agents in that area.

The DEA had already been alerted by the FBI when they got the call from the RCMP. The official story was that they were after a shipment of weapons grade plutonium. Absolutely no mention of a bomb.

The RCMP discussed the usual suspects with Candice. The usual suspects were fishing guides who had nice boats, nice cars, nice homes; but didn't seem to have a lot of charter business. One in particular, Mark Wapner, drove a Ferrari and had a new boat with state of the art electronics that would help smugglers avoid detection. Candice sent one of her agents to pay the man a visit.

When the DEA agent showed up on the Wapner's property, he took it in stride as he always did. He had been boarded by the best of them: the RCMP, the OPP, the Coast Guard, DEA, and Homeland Security. None of them had ever found a thing. True to form, Candice's man found nothing.

Candice quickly realized that pursuing this line of investigation would be futile. She and her Canadian counterparts could check all 79 charter captains on her "usual suspects" lists and probably come up with nothing. It was then that she took a secure call from the FBI in Washington. A gentleman named Michael Cornell was on the line.

They talked for over two hours. Candice had been cleared for the real story, so Michael told her they were after a bomb, not a shipment of plutonium.

Candice told Michael all she knew about the smuggling scene in the Thousand Islands. It was all too clear her disappointment that they hadn't made greater inroads against the drug smugglers. Arrests had been few and very far between.

Michael told her what he knew about the passage of the bomb from Russia to Kingston to Ganonoque and that there the trail had gone dead. Smuggling an atomic bomb across an international border was not the same as a routine drug run. Was there no buzz among the "usual suspects" about some big deal? Nothing unusual in any of their behavior? Smuggling a bomb would pay far more than a drug run. Nobody flaunting sudden wealth? The answers seemed all dead ends. Candice had set up relationships with all of the local bank managers. Most charter boat captains regularly made deposits of several thousand dollars a week. Most of their customers were groups of 4-6 avid amateur fishermen who pooled their funds to pay for their trip. So, most of the deposits were in cash. Her bank managers had reported nothing unusual in the last week. But she said she'd check again. Michael said he wanted to come up. Candice agreed to pick him up at the Watertown International Airport, about 35 miles south of the Canadian border.

"Candice, one more thing."

"Sure. What do you have in mind?"

"Can we search the boats of your usual suspects?"

"Sure, but we'll never find anything. They are too clever. They cover their tracks too well. We've never found anything."

"I may have a new wrinkle in mind."

"Oh"?

"What's the nearest military base?"

"Fort Drum. It's the home of the 10th Mountain Division. About 35 miles south of here. Near the airport you're coming into."

"I'll have my office contact them and get some Geiger counters. Let's search the boats with Geiger counters. Whoever brought the plutonium across won't be able to cover those tracks. The Geiger counter will tell us what he carried."

"Ok, sure. Have your office call me with the details. I'll call the Sheriff and see if he can get some of his men to pick them up."

"Oh, yeah, one more thing. This Sheriff, is he the local satrap?"

"Satrap?" Candice laughed.

"You know. The local poobah. The big guy."

"Poobah. Satrap. Yes." She laughed again. "He's not a bad guy. His name is Paul Demske. Big dude. He's the coordinator of all the drug work on the River. Both sides."

"You have a joint operation with the Canadians?"

"Yeah. Excellent relations. We're all on one team. There are three Canadian law enforcement agencies and five of us. We work well together."

"Ah, that brings me to my last point."

"You just *had* your last point: the Sheriff." They both laughed.

"No, really. Did the RCMP give you the dimensions of the shipping crate?"

"Yeah, about 3x3. Weighs about 100 kilos. So, 220 pounds. They said there was one dude who brought it up. He was big, but he had a dolly. All these charter boats have winches and dollies and other equipment to handle stuff. So, with all that, we can assume that one big dude or two little dudes can handle it."

"Candice, can we get a list of all boats registered on both sides of the border that can handle a 3x3 crate weighing 220 pounds?"

"I'm sure we can."

"Your Canadian brethren will come up with theirs?"

"Absolutely."

"Then, let's do it and check all of them."

"Ok. I'll get a hold of the Sheriff and set it up."

"Oh, yeah. Speaking of your friend, the Sheriff, can you arrange for me to meet him. Protocol. Gotta check in with the local poobah and brief him on the operation. I guess I gotta get him cleared to have that discussion too. So, I'll get on it."

"Not a problem. That'll be our first stop."

"Ok, Candice. I think were good. Did I miss anything?"

"Well, I assume you don't have a place to stay. End of the season. Everyplace is packed. But I'm sure I'll be able to get you a decent place."

"Great. That's very kind of you. Anything else?"

"Nope. I think we're good, for now."

"Then all I have to do is figure out how to get to the Watertown International Airport. I assume they don't have direct flights from National."

"Are you kidding me?"

"About what? Direct flights from Washington?"

"You're gonna fly commercial?"

"How else?"

"Your Bureau and my agency each own small airlines. Get a company jet."

"I thought those were just for the directors and the other brass."

"And for peons like us when we're on mega-cases like yours. Just ask your boss. They'll roll out a jet for you. And even a pilot who can find his way to Watertown! You gotta be new with the Bureau."

"Two months of brainwashing at Quantico and two months on the job."

"So, you're the junior officer on this case. You should be picking *me* up at the airport. And I should be riding in the private jet."

They both laughed and rang off.

Michael's next call was to his boss, the legendary Executive Assistant Director of the FBI who was the chief of the National Security Branch, James E. Slevin. Michael briefed Slevin on his conversation with Candice.

"Sounds like your DEA friend has her act together. Good. What's her name?"

"Candice Teresi."

"Candice, huh? Not Candy?"

"No, definitely not Candy."

"Is she pretty?"

"She sounds pretty. But it's tough to tell over the phone."

"Oh, yeah. It is, isn't it?" Said Slevin in his well-practiced, distracted tone of voice. "When are you leaving?"

"First thing in the morning. I was just going to ask if I could get a company plane?"

"Of course, not a problem. I'll call Flight Ops right now and authorize it. I'll call you right back." He rang off.

Five minutes later Slevin was back on the phone.

"You're all set. Just call Flight Ops and let them know when you'll be at National. They'll be there waiting for you. Oh, and yeah. I just did you a favor for which you will owe me the rest of your life."

"What's that"?

"I arranged for Laura Doughty to take care of you in the air."

"Who? What?"

Laura Doughty works for the contractor that flies our planes. She is the best. She's smart. She's nice and she's very pretty. But don't you get any ideas about her."

"Oh? Well, perish the thought Mr. Director. But do I detect a tone of unprofessional interest on the other end of this line?"

"You smart ass. For that insubordinate remark I sentence you to one day in Watertown, New York! Now, you better get out of here. And if you don't come back with an atomic bomb, don't bother coming back. And, as for Laura, my friend, it's all in my dreams. If she only had bad taste in men, I might have a shot at her." Slevin laughed and rang off.

Michael was lucky and he knew it. A direct report to so senior an officer as Slevin was unheard of. Slevin had only eight direct reports: his five division heads, the head of the Intelligence Directorate, the head of the Counterproliferation Center and Michael Cornel, new kid on the block. Furthermore, it was equally unheard of for an analyst or agent as new as Michael to handle so important a case. Slevin could have parked the case in any of three of the five divisions he commanded: Counterintelligence, Counterterrorism, or WMD. Slevin was literally putting his career on the line letting Michael handle the case. If Michael screwed up, both he *and* Slevin would be gone.

Michael caught himself. "Wake up man"! He said to only himself. "This isn't about you and/or Slevin. It's about an atomic bomb! Get over it and get on with it."

* * * * *

"Hi, you must be Laura." Michael said as he climbed the stairs of the Gulfstream 650.

"And you must be Michael Cornell. Nice to meet you."

Shaking Laura's hand, Michael said: "I bring you greeting from the distinguished Executive Assistant Director of the National Security Branch of the Federal Bureau of Investigation."

Laura giggled. "Jim is such a flirt."

Laura closed the door and took Michael's bag.

"Wanna meet your pilots before we take off?"

"Sure." As they walked toward the cockpit.

"Tom? Trish? Meet Agent Michael Cornell."

"Welcome aboard!" They both said, almost in unison.

"Nice to meet you!" Michael said.

"I'm Tom Young," the pilot said extending his hand "and this Trish Apple, my co-pilot."

"Nice to meet you both." Michael said shaking both their hands

"Buckle up, Agent Cornell. We're cleared to taxi."

"Will do. Please call me Mike."

"Please call me Mike." Laura mimicked as she showed him his seat. "You're just like Jim."

"I take that as a compliment. But don't tell him I said that." Laura laughed at this.

Michael thought that around the Bureau Slevin was renowned for his gracious informality. He had a reputation for knowing everyone's name and for calling them by name. This included the greenest admin types, the cafeteria help, and the folks who cleaned the offices and the restrooms. And everyone called him Jim. This was in sharp contrast to the other senior officers who insisted on being called by their titles and who addressed everyone as either Agent, or Miss, Mister, or whatever, but never by first name. Laura seemed to know what he was thinking. She said:

"You know one day he got on board with a cute little pink stuffed animal that he'd bought. Well, you know, Jim works late, so he gets to see the people who clean his office. And there was one guy – his name was Angel, I think – who cleaned Jim's office regularly. And, this guy Angel's wife had just had a baby girl. So, as busy as he was, he took the time to buy a toy for the new baby of the guy who cleaned his office. That's Jim."

Laura stowed his bag and was back in a couple seconds.

"Since you are new on this little bird, I need to go over the safety instructions with you." Which she proceeded to do and then took her seat for take-off.

Once in the air she came back. "Tom just told me we'll just barely be an hour - gate to gate. We're lucky to have Tom as our pilot."

"Oh?"

"Well, I guess not really. All of our pilots are excellent. But Tom Young is probably the best. He flew through hell in Afghanistan. I'm glad he got out of there alive."

"Yeah, I'll say."

"So, you must be the fair-haired boy in the company." Laura went on.

"Why do you say that?"

"How many guys do you think Jim makes flight arrangements for?"

"Oh, yeah. I never thought of that. I guess I am lucky."

"Not lucky. He must think very highly of you."

"That's very flattering. But, if that's the case, I wish he didn't think so highly of me."

"Why?"

"Sometimes I feel like I'm way in over my head."

"Yeah, with the case you're working on, that's pretty understandable."

"You *know* about the case I'm working on."

"I don't know any of the details. Jim just told me it had to do with weapons grade plutonium."

"He did?"

"Yes, I have a security clearance. I had to go down to your office to take my lie detector test."

"Did Jim at least buy you lunch when you were down there?"

"He did, indeed."

That sly fox, Michael thought. Polygraph tests were no longer required for security clearances. Slevin just wanted to get her downtown for lunch.

"Anything to drink?" Laura asked.

"Black coffee with lots of sugar would be great."

When Laura came back with the coffee, Michael said: "Laura, let me ask you something. Are Tom and Trish an item?"

"Oh, Lord no. They're all business. Tom's already married to one of his flying partners."

"Oh?"

"Yeah, they met in Afghanistan. She was an interpreter, I think, in the Army. Anyway, they were bringing this bad guy out of there for interrogation somewhere in the West. Their plane was shot down by a missile just after they took off from Kabul. Tom and this woman, who's now his wife, Sophia Gold, and this bad guy mullah were the only ones to survive the crash. They went down in the mountains that were controlled by the Taliban. So they had to hide in the daylight. Couldn't get very far in the dark with no guide and no lights. And they had to drag the goddamn mullah around who was always looking for a way to give away their position to his buddies. It took them forever to get out of there. After that, Tom got out of the Air Force. Then he married Sophia. Then he wrote a book about their escape from the Taliban with that mullah."

"Really? That's amazing."

"Yeah, the book is called *The Mullah's Storm*, I think. They're making a movie about it."

"Wow! I guess were lucky not just to have him as our pilot, but that he's here at all after that ordeal."

"Yeah. That's for sure. More coffee?"

"No, thanks. If we've only got an hour, I'd better get to work."

The flight was smooth as was the landing at the Watertown International Airport.

"Give us a heads-up as far as you can in advance when you want to leave." Tom said as Michael went to thank him and Trish.

As Michael climbed down the stairs, an unmarked car pulled up on the tarmac, and out stepped Candice Teresi, who stretched her hand out and introduced herself. Candice was about 5'6", had light brown/blondish hair, glasses, and a face that lit up when she smiled.

"Nice to meet you Agent Cornell."

"Candice, we gotta get something straight. It's either Mike or Michael, not Agent Cornell.

"Ok. Which is it, Mike or Michael?"

"Your call. I like both. My mother called me Michael. My dad called me Mike."

"You look more like a Michael to me." Candice smiled. "Let's shoot up to meet the Sheriff in Clayton. Then I'll take you up to Alexandria Bay where you're staying. By the way, Mike or Michael won't work with our Sheriff. He's quite formal. Don't even think of calling him Paul."

"Alexandria Bay. That's the resort town for the Thousand Islands, isn't it? Aren't rooms there hard to come by?"

"For sure. And Labor Day's coming up." But I have a friend who owns a place called the Bonnie Castle. It's the best place in the Thousand Islands."

"Nice to have friends like that."

Yeah. Her name's Cathy Garlock. I'll introduce you. She's only a couple years older than me. She owns the place and she runs the place. She's a lot of fun and she's very nice. You'll like her."

For the rest of the 30+ mile run up to Clayton, Candice talked mostly about how everything worked, who was who, and, inevitably about the dark underside of this otherwise sunny resort.

The Sheriff was, indeed, a big dude. Maybe 280 pounds. But no gut. Lots of muscle. Not someone to tangle with.

"Candice, nice to see you. And you must be Agent Cornell."

"I am, indeed, sir. Thank you for taking the time to see me, Sheriff. I appreciate it."

"What unit are you with at the Bureau?" The Sheriff asked.

"I'm not assigned right now. Just working for the head of the National Security Branch." Michael answered.

Michael told him the story that he had made up, and Slevin had approved, about how some plutonium had gone missing from a laboratory in Eastern Europe and had made its way to Canada destined for the United States. They had traced it to Kingston and then Gananoque and the trail had gone dead.

The Sheriff then took the floor and described how he coordinated the eight law enforcement agencies that patrolled the Thousand islands. Six agencies actually did the patrolling: DEA and Homeland Security went with the Coast Guard. He described how their anti-drug smuggling work was such an uphill battle. He said there were several thousand boats licensed on both sides of the River. What's more, he said, standing at a large map of the River, there are over 1800 places for them to hide. Almost any one of the thousands of boats could ferry a shipment of drugs across the River.

He then described how he had organized the search for the bomb – with the Geiger counters Candice had got from Fort Drum – on all vessels capable of handling a 3x3 crate containing 200+ pounds of cargo. He said that he had got the Ontario Provincial Police to organize the searches on the Canadian side of the border.

"Thank you very much." Michael said when the Sheriff finished. "You're doing a helluva job here, Sheriff, under seriously adverse circumstances. Even in big cities there aren't thousands of suspects and thousands of places to hide out.

"You have also done an incredible job coordinating the eight law enforcement agencies from the two countries. Talk about international cooperation. You've got the model here, Sheriff, that the rest of the world needs to follow. I'm certainly going to tell my people in Washington about your work here."

"Well you certainly impressed our Sheriff." Candice said as they got back in the car.

"I did? How so?"

"When you went to the men's room before we left, the Sheriff told me that you were the most polite FBI agent he had ever met." They both laughed.

"By the way, what happened to your 79 'usual suspects'? The Sheriff was talking thousands of suspects."

"I disagree. There may be thousands of registered boats and thousands of places to hide, but there certainly aren't thousands of happy boaters who know this River well enough to navigate the thousand little rocky places and the millions of rocks that surround the rocky little places – all in the middle of the night. No sir, I reckon there are no more than a hundred people that can do that and the 79 most likely are on my list."

As they got out of the car in front of the Bonnie Castle Resort, Michael said: "Where's your office?"

"Over there." Candice said, pointing out into the River. We and Homeland Security are holed up at the Coast Guard Station over there on Wellesley Island."

"Your office is on an island. How do you get there?"

"The Coast Guard always has a whaler at the city dock here. And, if you have all day you can drive down to the bridge and then back up on the other side."

"Can we go over there and talk?"

"Let's get you checked in and then let's talk here. I've got you scheduled to go on the first Coast Guard boat tonight to see how we do our patrols.

You should get a couple hours sleep before you go. The Coast Guard has two patrol shifts: 9 to 3 and 3 to 9. So, you'll go out at nine."

Candice disappeared as Michael went through the check-in formalities only to reappear with an attractive dark-haired woman with a radiant smile.

"Michael, this is Cathy Garlock, your host."

"How nice to meet you Cathy. Beautiful place you have here. Incredible view of the River. I'm looking forward to staying here."

"It's nice to meet you, too, Michael. Candice says you're going to be very busy, but I hope you have time to enjoy yourself a little. Here's my card. I put my cellphone number on the back. Please be sure to call me if there's anything you need or anything I can do."

Michael and Candice walked through the bar to the terrace and sat down in the calm before the happy hour storm. Candice was laughing.

"What's so funny?"

"Your Irish bullshit." Said Candice still laughing. "I thought I was going to drown in it back at the Sheriff's office. And now you put it on Cathy!"

"All right. You got me, Special Agent Teresi. But now we gotta get some work done."

Michael and Candice went back over all the ways that an atomic bomb could get across the St. Lawrence River. All were blind alleys.

"This makes no sense at all." Michael said when they finished. "They bring an atomic bomb across the Atlantic Ocean. They take it to Canada, because with heightened border security they could never get in through an American port. They take it to Kingston. Why Kingston? Because it's near a smuggling hub. Then they truck it back east to Gananoque. Why Gananoque? Because it *is* the smuggling hub. It would be absurd for the truck that brought the bomb to Gananoque simply to hand it off to another truck going somewhere else in Canada. The bomb simply had to have crossed the River within a few miles of where we're sitting. And the only people the terrorists would have entrusted their bomb too would have to be pros. People who know the River. People who know where the water is shallow and where the rocks are. People who know how to avoid the patrols. It has to be one of your 'usual suspects.'

"So you searched all of the boats with your Geiger counters and nothing turned up?"

"That's right."

"Damn, that's impossible. What about money? Could we check the banks to see if any of the 'usual suspects' have deposited a large amount of cash in the last few days? Doubtful our smugglers were paid with a personal check. Must have been cash. Anything over $10k has to be reported to the IRS. So, the banks would know."

"That's a 'yes' on checking the banks. I said I'd do that and it's already done. And a 'no' on any unusual cash deposits. One the first things I did here was to get to know the bank managers. There aren't that many banks around here. I asked each of them to let me know when any of the 'usual suspects' made a large cash deposit. Problem is that these guys are charter boat captains. Most of their charters consist of amateur fishermen who all chip in for the boat. They almost always pay in cash. At $250-350 for a half-day, these captains take in some fairly significant cash each week. That's what the managers all told me. So, I just told them to give me a shout if they noticed anything unusual or suspicious. My phone hasn't rung. But I'll check one more time, first thing in the morning. Now get some sleep. I'll ask the Coast Guard to pick you up at 9:15 PM at the Bonnie Castle's boathouse."

Michael slept. Then he ate. Then he went to the boathouse where he was picked up by the Coast Guard patrol boat. Then he shivered for the next hour. He had packed for daytime DC, not nighttime Canadian border. After an hour, one of the crew heard his teeth chatter and gave him a suit of foul weather gear to wear. And so he survived without incident until 3 AM when they let him back off at the Bonnie castle boathouse.

"Totally useless." He thought as he walked back to his room. Didn't see or learn a thing of any importance. He chalked it up to team spirit.

Next morning Candice let him sleep till 10 AM before showing up. They met back on the bar terrace.

"Any luck with your bankers?" He asked.

"No, none of the usual suspects made any unusual deposits in the last few days."

"Damn," Michael said.

"Yep. No luck again. But my manager at Key Bank did have one large cash deposit - $9,000. It wasn't one of the 'usual suspects,' though; it was a 93-year old woman named Rosemary Brady." "Yes," Candice read from her notes: "Rosemary D. Brady."

"What was that all about? Rosemary's big deposit?"

"Don't know. I didn't think to ask about a 93-year old."

"Would you?"

"Sure. I can do that. Do you really think our 93-year old Rosemary D. Brady smuggled an atomic bomb across the St. Lawrence River?"

"I guess I'm just curious what a 93-year old woman is doing with $9,000 in cash – just under the IRS 8300 reporting limit – at a time when we know someone paid someone else a lot of cash to smuggle a bomb within a few miles of here."

"Ok. I'll call my manager-friend."

"By the way, what does the 'D' stand for in Rosemary's name?"

"I'll ask." Said Candice as she got up to get some more privacy for her call. When she returned, Candice and Michael discussed exactly how the river patrols were organized, something that was not apparent to someone – like Michael – who was actually on a patrol.

Candice's phone rang.

"Hi Joyce," Candice said. "Find out anything?" Ten seconds of silence, then: "Oh, my God. Her middle name is Demske. That's with an "e," not a 'y'? Hang on a minute. Let me go outside where I can talk."

Michael signed the check to his room. When Candice returned she confirmed that Rosemary Demske Brady was, indeed, the mother of the Sheriff. The bank manager had checked with her teller who confirmed that it was the Sheriff himself who had made the $9,000 deposit.

"I'm going over to the bank. I told Joyce I wanted to see all of the records." Candice said.

"Ok. I'll get onto my office and see what all I can learn about Rosemary's Baby, our Sheriff."

As Candice got out of her car, she called her office and told her two agents to stand by close to Alexandria Bay. She said she'd be needing them.

An hour later she sat in Joyce Neve's office shaking her head. Not only had the Sheriff deposited the $9,000 in cash in his mother's account three days ago, but he had been making cash deposits in the $1,000-$1,500 range every week for the last year. It was about that time that drug smuggling arrests had fallen off sharply on the River. A few months later the DEA had sent Candice to find out why. Now she thought she knew. But she needed proof.

"Joyce, Mark Wapner banks here, doesn't he?" Mark Wapner was the arrogant charter-boat captain with the Ferrari.

"Yeah." Joyce said with hesitation.

"Can I see his account records?" Candice asked.

"Uh. I'm not supposed to do that. Are you going to cover my butt?"

"My Resident Office in Syracuse will have a grand jury subpoena in your hands today."

Joyce produced Wapner's account records that showed cash deposits of $3,000 to $6,000 every week for the last year even during the Winter months. "Oh, my God." Candice said to herself. "I never thought to look at the Winter months. How could Wapner earn thousands of dollars a week during the Winter. Who'd charter a fishing boat on the St. Lawrence River in January?" Candice made a call.

"Kevin. Two things. Get onto Syracuse and get a Grand Jury subpoena for the bank records of Mark Wapner and search warrants for Wapner's home and for the home of Paul Demske. Yes, that's Paul Demske, the Sheriff And don't say a word about this to anyone. Please ask Syracuse to fax the subpoena directly to Joyce Neve, the manager here at KeyBank. Second, tell Danny to go to Wapner's house the minute we get the warrant and let me know so I can meet him there." She rang off. Looked down at Wapner's records again and made another call.

"Kevin? Forgot something. Can you get me the temperatures in Alex Bay over the Winter months? Say December through March? Call me as soon as you find the data. Thanks."

"You think you got something on Wapner?" Joyce asked.

"Maybe so. But I gotta trust you not to say a thing to anyone."

"Your secret's good with me. But watch out for Wapner's wife; she's a real head case. My tellers say she's a real pain in the neck."

"What do you mean?"

"She's Mark's – what should I say – business manager? She handles all the books and all the money. She makes all his deposits. She's a stickler on everything. She hounds my tellers about the overnight interest she loses if she doesn't make deposits before 3 PM. Overnight interest! Like two milli-frickles! Can you believe it?"

"You call him "Mark." Do you know him?"

"I've met him and his wife socially. I've seen them out a few times. He's a good guy. She's the one who's nutso for the money."

"Really? He's the one with the Ferrari."

"Yeah. That's Mark. He's a big little boy. That's his toy. But, it's her that's money crazy. She got her big palazzo of a house. She's the country club lady. She even flies to New York to buy her clothes. Mark's the kind of guy who's happy with an old pair of jeans."

Ninety minutes later Candice met Special Agent Danny Arevalo in the driveway of charter-boat Captain Mark Wapner's home: "Put your spikes on, Danny, today we're playing hardball."

"Mr. Wapner, Special Agents Candice Teresi and Danny Arevalo. We'd like to talk to you."

"Not again! Can't you goddamn people ever stop? You've been through my place, my car, my boat – a hundred times. So, you want another look?"

"We want to talk to you, Mr. Wapner. We have a warrant, if you'd like to see it. And, if you don't let us in, Special Agent Arevalo will handcuff you and take you to our office for questioning. Your call, Mr. Wapner."

Wapner opened the door and walked into his living room and sat down in an armchair. Candice and Danny sat down on the sofa across.

"Mr. Wapner, I have subpoenaed your bank records. I have noted that you regularly deposit $3,000 to $6,000 each week. That seems like good money for a charter boat."

"Not surprising, Agent Teresi. I have the nicest and biggest boat on the River. I can accommodate 10 fishermen. I also charge the most: $750 for a half day, $1,200 for the full day."

"Still that's a lot of charters. Strange that you have so much business when we see you driving your pretty car around so much during the Summer."

"I specialize in night charters. Few people know that night fishing is far more interesting and fruitful than day fishing on this River."

"I see. What about Winter fishing?"

"What?"

"Mr. Wapner, your records show a $4,900 deposit on Monday, February 11th this year. It was the coldest week of the year. The temperature never went above 5 degrees in the preceding 10 days. Could you please tell me where you got the $4,900 from? Did 49 avid fishermen pony up $100 apiece to ride on your beautiful unheated boat for three hours or more in zero degree weather. And, if you tell me they did, you'd better have their names and addresses and the signed receipts for their payments because I am going to call every one of them from right here in your living room. And when we find out who the avid fishermen were that week, then we'll look at who chartered your boat on the other sub-freezing days last Winter"

"I don't remember who any of these people were."

"Well, you'd better ask your wife. The bank says she keeps all your records.

"Let me tell you something, Mr. Wapner." Candice continued. "I'm sure you know about the IRS's $10,000 reporting rule. What you may not know, however, is that when there are a series of large *cash* deposits and you cannot account for the source of that money, then there is a legal presumption that you are avoiding the reporting requirement, that you are breaking the law. So, let me tell you what I am going to do: if you don't tell me what I want to know I am going to arrest you for failure to report your weekly multi-thousand dollar deposits to the IRS. Furthermore, I am going to squeeze you until I find the source of those deposits. And if they didn't come from legitimate fishermen, I am going to put you in prison for the rest of your life.

"You bastard, you're going to put us *both* in jail!" Mrs. Wapner shrieked as she lunged into the room pointing a rifle at her husband. Danny hit her with a cushion deflecting her aim before the shot went off and then tackled her. Candice pulled her gun and held it on Mrs. Wapner until Danny had her handcuffed.

"Mary, what are you doing?" Wapner had screamed as the bullet went over his head.

Candice called the State Trooper barracks just outside of town and asked for immediate assistance.

Before the Troopers arrived, Candice went over to Wapner and stood right in his face.

"Listen, you son-of-a-bitch, you'd better tell me what I want to know."

"What?" Wapner gasped.

“I want to know why no drug smugglers have been arrested in the last year.”

“It’s because we know where the patrols are.” Wapner said in a weak voice.

“How?”

“He tells us.”

“Who?”

“Demske.”

“The Sheriff?”

“Yeah.”

As the Troopers led off Wapner and his wife, Danny turned to Candice.

“Was that stuff about the IRS true?”

“I don’t think so. But it sure worked, didn’t it?”

“Yeah. Why didn’t you call 911 instead of the Troopers?”

“Because the 911 operator would have called the Sheriff’s office.”

“Oh, yeah. That’s what I figured.”

* * * * *

“I’ve had a very exciting afternoon.” Candice said in answer to Michael’s question. “In addition to putting the final nails in the Sheriff’s coffin, I broke up a drug ring and was shot at.”

“Shot at?” Said Michael with alarm.

“Well, close. Let me tell you what happened.”

She told him about the bank accounts. She told him about Wapner's account with all of the money deposited in the dead of Winter when no one in their right mind would charter a fishing boat. Candice told Michael about confronting Wapner whose wife tried to kill him for talking. Wapner told Candice that as soon as the eight law enforcement agencies had agreed on their patrol schedule, the Sheriff would pass the information along to the several charter boat captains that did most of the drug smuggling. This provided the Sheriff with a nice second source of income. He got a percentage of what every smuggler got on every shipment. He hid the money in his mother's account over which he had power of attorney. Wapner said he heard a week or so ago that there was big money coming up for a big shipment – not of drugs – that needed to be brought in. Wapner heard the pay would be $50,000. He said that the Sheriff had caught wind of it and did the crossing himself. What were the smugglers going to do, bite the hand that fed them?

Candice said that she and Danny had tossed the Sheriff's house and found the other $41,000 in a dresser drawer.

"Do you think we have enough to arrest him?" Candice asked.

"No but we should in a few minutes."

"Really, then we'd better find him." Candice said.

"No need. Cathy said he's here. It's the Chamber of Commerce end-of-the-season reception. All the civic poobahs are here, including our Sheriff."

"He's here? Michael, are we going to bust the Sheriff right in front of everyone at the reception?"

"No. Isn't that the Sheriff's boat down there?" Michael asked pointing to the large boat parked at the Bonnie Castle's dock.

"I want to check out the boat. I'll be right back."

About 30 minutes later, as Michael poked around on the back of the Sheriff's Department boat, the Sheriff appeared on the path leading to the boathouse. Michael saw him and sat down on the engine casing facing him.

"Agent Cornell, what brings you here?"

"Nice boat."

"Yeah… it is. What can I do for you?"

"Remember those clumsy World War II Geiger counters that Candice Teresi got from Fort Drum?"

"Yeah."

"Well, this is the latest version." Said Michael pointing to a metal device the size of a cellphone sitting on the floor of the boat. "Know what the flashing red light means?"

"I'll bet you're gonna tell me."

"It means there's been a large amount of radioactive material – probably weapons grade – that's been here in the last few days."

"That's not possible. This is a Department boat. Nothing happens on this boat that I don't know about."

"I think that's what we should talk about."

"Oh?"

"Yeah, but first let me say how impressed I am with your generosity to your mother."

"What the hell are you talking about?"

"I'm talking about the $9,000 cash deposit you made to your mother's bank account this week – all in $20 bills. And I am talking about the other $41,000 in $20 bills in your top dresser drawer."

"You searched my house, you son-of-a-bitch?"

The Sheriff began to raise his right hand to his holster.

"I wouldn't do that, Sheriff."

"Candice?"

"I have my gun pointed at the back of your head. So do the two Troopers with me. If you touch your weapon, you're a dead man."

* * * * *

Candice drove Michael out to the State Police barracks just outside of town on Route 12.

"That was nice work." Michael said as they got in the car."

"When you went down to the boat I called the troopers for back-up. Fortunately, those two were in town and came right over. A few minutes later, I saw the Sheriff come out of the reception and head on down to the boathouse. So, I signaled the Troopers and we followed him."

"I've gotta say, if I hadn't seen you behind him I wouldn't have been so brave."

"What would you have done?"

"Jumped overboard and floated out to sea." Candice laughed at this.

"You know, just for an instant – when you told him he'd be a dead man if he went for his gun – I thought he'd do it. I thought he'd pull his gun and you and the Troopers would have shot him."

"You mean 'suicide by cop'"?

"Yeah, just a feeling."

Candice, Michael and one of the Troopers sat with the Sheriff in the interrogation room.

The Sheriff told them all he knew, which wasn't much. He said he had been contacted by one of the Canadian drug smugglers. The smuggler told him there was serious money involved: $50,000. The Sheriff had told the smuggler that this time he wanted the big money, not the usual percentage he got for protecting the smugglers. What could the smuggler say?

So, the Sheriff picked the crate up at a public landing just west of Gananoque and brought it to the public landing in Clayton. The crate had been delivered by a big man in a flatbed truck. Another man met him at the landing in Clayton where they loaded the crate onto his pick-up truck. He said he didn't know anything about what was in the crate. He didn't know anything about radioactivity till Candice showed up with her Geiger counters. Then he looked at Candice and at Michael and broke down in tears.

"You think that's all he knows?" Candice asked as she and Michael went to get the sobbing Sheriff a coffee from the kitchen.

"Yeah. The tears tell me he'd told us everything."

"What do you mean?"

Just then there was a loud crash and a thump in the interrogation room. Candice and Michael turned back to run. Then they heard the shot.

When they got the door open they saw the Trooper staggering to his feet and the Sheriff lying on the floor with a pool of blood under his head and the Trooper's pistol in his hand.

"You ok?" Candice said to the Trooper.

"Yeah." He said shaking off the pain of the fall.

"So it wasn't 'suicide by cop,' just plain suicide." Candice said as the other two Troopers in the barracks barreled into the room and began to call 911.

"Yeah. We shoulda never left the room." Michael said. "I was afraid something like this would happen when he started to cry."

"What do you mean?"

"I think he knew his life was over. Disgrace. Prison. A man like that. He *was* his badge. If he wasn't the Sheriff, he was nobody. He didn't want to be a nobody."

It was a long night. A suicide in a State Police barracks was not something anyone was going to take lightly, especially when it was a well-known County Sheriff. The Troop D Commander of the State Police flew up from Oneida in a helicopter. The Undersheriff drove up from Watertown. By the time the interviews were over, and the official statements taken and signed, it was almost dawn.

Candice and Michael went to her car. She started the ignition. Then she just looked straight ahead for a few seconds. Then she turned to Michael, grabbed his tie, pulled him toward her and put her face about six inches from his.

"Listen, Agent Cornell, you shoulda said something. We mighta saved the Sheriff's worthless life. The Trooper might have been killed. *We* might have been killed. You may be the new kid on the block; but you gotta learn to rely on your instincts. Next time, say something."

# CHAPTER 20 – THE USGS

The trigger mechanism of the bomb had been unloaded at Port Weller in St. Catherines, Ontario, and taken away in a rental truck. But this time the terrorists took the crate to a freight consolidator who routinely took shipments over the U.S. border. It was labeled "farm machinery" and was consigned to a commercial warehouse in Buffalo, New York. The men quizzed the consolidator as to which of the four bridges across the Niagara River between the US and Canada he would use for the crossing. He told them he would cross the Peace Bridge at Buffalo. Mustafa thought that crossing the Peace Bridge with the bomb detonator was a nice piece of poetry.

Two days after the crate arrived at the Buffalo warehouse, the leader of the terrorists, Jamal, picked it up with an SUV that he had rented. He drove it about 50 miles south on the New York State Thruway, I-90, to a small warehouse the locals call the DuraMold Hangar, which he had rented near the Jamestown Airport. There he would rendezvous with the other two terrorists who were bringing the radioactive core from Alexandria Bay.

Mustafa originally thought that moving the bomb from the DuraMold warehouse to Yellowstone would be easy. The direct route almost all the way to the park was I-90.

Interstate Highway 90 – at just over 3,100 miles – is the longest highway in the United States. It runs from Seattle in the West to just near Logan Airport in Boston in the East.

Mustafa's men had to get the warhead from Jamestown to Livingston, Montana, a town just north of Yellowstone Park. The driving distance between Livingston and Jamestown is 1,827 miles on I-90. Much of I-90 in the Midwest and West has a speed limit of 70 mph. Mustafa had originally instructed his men to stay on I-90 and keep right to the speed limit. He didn't want them stopped for speeding. But he didn't want them attracting attention by driving too slowly, either. So, with meals and rest stops he figured about an average of 50 mph. So, he thought it would take them about 37 hours to get the bomb to Livingston.

Then Mustafa got a message from Jamal, who was already in the US. The message asked if there was an address that could be used for a thing called an E-ZPass. This was an electronic device that drivers mounted on their dashboard. It was used to pay tolls. A sensor at each lane at toll barriers probed the E-ZPass for the vehicles account number, to which it then charged the toll.

The E-ZPass system sent the owner of the vehicle a hard-copy statement of how much had been charged to the owner's credit card the preceding month. The E-ZPass application required a mailing address. So, Jamal asked Mustafa had an address that he could use in the US.

*Good thinking.* Mustafa mused. A foreign address might arouse suspicion.

But Mustafa didn't have an address in the US. So he queried his contacts at the *Stiftung Erdlust* in Munich. They might have an address in the US that he could use.

What did he need the address for, the Germans asked? Mustafa told them that it was just for some American driving toy called an E-ZPass.

Was it an electronic toll collector, the Germans asked once more? And was it a passive device? Yes, Mustafa replied to the former, and said he would find out about the latter. So, he messaged Jamal asking how E-ZPass worked. Jamal confirmed that E-ZPass was, indeed, a passive electronic device. That meant that the E-ZPass was actually a transponder that could pick up signals from the E-ZPass device on the car's dashboard. Electronic signals are actually a form of radiation. What other forms of radiation could the transponder pick up?

That is exactly what the Germans were thinking. Mustafa knew there was a low grade residual or radiation coming from the bomb. Not enough to give anyone radiation poisoning. But detectable, certainly by devices like a Geiger counter.

Could the E-ZPass detect the bomb? The Germans said they would investigate and get back to Mustafa.

When they came back the answer was "yes". E-ZPass could definitely detect an atomic bomb passing through a tollbooth on Interstate 90. This presented Mustafa with a serious setback. Much of I-90 was toll road. The E-ZPass sensors would detect the residual radiation from the bomb. E-ZPass would notify the State Police that a radioactive cargo had passed through the toll barrier. The State troopers would begin hunting. It was a game Mustafa didn't want to play.

So, Mustafa's men couldn't travel those road segments. That meant they'd have to take many secondary roads that went through cities and towns. This dramatically increased their chances of being stopped. It also dramatically increased the time for the trip.

The New York State Thruway is I-90 and it is a toll road. Mustafa's men didn't have to worry about it. Jamestown is just north of I-86 which runs east/west across the Southern Tier of New York and joins I-90 in Pennsylvania where it is not a toll road. From Jamestown to Cleveland, they'd be ok. Then much of I-90 was toll road all the way to Wisconsin.

Coming down from the Thousand Islands with the radioactive core had presented the same problem. From Alexandria Bay on the Canadian border, the men had driven I-81 south, which isn't toll. But at Syracuse, they couldn't turn west onto the Thruway toward Buffalo because of the tolls and the E-ZPass sensors. So, instead, the men kept on I-81 south to Binghampton and then took I-86 west to Jamestown. Much longer, but safer. No tolls. No toll barriers. No E-ZPass sensors.

* * * * *

While Candice Teresi had done the great job of flushing out Sheriff Demske as the bomb smuggler, Michael had worked in his room at the Bonnie Castle. Michael was hoping desperately that someone up here in the Thousand Islands had talked to the terrorists who picked up the bomb, seen them, seen their vehicle – something – anything – that might point to where they were taking the bomb.

What in the hell was he going to tell Slevin? What could Slevin tell the White House? That they got tipped off by the Russians. That they traced the bomb from St. Petersburg to Murmansk and then to Polyarny. Then they tracked the little freighter from Polyarni to Rotterdam and then the Med. Then they were fooled by a decoy freighter carrying nuclear waste. Then they found a passenger ship that brought the bomb from Europe to the Canadian coast, rendezvoused with a U.S. freighter who delivered the bomb in two pieces to Ontario. Then they caught the bastard – a fucking County Sheriff – who smuggled the bomb into the U.S. All of this; and then the trail went dead? Dear God! After all that, the trail goes dead in upstate New York!

Finally, just before Candice returned, Michael took a call from Jim Griffin.

"Mike, the USGS people want to see you as soon as possible when you get back; but their preliminary analysis is that your bomb is headed for the San Andreas fault and the City of San Francisco."

*Dear God, not one disaster, but two. First a blast that could kill millions and poison millions more, then an earthquake that could kill even more millions of people.*

*When most Americans think of earthquakes they think of San Francisco. In October 1989, the World Series was being played by two teams that lived across San Francisco Bay from each other: the San Francisco Giants and the*

*Oakland Athletics. At 5:04pm on October 17, during the warm-ups for Game 3, a 6.9 magnitude earthquake hit about 60 miles south of San Francisco. Because almost all sentient beings in the Bay area were glued to televisions sets instead of in their cars on the way home from work at 5:04pm, the quake killed only 63 people.*

*Millions of people were watching the pre-game show. When the quake hit, the power went out at the stadium; TV screens around the world went dark. The World Series went off the air, and because of the damage done to bridges and elevated highways in the Bay area, did not resume for 10 days.*

Michael was stewing on all this horrible information when he got the presence of mind to call Griff back.

“Griff, ok, there’s no denying that setting the bomb off in San Francisco would be a monumental shit-show of the first order; but if they want to destroy a chunk of California, why bring the bomb in through upstate New York? Why not Charleston or Savannah or a port on the Gulf? Or why not even go through the goddamn Panama Canal and take it straight to the West Coast? I don’t like it when things don’t add up - like this.”

“Mike, I’ve been thinking the same thing since I got the good news from the USGS. I don’t know the answer. But the facts are that the bomb was in upstate New York the day before yesterday and sooner or later it’s supposed to show up in California. I don’t know. But maybe our FIGs guys can help figure this out.”

“Can you contact them?”

“Sure thing, their National Coordinator is one floor down. When are you back?”

“Dunno yet.” Michael said. “I’ll let you know when I know.”

* * * * *

"Ok, Mikey boy, let's find your bomb." Griff said as Michael Cornell walked in the door to their offices at FBI headquarters. Griff knew Michael hated being called "Mikey boy", but he liked to rattle him once in a while.

"You fucking geezer." Michael came back, knowing Griff didn't like to be reminded of his age. "What do we do now?"

"Off to the USGS. I talked to my friend, Hank Heasler, who is the chief geologist out in Yellowstone Park. The person to talk to at USGS is Virginia Green." Griff said. "She's the Chief of Staff over there. Hank says she knows everyone. She'll put you on to the right folks in their shop. Hank said he'd call her and ask her to call you. I told him you'd be back around now. So, be expecting a call from Virginia Green. Ok, sunny boy? Got that?"

"Got it. Thanks, Griff."

Michael's phone interrupted. It was Virginia Green, the USGS' chief of staff. She asked if Michael could come out to meet with their Director, Dr. James F. Davis.

"Shit," Michael thought. He knew this was important. But he also knew that titles get in the way. Reluctantly he agreed. Two hours later he was ushered into Davis' office at USGS headquarters in Reston, Virginia.

"Agent Cornell, I'm Jim Davis."

"Do you prefer 'Director,' or 'Dr. Davis?'"

"Actually, I prefer 'Jim.' I think titles get in the way. And you? Do you prefer Mike or Michael?"

"Actually, I like both. But Mike will do fine." He smiled. He liked Davis instinctively. Davis grinned back.

"Mike, the reason you're talking to me right now is that my staff have concluded that a possible earthquake is what we are most likely looking at. Before I came here I was the State Geologist in California. Earthquakes are what geologists do in California. I built a whole seismic network out there to keep track of them. So, if it's ok with you, I'd like to have one of my senior seismologists give you a little course in Earthquake 101, while I take a call from the Secretary. Then I'd like to talk to you about California and the San Andreas fault and what just could happen. Ok?"

"Sure thing."

The San Andreas fault seemed logical, Michael thought. A 16-kiloton bomb, detonated at 2,000 feet above downtown San Francisco would flatten about 5 square miles of the city. That's what happened in Hiroshima. Radiation poisoning would kill millions more. It would also set off a major earthquake that would kill tens of millions of people as it ripped up the coast of California.

The door to Dr. Davis private conference room opened and in walked an attractive 40-ish redhead with freckles and the whitest teeth Michael had ever seen glowing through her smile.

"Agent Cornell, I'm Dr. Cheryl Jaworowski."

"Will you call me Michael if I promise to call you Cheryl?" Michael joked.

"I see our straight-laced and formal director's attitude has rubbed off on you." Cheryl joked back.

"Ok, Michael. Jim said to do Geology 101 and then Earthquake 101. Is that good with you?"

"Sure thing."

"Ok. Here we go. Now, the earth is round….." She laughed again.

"At the center of our planet is a solid iron core about 1600 miles across. On top of that is an outer core that is about 1400 miles thick, which is made up of molten iron. On top of that is another 1800 feet of mantle. The mantle is made up of several elements such as iron, aluminum, silicon and magnesium. It is plastic, viscous. It moves – geologically speaking. Finally, at the surface of the earth is the crust, which is from 5 to 25 miles thick. The boundary between the crust and the mantle is called the Mohorovicic discontinuity….."

"Whoa! The what? I gotta write this one down."

Cheryl laughed and spelled it for him as he wrote.

"Gotta remember to use this at cocktail parties." The both laughed again. "Back to business."

"The crust is not a single, brittle cap on all of these boiling minerals. Rather, it is composed of many – what are called – "tectonic plates" that sort of float on the asthenosphere, which is what the top part of the mantle is called."

"'Tectum,' in Latin, means roof." Michael said.

"Yes, that's it. The tectonic plates are like a series of roof panels on the planet's surface."

"Most earthquakes occur along plate boundaries. Most, but not all. As a matter of fact, most people think that the San Andreas fault earthquake that destroyed San Francisco in 1906 was the largest one in American history. It was; but it wasn't the most significant. The most significant earthquake occurred in 1811 in Missouri.

"Missouri?"

"Yes, to put this in perspective, the San Francisco event was felt over about a 6,200 square mile area. The earthquake in Missouri was felt over one million square miles."

"Whoa!"

"Whoa, indeed!"

"What was going on in Missouri that made that happen?"

"Well, we aren't absolutely certain. But here's what one humble scientist believes.

"Think of pressure from the mantle welling up under a plate on the crust. Sooner or later the crust is going to fracture and the plate will break in two. Think of the 'peace sign' – three 120 degree angles inside a circle. Well, the fracture is along each of those three lines. That chunk – two-thirds of the circle – breaks away – along two of the three fracture lines - from the other third. But the big piece now has a fracture line going right down the middle."

Cheryl took Michael's pad and drew on it. "Here, it's like this."

"Now, as the pieces move apart, the pressure eases and the bulges sink. As they do, the crust can break causing massive earthquakes. The axis of the fracture is called the 'failed arm'. This slowly sinking structure is called an 'embayment'. When you look at a map of the center of the country, most people call the primary feature the Mississippi Valley. We geology nerds call it the Mississippi Embayment. So, that's what happened in Missouri. A huge piece of crust one day just sunk.

"That type of earthquake is what we call a 'dip-slip' quake. They are the biggest quakes. The more common form of earthquake is the kind that happens along the San Andreas fault. Those are called 'strike-slip' quakes. There one plate is 'slipping' by another one. In this case, it is the Pacific Plate that is moving north along the edge of the North American Plate. Needless to say, these plate boundaries are never smooth. So, 'slipping by' is definitely a misnomer. It's more like they're grinding into each other. When there's no give, the pressure builds up. When the pressure builds up to the point where the rock formations can no longer take the strain

– bingo – one plate shoots by the other and the ground shakes like hell. Major earthquake!"

Suddenly the door shot open and Jim Davis came in. "How's your student doing, Cheryl?"

"Well, he totally lost it with the Mohorovicic discontinuity. And, I could tell by his funny little grin that he was going to say something smart about dip-slips and strike-slips when you just came in." She said with her nice white smile.

"Mike, you got all the good stuff in one day. It took me eight years. We usually require students to show ID before we discuss the 'Moho.'" They all laughed one more time.

"Cheryl, I need a few minutes alone with this federal law enforcement officer."

"No problem, Jim. Michael, it was really nice to meet you. If you have any questions," she said handing him her card, "please don't hesitate to call."

"I enjoyed meeting you too, Cheryl. Thank you for all your help and patience."

"Michael, I just talked to Hank Heasler out in Yellowstone. Yes, geology is a small world. Hank and I go back to graduate school. He's one of the brightest guys in the business. Don't know how he got mixed up with that National Park Service crowd. The word Hank passed to me is that you have some bad guys that want to set off an explosion that will create a natural disaster. Is that right?"

"Right."

"Well as I said when we met, I think you should focus on the San Andreas fault."

"Ok. But what about that earthquake in Missouri? Cheryl said it was far more powerful than the one in San Francisco."

"It was. But we don't know – for sure – what happened. We certainly don't know what caused it. And, if we don't know, you can be sure that your bad guys don't know.

"No. Setting off another San Francisco earthquake would be a very major disaster. Much, much worse than the World Trade Center.

"Michael, most people remember the relatively small earthquake that struck San Francisco a few years ago during the World Series. Relatively speaking, that was nothing.

"The real San Francisco earthquake happened at 5:12 in the morning on April 18, 1906, when the world out there was asleep. The real damage was not so much the earth tremors as what happened as a result of those tremors. In those days there were gas mains and there were plenty of gas and oil lamps. As the buildings shook, the gas mains broke. As the buildings shook more they knocked over the gas and oil lamps. Some 2,831 acres were burned to a crisp. A total of 28,188 buildings were destroyed. In those days there were about 400,000 people in the city. Only about 3,000 died. But more than half of the total population were left homeless. Today, in the nine-county bay area, there are about seven and a half million people. Miles and miles of bridges, tunnels, and roads. Thousands of high rises. No, Mike, a major quake on the San Andreas fault today would easily kill more than a million people. If that's what your terrorists are up to, they've simply got to be stopped."

"Who said anything about terrorists?"

"C'mon. Whaddya telling me? You've maybe got a bunch of bank robbers going to set off an earthquake so they can knock off a couple of banks?"

"You didn't hear it from me."

"Deal."

"So, Jim, how do we stop them?"

"I think we have to assume that they will attack one of the asperities along the northern leg of the fault. Somewhere between Santa Rosa in the north and Santa Cruz in the south."

"Uh, sorry. Asperities?"

"I guess Cheryl didn't get that far in the lesson plan." Davis said with a kind smile. "She did explain strike-slip earthquakes, yes?"

"Yes."

"Asperities are the points along the plane of a fault where the 'slip' occurs. It's where the earthquake, itself, starts – the epicenter of the quake. Plates are trying to move past each other." Davis said, illustrating with his hands. "Then they get stuck and don't budge. It's that precise point that we call the asperity.

"When the plates stick, pressure builds and builds and eventually releases when the plates slip. That's what a strike-slip earthquake is.

"So, if you want to cause a serious earthquake, you would attack one of the asperities where the most people are – between Santa Rosa and Santa Cruz.

"How many asperities are there in that area?" Said Mike going back to his notebook.

"I wish we knew."

"Oh, God. I was afraid you were going to say something like that!" Mike said wincing.

"Mike, let me explain. When I was State Geologist in California, I set up a network of over 1,200 earthquake monitoring stations with over 8,500 instruments. The State Government didn't give me the money to do that because they think geology is cool. They wanted my people to learn more about strong ground motion so that we could inform building codes. The State wanted buildings to be more resilient to earthquakes. We know there are going to be more. And we know that some of them will be big quakes. But, most of all, we want people in buildings to survive them.

"I guess what I'm saying is that my 8,500 instruments don't look for where the plates are stuck; they are looking for where they are slipping – albeit begrudgingly – by each other. That's how we learn the effects of ground motion on buildings. If the ground's not moving, our sensors pick up zippo and we don't learn anything."

"Shit. Is there *anything* they can tell us?"

"Maybe. Maybe."

"Let me ask you something. If you were standing at a surface offset and dropped a firecracker – or even a couple sticks of dynamite – down the fault, there would be a boom but nothing else. Nothing at all would happen.

"What I am saying is that there are millions of tons of rocks on both of those plates that are pushing on one another. You would have to have one hell of an explosion to get them to slip. One absolutely enormous explosion! Are your bad guys capable of that? Are they capable of an explosion that would budge several million tons of rock?" Davis looked Mike straight in the eye for a very long second.

Michael stared right back. "They are." He said very deliberately. Davis had guessed they were dealing with a nuclear device. Thankfully, he didn't say anything that Mike would have had to lamely deny.

"Well, if that's the case then they're going to have to do some serious digging somewhere along that fault – wherever they think there might be an asperity. And, when they dig, my 8,500 little seismographs will hear them. That's absolutely for sure.

"In addition to whatever the instruments can tell us, I'm sure my old crew out in Sacramento can also help. They certainly know where every inch of that fault is in the Bay Area. If your people are looking for people messing with the fault, my people can certainly tell them where to look.

"And, second, I'll have my people all over the country – as well as the California people – comb the literature. Some scientist just might think that he has identified a possible asperity. If so, he would have written about it. If so, we'll find it.

"What are your next steps, Mike?"

"I actually report to a guy named Slevin." Michael said to Dr. Davis. "He's the #3 at the bureau. I will brief him and I am certain he will get on to our San Francisco office immediately. He will also send them all the reinforcements they will need."

"Ok. On my end I will brief everyone here as USGS and get them hunting for asperities and even any theories on how to find asperities. I will have Virginia get onto you with whatever they come up with.

"I will also call my successor in California and impress upon him how serious this matter is. He is a good man. I am sure he will assemble everyone possible who can help. I'll find out who's in charge of his team and get it to you through Virginia."

"Thanks so much, Jim. I really appreciate both the education as well as all your help."

Virginia called a cab for Michael, which took him to the Reston station of the new Silver Line on the Metro. Michael loathed DC traffic. He took the Metro whenever possible. Tonight he took it from Reston to Metro

Center, a few blocks from the J. Edgar Hoover Building at 9th Street and Pennsylvania Avenue.

He hadn't eaten all day. He wished he could go to the Old Ebbitt, one of his hang-outs. A couple of cocktails – Mojitos since it was Summer – and a good meal was just what he needed. But he couldn't. Cocktails weren't on the agenda with what he was up against. Maybe a good British beer – just one – at the Elephant & Castle. Maybe. But nothing was going to happen till he got back to the Navy Intelligence people at Ft. Meade. But first, Jim Griffin.

On his way back in, Michael called Griff and asked if they could meet in one of the Bureau's SCIFs as soon as he got back.

"Griff, humor me for a minute, will you? Let me ask you: there are three ways you could get a bomb from Rotterdam to San Francisco. First, take it through the Panama Canal. Second, take it around South America through the Straits of Magellan. Third, land it somewhere on the East or Gulf coasts of the US and truck it, or whatnot, out to California.

"I've got to think that the Straits of Magellan is the least likely. First, it would take the longest by far. And, second and more importantly, it would be easy for the Navy to trace. Of the 56 ships the Navy was looking at, how many do you think were headed for the Southern tip of South America? Maybe one? Possibly two?"

"Agreed." Griff said. "But the other two options aren't good either."

"Why?"

"There are radiation sensors all over the Panama Canal."

"There are?"

"Yep. They're not looking for atomic bombs. They're looking for illegal shipments of hazardous nuclear waste. There is a burgeoning business in the illegal disposal of hazardous nuclear waste. There isn't much publicity about it; but its there. Countries, other than the US and Western Europe, that have nuclear reactors often engage in side businesses of selling nuclear materials rather casually. The buyers of these materials need to get rid of them when they're spent. It's not easy to do. Hence, a bunch of entrepreneurs on the dark side have started up a highly lucrative business of taking this radioactive material to some deserted areas all across the globe and burying the stuff. Nasty business. We, Interpol, and other agencies in developed countries, are just catching onto this. Some countries obviously don't care. They're in the business. But we have been able to put sensors at some critical points along international trade routes. The Panama Canal is definitely one of them.

"Our little bomb is undoubtedly packed in lead shielding. But the lead doesn't absorb all of the radiation. The sensors at the Canal would definitely pick our bomb up.

"That brings us to the third option: landing it on the East or Gulf coasts and trucking it across the US. Unfortunately, that's not easy either."

"Why? I mean driving an atomic bomb a couple thousand miles across the US doesn't sound like a smart idea; but what's your take on this?" Michael said.

"Same problem as the canals: sensors. We have – through our network of Fusion Centers – clued the state highway patrols in about the hazardous nuclear waste problem. Oh, yes, we have it here in this country as well; but to a much lesser degree than around the world. You know how every State has truck weigh stations? Well, now every state police unit manning those stations has those cute little portable radiation detectors – PRDs – like the one you have.

"Of course, trucks below a certain weight don't have to pull in to those stations; so most States outfit all of the commercial vehicle division units of their highway patrols with PRDs as well. If they don't catch them at a weigh station, they can catch them on a routine stop. Or a not-so-routine stop, if you get what I mean?

"And, Mike, there's one more thing. Something the general public knows nothing about – but I am sure that our terrorist friends do – is that the E-ZPass machines on all toll roads can detect nuclear radiation as well."

"They can?"

"Yep. They're sensors. When you pass under them, they send a message to your unit to identify itself, so they can bill you for the toll you are going through. Your unit responds with a signal of its own. That signal is radiation. All we had to do was ask the E-ZPass people to tune their receivers to x-ray frequencies as well, and bingo, the E-ZPass now knows when Michael Cornell's car is going through the toll barrier and it also knows if Mikey Boy is transporting nuclear material. Neat, huh?"

"So what you're saying is that the Panama Canal is totally unlikely and that the other two alternatives are unlikely too?"

"I'm afraid so."

"Shit. Back to square one."

# CHAPTER 21 - THE ROAD WEST

"So, what do we do, my friend?" Michael asked Jim Griffin when he got back from the USGS. "A bomb comes ashore in Alexandria Bay, New York and has to find its way to San Francisco. How do we find it?"

"Way ahead of you – as usual." Griff said with his usual twinkling eye. "We go see the FIGs."

"The Field Intelligence Groups, huh?" Michael knew there was a Field Intelligence Group in each of the FBI's 56 field offices. They were responsible for gathering information about threats to the United States and for disseminating that information within the intelligence community and, as appropriate, to state and local law enforcement agencies.

After 9/11 the FBI had worked with the States to create centralized offices to gather and coordinate information about threats. These offices were called "fusion centers". There were 75 of them throughout the United States. The FIGs in each field office worked closely with the fusion centers in their States.

Griff had already briefed Gerry Martinez, the National Coordinator of all of the Field Intelligence Groups. Gerry's office was right down the hall. "He's in and waiting to talk to us." Griff said putting down the phone.

* * * * *

"Nice to meet you." Michael said to Martinez as he and Griff entered his office.

"Nice to meet you too, Mike. I've done a little homework since Griff talked to me. I hope it'll be helpful.

"As I understand it, your device entered the U.S. at Alexandria Bay, New York, in about a 3x3 container that is relatively lightly insulated. Griff also tells me you think it's heading to San Francisco. That said, they are probably driving the bomb down 81 to 83 to 95 all the way to Raleigh. Then they're getting on to I-40 and taking it all the way to California."

"Wow! Isn't that the long way? I looked at a map, myself, and it looks like I-80 is the shortest way to San Francisco."

"It is, for sure. But for your terrorists, it's not safe. As you already know, the device gives off radiation. That radiation can be detected; and we have to assume your terrorists know this. I-80 is pocked with tolls. Nowadays, every lane at a toll barrier has an E-ZPass transponder. These transponders will detect your device. They will then inform the state highway patrol who will, based on the timing of the toll passage, be able to close in on the vehicle carrying the radioactivity. I think we have to assume that your terrorists know this. So, we need to focus on I-40.

"I have sent priority one alerts to each field office on the I-40 corridor, including the States along the east coast between Alexandria Bay and Raleigh. Those States are New York, Pennsylvania, Maryland, Virginia, North Carolina, Tennessee, Arkansas, Oklahoma, Texas, New Mexico, Arizona and, of course, California. I have told them that we are searching for a shipment of weapons grade plutonium that is radioactive, that is approximately 3x3 and weighs 220 lbs. I have told them this is priority one and that they should contact all fusion centers and seek out any reports of any suspicious vehicles or incidents. I have told them to report to me immediately with any leads. That was about an hour and a half ago. So far, nothing."

When Michael got back to his own office, he had two messages. One was from Slevin, of course, wanting to know what he'd learned at USGS. The other message was from Jim Davis. Davis' number didn't have a 703 area code. It had a 916. That's Sacramento. It wasn't Davis' office number; it was his cell. Why did he want to talk to Michael? Michael figured that Dr. Davis might have some more information, so he dialed the number.

"Mike?" It had never occurred to Michael that his number would register on caller ID. He had just assumed that all Bureau phones had their caller IDs blocked.

"Yeah, Jim, what's up? Shoot, so to speak."

"Mike, there are two things I totally missed when we were talking. After you left, it finally sunk in how vitally important your questions were. After thinking about what we talked about, I realized I missed two huge points.

"First, is the asperities. Your bad guys have to know where there's a major asperity in the Bay Area! Or think they know. Otherwise they'd just be shooting blind! I can't imagine they would go to all of the effort they must already have gone through without knowing where to put the bomb.

"So, Mike, I'm sure the FBI has relationships with sister agencies all over the planet. Ask them to put every ounce of muscle they can – look at every university, every consulting firm, every earth science laboratory – all over the world – not just this country - for a theory – no matter how daft it might sound – for identifying asperities. Or for anyone who thinks they've identified an asperity along any fault anywhere on the planet. We here at USGS have good relations with our sister agencies around the world. I will put out the same requests to all of them. The terrorists must know where an asperity is. We absolutely need to find out what they know. If we can just find out what the terrorists know about asperities, that will lead us right to them."

"I understand. Thanks very much. I'll get right on this. Oh, and what was the second thing you were going to say?"

"Mike, this may be some good news for a change. I think my 8,500 seismographs probably do know where the asperities are."

"Say again."

"I thought you said they listen for slips, right?"

"Right."

"Mike, listen: the asperities aren't where the slips *are*. They're *where they aren't*."

"Whoa! What?"

"Every time those plates move an inch, my instruments hear them. And, more importantly, they record exactly what they hear and calculate the exact coordinates of each slip.

"Mike, if there is an asperity, then the plates aren't slipping. The machines hear nothing. And, again, most importantly, they record nothing.

"So, if I get all of the records from all 8,500 seismographs, tune them to focus on the plate boundaries between Santa Rosa and Santa Cruz, and tell them to plot where all of the slips have been; the resultant map will also tell us where there have been no slips. Where there are no slips, there must be asperities. In other words, the map should tell us where the asperities are."

"Jim, that is the best news I've had in days."

"Yeah, but don't start popping the champagne corks."

"What's the problem?"

"It's just that this has never been done. We've never tried to harness and coordinate the data from all 8,500 seismographs, especially going back over 10 years. It's going to take a while. But I'll get right on it. I know the best IT people in the business. I'll get them out to California right away. We'll do it."

As they hung up, Michael thought: "Dear God, how am I going to explain all this to Slevin?!!!"

* * * * *

"What's a matter, Mike? You don't look so good."

"I'm not."

"Well, you better get your act together. We've got to go tell the White House. You'd better get your story straight as a pin." Slevin told him. "I'm pretty sure you're going to have to tell the President."

"The President?! Of the United States?!" Michael choked.

"An atomic bomb? On US soil? Damn straight, you've gotta tell the President. But, don't soil yourself, Mikey; this President's a good guy."

So, it's "Mikey" again is it, Michael thought. And "This President's a good guy." *Oh, spare me*, he thought.

"I'm going to call the national Security Advisor. I'm sure we'll meet in his office at the White House. I'll let you know when. So, stand by."

"Ok, but Jim, 'get my story straight as a pin'? What story? What on God's green earth are we going to tell the President? We get a tip from the Russians. We track this bomb half way around the world. It comes in through Canada. The USGS thinks it's headed for California and San Francisco. And then we lose it! We lose it! We lose the fucking atomic bomb!"

"Ok, ok. Easy, Michael, my boy. I understand the FIGs and all the fusion centers in the country are on it. We'll find it. Something will come up."

"That's just it Jim. You just said what's really been bothering me that I couldn't articulate. All of the FIGs and all of the fusion centers in the country *aren't looking for the bomb!* Only the few that are along the Interstate 40 corridor are looking. Those are the only States that Gerry Martinez has alerted."

"You're shitting me? Really? Just a handful of States, not all of them?"

"Yes. Just the ones on the I-40 corridor. Gerry is certain that the terrorists are taking the much longer I-40 route just to avoid the sensors at toll barriers on I-80 – when the I-80 route is much shorter.

"Jim, I'm not happy with this. I watched the terrorists make fools of us and the entire U.S. Navy about bringing the bomb across the ocean. I don't think a couple of sensors or a couple of toll barriers are going to bother them. They've certainly gotten around bigger difficulties than that."

"So, what are you saying?"

"Jim, what am I gonna do. Tell Gerry Martinez he doesn't know what he's doing? Order him to alert the whole goddamn country? I don't think so."

"Calm down, Mikey."

"Aw Jim, gimme a break with the Mikey shit. This is goddamn serious."

"Michael, calm down. I am agreeing with you. The whole country does need to be on alert. You can't order Martinez to do that. But I can."

"Barbara?" Slevin called to his assistant. "Get me Gerry Martinez on the phone, please."

* * * * *

"Mike?" Slevin said before Michael could even say a word into his phone. "I talked to Martinez. He is putting the whole country under a priority one alert. The reason he wanted to limit it was to avoid anyone panicking or anything like that. After I told him to alert the whole country, he still wanted to exclude the East Coast because he thinks the bomb couldn't still be here. But I told him to forget it and alert the whole damn country.

"Are you happy?"

"Yes. Thank you for doing that."

"Ok, so now that you're a happy boy, get your act together. The National Security Advisor's office called. We're due there in 90 minutes."

# CHAPTER 22 - THE ROUND BAR

"Why do you always call this place 'The Round Bar'?" Richard Albion asked. "It's actually the 'Round Robin Bar.'"

"The 'Round Robin Bar' makes no sense at all." Nicholas B. Davis said. "What's it got to do with a 'round robin'? No sports going on around here. No, it's just a bar. And it happens to be round. Hence, the 'Round Bar' in my parlance. Besides, a nice name like the 'Round Bar' suits a lovely old dame of a hotel like The Willard.

"So, what brings you into this town that is the center of the universe, old friend? My company, I trust?" Davis said pompously.

"Always your company, Nicholas; but this time something more."

"Oh?" Davis said, genuinely surprised.

"Yes, but first things first. Will you be joining me here this evening?" Richard asked.

"Yes, I have our usual room reserved as my usual cover. And, I thought we'd have a relatively early dinner at a new place, Le Diplomat, just up on 14th Street. I hear the food's great. A little noisy, perhaps, sometimes. But I think you'll love it."

"Sounds fine."

"So, what's this 'something more' you spoke of?" Davis asked.

"Nicholas, we have been more than just good friends since our school days at Bruton. Even so, all this time we have gone our separate ways. You to your career in law enforcement; me to my shipping business, where I have made tens of millions but have not found happiness.

"I am now going to seek that happiness and the one I want to share it with is you."

"Oh dear God, Richard." Davis said into his napkin.

"No, you listen now to me, Mr. Nicholas B. Davis. Hear me out. I have several things to say that you need to hear.

"The first is that I have more than enough money for both of us. I have bought an island off the south coast of Thailand. Never rains. Never too hot there.

"Second, is that you have nothing in your life. You have no money. I furnish you with your Patek Phillippe watches and your Armani suits. You tell your suspicious colleagues – who can guess that you can't afford them on your Bureau salary – that you come from family wealth. That we know is rubbish. Your father was a civil servant like you.

"No money." Richard said raising one finger. "No future." He said, raising a second.

"You were passed over for that number three position at the Bureau the year before last. That means the end. There won't be any more promotions; and you know it. Your career has come to a dead end. You know this, Nicholas!

Davis had turned deep red and his breathing was heavy.

"So, you need to come away with me to Thailand. I will take care of you for the rest of our lives."

"Richard, I.....I.....I....."

"You will come with me. And there is one important thing you will do for me before we depart." Richard just sat there as Davis tried to take all of this in.

"Nicholas, you may recall that on that unfortunate weekend with the young dead girl in my apartment, I mentioned to you that young girls would be your undoing. I didn't realize it then; but that statement has come to be a self-fulfilling prophecy.

"Nicholas, look at this picture." Richard said handing his phone across to Davis. It was a picture of Davis and the dead girl naked together in bed. There was the belt around her neck. There were the golden handcuffs. There was a close-up of the handcuffs where you could see both the girl's dead eyes and the inscription 'To Nicholas B. Davis on his 25th Anniversary with the Federal Bureau of Investigation, from his Loyal Staff.'

"You may recall that I said my men from the docks would take care of the girl's body? Well, they did; but not in the way you might think. In fact they put the girls naked body under a bridge on the Hudson River Park bike path – where it would certainly be found. And, indeed, it was found. The police, of course, have no idea of her identity. But the medical examiner said she died of asphyxia from a cloth belt around her neck. That cloth belt sound familiar, Nicholas?

"The coroner also determined she had been raped. They found semen inside her. Guess whose?

"As I said, they don't know her identity. But they certainly would if I showed them these." Richard again proffered his phone with a picture of Nicholas and the girl lying together naked, but where their faces were clearly visible. No mistaking who they were. Davis and the police's Jane Doe.

"So, my friend," Richard went on to an ashen and trembling Davis. "Not only is your career over; but if these photographs ever get into the hands of the press – right across the street at the National Press Club – your entire life is over. Rape and murder of a fifteen-year old girl by a senior official of the FBI. You know, New York just reinstated the death penalty.

Their new Governor is dying to use it – so to speak. You will end your days in the electric chair at Sing Sing."

"Richard, you wouldn't……"

"Oh yes, I would." Richard came back. "I want you that badly. And I have seen you make a fool of yourself too many times with these flings with young girls. Never again! Oh, yes, I definitely would." Richard said raising his voice a bit too much and wincing from it.

"So, Nicholas, you are coming with me. And we are going to get you an entirely new identity. You will need one after what you are going to do for me."

"What do you mean? What am I going to do for you?"

"I'm going to tell you. But first, I am going to tell you a story that will explain why we are going to do what we are going to do.

"Do you know what my name means?"

"Albion? Yes, of course, it's the Roman name for Britain."

"Originally, it wasn't a surname; it was an eponym."

"So, you mean, like, 'Richard, the Briton'?"

"Exactly. I am descended from crusaders.

"Really?"

"Yes. The story is that one of my forebears commanded a unit of non-Britons in the First Crusade. You may recall that the Pope summoned crusaders from all over Christendom to 'liberate' the Holy Land. So, it was given to one of my ancestors to command a unit made up of warriors from other European countries.

"My Christian name, of course, comes from the most famous of the Britons who fought in the First Crusade, Richard the Lion Hearted.

"This is all a very charming story, Richard, but where are you going with this?"

"I don't know if you know that my mother was Lebanese. They have a very different take on the crusades. Oh, certainly, the Muslims took the Holy Land by force. But they lived there. As you know, tribal wars had been going on in that part of the world for millennia before the Christian era. As the Muslims see it, when they captured Jerusalem in the seventh century, it was just their turn, in the natural course of events.

"The crusades, on the other hand, were, to them, pure unwarranted aggression by an arrogant foreign power. Did you know that when the crusaders conquered Jerusalem in 1099 they massacred not only the Arabs, but the Jews *and* the Christians living there? The Islamic rulers in the Holy Land never molested the Jews nor the Christians. They all lived in peace. When the crusaders came, the local Christian population had no reason to rise up against - what were to them after 461 years – their Arab neighbors. For this reason, my arrogant ancestors on my father's side put them to the sword."

"Again, Richard, is this going somewhere?"

"Don't be so condescending, Nicholas. Yes, it is going to the reason you're leaving this town with me. Let me continue.

"When I first got into the shipping business in that area of the world, I looked up my mother's people. It turns out she came from a powerful family. They were very good to me. They arranged many shipping contracts. My business between Lebanon, Cypus, Turkey and the North African coast flourished because of them. They made me a multi-millionaire many times over. That is how I can afford your expensive tastes in jewelry and clothes – and virtually anything else I want.

"In time they introduced me to a group called Ada'ala, which means 'justice.' It is because of Ada'ala that I am here with you today." Richard said staring intently at Davis.

"Ada'ala wants a little piece of justice from this miserable country of yours which has done you no good, and which buys oil from the Muslims on the one hand and then publicly reviles them on the other."

"What do you mean, 'a little piece of justice'?" Davis said squinting back at Albion.

"Embarassment, Nicholas, embarrassment. A major embarrassment for the great United States of America. We had originally thought of blowing off the torch arm of the Statue of Liberty. We found that to be – technically – almost impossible because of the security. But, more so, because it could be repaired. In less than a month, a new arm would no doubt appear.

"So, the plan we settled on was to destroy the largest national park in the country. The crown jewel of the National Parks – Yellowstone."

"What in the hell, Richard?" Davis said shaking his hear as if he hadn't heard right.

"Allah has given us – Ada'ala - a gift. Yellowstone sits on a volcano. My colleagues are going explode a low yield nuclear warhead at Yellowstone. The bomb itself will do some damage. Kill many of the visitors in the park. It will be about the size of the bomb that your countrymen dropped on the Japanese at Hiroshima. Flatten several square miles of terrain. In Yellowstone, terrain is mostly trees and wildlife. The real beauty of this idea is that the bomb will waken the volcano. The caldera is over three miles below the surface. The bomb wont cause it to erupt. But it will cause large pools of lava to surface, inundating the park and turning the country's crown jewel into a thousand mile black scar of magma. No more Old Faithful, no more tourists, no more Yellowstone.

"Nicholas, you are going to help me make sure this venture succeeds."

"You know something, Richard, I have done a little research of my own. You my friend, are an old homo." Davis held up his hand to stop Richard from interjecting. "Your Ada'ala people aren't your friends. Allah doesn't tolerate queers like you – or me. They are blackmailing you.

"After that incident in your apartment with the young girl, I came to my senses and did some checking. It occurred to me that, although we are old friends – and, as you say – more than friends - what happened that night might not be what it seemed. Richard, your fucking Ada'ala friends blackmailed you into setting me up. Sure I fucked that girl. But I didn't kill her. Your fucking thug employees from the docks probably killed her and then set up the pictures with my belt and my handcuffs.

"Nicholas." Richard said coolly. "Regardless of how you may characterize my friends in Ada'ala, they have the pictures. Ada'ala has the medical examiner's report and the pictures of our little 'Jane Doe'. And, what is more, Nicholas, is that if I do not signal them that you are *in* by 2 o'clock this afternoon, the pictures and the reports and everything else will be delivered right across the street." Albion said pointing up to the National Press Club across the street.

"You will be the headline story in every newspaper and newscast in the country. Probably the world. And you will have begun your march to the electric chair at Sing Sing.

"What say you, Nicholas B. Davis? What shall I tell my friends at Ada'ala?

# CHAPTER 23 - THE NATIONAL SECURITY ADVISOR

To the professional political soothsayers in the Washington news media, President William Blaine Richardson III, better known as just Bill Richardson, and his Vice President, Jeremy Mahikane, were anomalies. The word among the political pros in Washington was that these two didn't stand a chance. But, unnoticed by the pundits, the country had tired of the big-city, spendthrift, entitlement-enthralled Democrats. And they had also tired of the anti-woman, gay-hating, poor-hating, big-business-ass-kissing Republicans. So when the Republicans nominated two of their best hacks in the Senate, the Democrats turned uncharacteristically to a Democratic Governor from New Mexico – one of two blue states in a mid-country sea of red - and his counterpart from – of all places – Hawaii. Anomalies?! Richardson was Hispanic! Mahikane was native Hawaiian! A Democratic ticket with two minority candidates, both Governors, both from small states: no way they could get elected.

Richardson and Mahikane won by the greatest margin since 1964.

President Richardson had not only been a two-term Governor of New Mexico, but had served in Congress from there for 14 years and had been both Ambassador to the UN and Secretary of Energy at various times under President Bill Clinton.

Vice President Mahikane was a Ph.D. in Geology and a Professor of Volcanology at the University of Hawaii. He was a recognized expert on volcanoes, which is, of course, where the Hawaiian Islands came from. Not seeing anything he liked among the local politicians, he ran for Mayor of Honolulu and won. He went on to be elected Governor of Hawaii. Richardson and Mahikane worked together at the National Governors Association, which Richardson was president of, and the Democratic

Governors Association that Mahikane was president of. They liked each other and trusted each other. So, when the Democratic Party turned to Richardson, he persuaded them to nominate Mahikane as his runningmate.

* * * * *

At 11am the next morning Slevin and Michael were at the White House in the office of Gary Gill, the National Security Advisor to President Bill Richardson.

"Is this a meeting or a Mongolian Cluster Fuck?" Slevin said to Gill looking into his conference room. "Who's the cheerleader in the admiral's outfit?"

"Be quiet, you stupid bastard!" Gill hushed Slevin. "That's Admiral Molly McNamara. She's the Chief of Naval Operations. Molly's people are the ones trying to help you find your goddamn bomb."

"Yeah? Isn't she a little too young and definitely too pretty to be an admiral? What does she do?"

"What does she do? God, you *are* a stupid bastard. Molly McNamara *is* the "US CyberNavy." She has almost singlehandedly brought the Navy – kicking and screaming - into the 21st century. Without her there would be no CyberOps. They'd probably still be using signal flags. You'd be looking for your bomb with a deerstalker hat and a magnifying glass."

"I guess I'm impressed."

"Well, you ought to be. Let me tell you this quick story about Molly. How she made page one in the Navy, so to say. Are you ready for this? During some war games, she was the communications officer on a destroyer. The flagship of the 'enemy' fleet," Gill said making quotation marks in the air, "was the aircraft carrier *Nimitz*. Apparently, the *Nimitz* team was winning the war game and everyone on Molly's team was completely bummed out.

So, Molly takes out her laptop, hacks into the *Nimitz*' system and shuts the entire ship down. Everything. No propulsion. No communication. No lights. No running water. Five thousand sailors in total darkness and silence. As each of the *Nimitz*' emergency generators came on, she left them on for 30 seconds each and then shut them down too. Total chaos on the *Nimitz*. She left them all that way for 30 minutes before turning the lights back on."

"Whoa, the brass must have shit a brick!" Slevin said laughing.

"They didn't know whether to shit or go blind - literally." Gill said. "They didn't know whether to court martial her or promote her. Mo Zumwalt was the Chief of Naval Operations then. He finally got them to wake up and realize that if Molly McNamara could do it, so could the Russians and so could terrorists. So, Zumwalt promoted her and put her to work finding a way to keep hackers away from the fleet. Since then she's been on the fast track to the stars – the ones on her shoulders."

"That's a hell of a story."

"Yep. And Molly's one hell of a woman. You'll like her, Jim. She is to today's Navy what Hyman Rickover was to the Navy 50 years ago. Rickover was the father of the nuclear Navy. Molly is the father – or mother, I guess you might have to say – of the new cyber Navy. And, between you and me, old friend, Molly is going to be the next Chairman of the Joint Chiefs of Staff – the first woman to come anywhere near that job."

"Really?!"

"I'd put money on it. When he promoted her to CNO, the boss told her he would make her the first woman Chairman - if you will - of the Joint Chief of Staff. Get this: he told her he wanted her to grab the other four services by the hair and drag them kicking and screaming into the 21st Century, just like she did to the Navy. Can you believe that? His exact words! What a piece of work our President is. That's why I love working for him.

"Well, since she is obviously a favorite of yours and the President's, I will show dutiful respect towards the Admiral, Mr. Gill." Slevin said bowing slightly and following Gill into the conference room.

"Do you give every National Security Advisor so much shit?" Said Michael quietly.

"No, I save it for Gary. We went to law school together at Fordham. He deserves it." Slevin said grinning broadly.

Michael and Slevin entered the conference room. Slevin turned toward the Secretary of the Interior. Michael turned toward Admiral McNamara.

"Who is that fat, balding wanker you are with?" The Admiral asked, her face flushed.

"You know you're really pretty when you blush." Michael said, winking at the Admiral.

"Again." She said, referring to the wink. "You insubordinate bastard."

"I'm not subordinate to you, Admiral McNamara; therefore, I can't very well be insubordinate. Which fat, balding wanker?"

"That one." Admiral McNamara said pointing to Jim Slevin

"Oh, that fat, balding wanker is my boss, Jim Slevin." Michael said loud enough that Slevin could hear. "You're right about him being a fat, balding wanker, of course, but I think you'd like him anyway. What did he say to piss you off so bad, Admiral?"

"He referred to me as a 'cheerleader in an admiral's outfit.'"

Michael laughed. "Oh yeah, he did, didn't he?" A brief pause… then. "What's your problem?"

"What's my problem? I'm the goddamn Chief of Naval Operations."

"Yeah, but you're still young enough and plenty pretty enough to be a cheerleader." Michael said under his breath.

"You're just as big an asshole as he is."

"And you're blushing again." Michael said. The Admiral stormed off; but Michael knew she was laughing inside.

Mary Munson, the Secretary of the Interior, said "Why do you look so surprised to see me, Jim Slevin? You didn't think that my guys at the USGS were going to tell you, but not me, did you?"

The surprised look turned to one of shock when Nick Davis walked in. Davis worked for Slevin. He was head of the Counterterrorism Division. He had been passed over for Slevin's job, a slight he couldn't forgive that had become a grudge he held against Slevin.

"What are you doing here?" Slevin asked.

"I have come to tell the President that the bomb you are so concerned about is a dud."

"A what?" Said Slevin turning to the stunned looks on both Gill's and Michael's faces.

"Mary, how nice to see you! You look stunning as usual!" Said Davis as he oiled off to schmooze the Secretary.

Gill spoke first. "You didn't know he was going to say that? You didn't even know he was coming?"

"No."

"Is there something going on here that I should know about?"

"It's a vendetta going back to my appointment that he thinks should have been his."

"Dear God! We're talking nuclear weapons and he's talking office politics!

"Mr. Davis? What did you mean that the bomb is a dud?" Gill asked in an official tone.

"Just what I said, Mr. Gill. The bomb that the would-be terrorists bought from the two Russian colonels is a dud. It has a defective trigger mechanism. The trigger is frozen. It cannot be detonated. The Tactical Weapons regiments of the 20th Guards have been vexed with several shipments of defective warheads. There's more than one. Here is the list." Davis said producing an email in Russian. "Note the serial numbers." He said. "The one with the check next to it is the one the Russians gave the terrorists."

"How did you learn this?" Gill asked.

"I have extensive contacts among the GRU. The GRU is the *Glavnoye Razvyedyvatelnoye Upravleniye*, the Head Intelligence Department, that is, of the Russian Army. It's Russian Army intelligence." He said turning condescendingly to Secretary Munson.

"This communication is from one of my contacts. He has assured me that this information is held very closely. Only the safety officer and the commanding general and his staff at the Western Military District know about it. The Guards officers – including the commanding officers – don't know. No need. Bad for morale if they did. And, you should appreciate that it is no coincidence that the warheads on this list are the one's selected for decommissioning. There was no possibility that they could defend the Motherland; so why not "decommission" a defective warhead? Furthermore, the frozen trigger mechanism cannot be detected or corrected by the military units. They haven't the sophisticated equipment. The only time one would know if a bomb were defective is when one tried to detonate it."

Turning to Michael, Davis said: "Your colonels didn't know they were selling defective goods and your would-be terrorists didn't know they were buying them."

"Well, I'll be damned. This might not be the worst day of my life, after all." Gill said. The little group—except Davis—forced short smiles. Gill signaled Slevin to stay back as they departed.

"What do you think, Jim?"

"Gary, I hope I am not stooping to Davis' level, but I just don't trust that son-of-a-bitch. I am going to check and double check everything that bastard said. And, until I get confirmation that he's right, I am not going to call off the investigation."

"That's what I hoped you'd say. I need to tell the President. But what I am going to tell him is: one, that a bomb has been purchased by a group whom we believe to be terrorists. Two, that we believe that it cannot be detonated. Three, that we believe that the bomb was intended to be detonated over San Francisco destroying the city and setting off residual earthquakes along the San Andreas fault causing unimaginable destruction. I am going to tell him that you are pulling out all the stops and proceeding as if the bomb were real."

"That's certainly true."

"Ok, I'm going to see the boss. And good luck to you, man."

As Slevin opened the door, he almost pulled Admiral McNamara into Gill's office.

"Oh, excuse me, Director Slevin."

"Excuse *me*, Admiral."

"Gentlemen, something's been bothering me since that little speech by Mr. Davis."

"What's that, Molly?" Gill said.

"I'm not an expert on nuclear weapons. But something didn't sound right. 'Defective trigger mechanisms?' I haven't given a thought to nuclear weapons since the Academy. But if I remember correctly, I nuclear warhead is an almost critical mass of uranium, an additional piece of uranium a few inches away, that would make the mass go critical. And a charge or C-4, or something that would ram the small uranium bullet, if you will, into the larger uranium ball setting off the chain reaction that constitutes an atomic explosion. So, I don't see any trigger 'mechanism,' much less room for a 'defective mechanism.' You detonate the C-4, you detonate the bomb. As far as I know there are no moving parts to make a 'defective detonator.' But as I say, I'm not an expert. I'd like to do a little digging and I may need your help, Gary."

"Sure thing. What are you thinking?"

"Let me ask my nuclear weapons people a couple of questions. Then, depending on what they say, I may like to pose some questions to our Army Intelligence people in Europe assigned to the NATO command. They're the ones that watch the Russians. They should be able to tell us what we need to know, if we need to know anything. I will need your help with those inquiries, Gary. But, let me quiz my weapons gurus first."

"That would be terrific, Admiral." Slevin cut in.

"Don't let my uniform fool you, Mr. Slevin. I'm just a cheerleader."

"What do I know, Admiral? I'm just a fat, balding wanker."

They both laughed.

Michael waited for Admiral McNamara to come out of Gill's office, and then walked up to her.

"I thought I'd come over and wink at you one more time." This time the Admiral laughed and said very quietly – her eyes darting around to see who was watching: "Are you just going to keep flirting with me, Agent Cornell? Or are you going to ask me out?"

"It never occurred to me that her admiralship would even consider going out with a lowly FBI agent."

"Well, there is *one* that her admiralship would go out with."

"What would happen if I called your office and I told Chief Montoya that the reason I wanted to talk to you was to make an appointment to make love to you?

"What they say about you law enforcement guys is true. You are all truly assholes. Give me your phone.

"I am putting in my super-secret personal cell number into your phone. Even the White House doesn't have this number. When you want to make love to me, call this number. I guaranty you, Chief Montoya won't answer. And if I don't pick up, tell me it's you and I'll get back to you as soon as I possibly can. Ok. My number's in your phone. Call me now to make sure I know it's you calling.

"You know, Admiral, I have always had trouble falling in love." Michael said quietly as he waited for the test call to go through.

"You know Agent Cornell, so have I. Probably being around so many hyper-testosterone military guys has had something to do with it."

The Admiral's personal phone began to chirp.

"Cute ring tone." Michael said looking up and turning off his phone "So, all I really have to do is call this number and I get to make love to you?"

“Yep. As long as you say the secret passwords.”

“And that is?”

“I-love-you.”

“Won’t we be investigated if we’re caught?

“Probably. They Navy will investigate you. And your FBI people will investigate me. Hopefully the two investigations will just conclude that we are no threat to national security threat, but that we are probably good in bed together.”

“I’ve always liked the way you think, Admiral.”

“Well, Agent Cornell, since you are soon going to slip into my bed, it might be appropriate for you to call me something other than Admiral. How about Molly?

“You know, ever since I laid eyes on you the first time we met, I thought how Molly suited you. It is such a young and pretty name, and you are such a young and pretty girl, Admiral….. er, Molly.

“And you, Agent Cornell, is it Mike or Michael? I’ve heard you called both.

“I actually like both. You will probably wind up calling me Mike when were working and Michael when I’m trying to make love to you.

Molly laughed.

“I hope you wind up calling me Michael a lot.”

Molly just kept giggling.

# CHAPTER 24 – STACEY

When she was a little girl, Stacey Coleman was, what-used-to-be called, a tomboy. When the girls in her neighborhood played dolls and made tea parties for their stuffed animals, Stacey played guns and touch football with the boys.

She grew up on Ewa Beach Road right on the beach, just southwest of the Pearl Harbor Naval Base on the Island of Oahu. Her stepdad had a good job at the World War II Valor in the Pacific National Monument, right on the base. Her mom was – what they called then - "a homemaker". She was a stay-at-home mom. She didn't work. She just took care of Stacey and her two older brothers.

Stacey went to elementary school right up the road in Pearl City. She did so well that the Principal brought her to the attention of the Director of the Priory Upper School at St. Andrew's Priory School for Girls in Honolulu. "The Priory", as it was called, was founded by Queen Emma, the wife of King Kamehameha IV, with the help of the Archbishop of Canterbury, in 1867. The Priory was the best, and most exclusive, school in Hawaii. Stacey played soccer, tennis and was on the swimming team. Stacey also surfed and got up to the north coast, where the monster 40-foot waves were, whenever she could. She was a straight-A student in science and got As and B+s  in her other courses, as well. So much so that at the end of her junior she was invited to take an AP summer course in geology at the University of Hawaii.

The teacher for the summer course was a young gentleman named Jeremy Mahikane, who was a Professor of Geology. The course was co-ed. As a treat for his students, Jeremy took them on a snorkeling trip to Hanauma Bay. As soon as Stacey saw the Bay, she became a geologist, or to be precise, a volcanologist!

Hanauma Bay was the semi-circular remains of an ancient volcano. It was now a state park. After the fires and the lava flows had dwindled, the sea kept pounding mercilessly on the sea side of the volcano until it collapsed into the ocean. This happened slowly, of course, and as the walls of the volcano were collapsing into the sea, a doughnut-shaped coral reef was building up right in the middle of the caldera of the had-been volcano. The water there in the newly-created bay inside the volcano was only about 40 feet at its deepest. An ideal spot for snorkeling. The reef abounded in all kinds of marine creatures – fish, crustaceans, eels, jellyfish – everything.

The class loved it. Most all of them loved the marine biology aspects. Stacey was infatuated with the volcano itself. *She had actually swum in a volcano!*

The next day in class Jeremy regaled the class with stories of doing night dives onto the coral reef in the volcano. He unscientifically described the many creepie-crawlies that lived in the coral, who would come out at night to investigate whenever light was shined into their hiding places. About 75% of the 16-year olds in the class, including Stacey, were certified scuba divers.

State parks closed at dark. So, it took lots of wheedling and gentle badgering, before they finally got Jeremy to prevail on the State Department of Land & Natural Resources to let his class do a night dive.

It was all that Jeremy said it would be. The coral was teeming with thousands of creatures of all sorts of colors and shapes and spines and scales and shells. Stacey figured that 90% of those who made the night dive would go on to become oceanographers or marine biologists. She, however, was infatuated by the volcano itself. *Once again, she had swum inside a volcano!*

Stacey stayed in touch with Jeremy. When it came time for college, Jeremy steered her toward the geology department at the University of

Hawaii and her stepdad steered her toward a NROTC scholarship, which she won.

While in the NROTC program at the University of Hawaii, she organized a marksmanship team that competed for the University and won several titles. Stacey, herself, even tried out for the Olympic team. After graduation she was commissioned and sent to the Naval Postgraduate School at Monterrey where she got a Masters in Oceanography. She was a star at basic training where she won more awards for marksmanship – the Distinguished Rifleman, the Distinguished Marksman and the Distinguished Pistol Shot Badges. Stacey volunteered for a stint with the Naval Marksmanship Team. While on that team she tried out for the Olympics again. This time she made it and came home with a Silver Medal in the Woman's 25 Meter Pistol competition.

From Basic, Stacey went on to the Army jump school at Ft. Benning. Then back to the South Pacific for five years doing marine science for the Navy. She was the only officer in the marine science division with jump wings and marksmanship badges. Stacey made a point of volunteering for sea duty. She figured she might spend the rest of her career in science – even, maybe, in laboratories; so she wanted to take full advantage of the opportunity and excitement of serving with surface warfare units.

After her discharge from active duty as a lieutenant, Stacey went back to the University for her Ph.D. in volcanology. But she stayed on in the Navy's Active Reserve frequenting the facilities and the Officers' Club at the base at Pearl Harbor.

As part of her studies, Stacey needed a second foreign language, other than Spanish. So, she took French. One of her classmates was actually an M.D. from the mainland who was an attending physician and assistant professor at the University's medical school. Her name was Caroline Gorn. What was a medical doctor doing taking French and juggling a full-time job in the hospital and at the med school on top of it all? So, next time Stacey ran into Caroline on the way to class, she asked her.

"It's for *Médecins Sans Frontières*." Caroline said.

Stacey had heard of *Médecins Sans Frontières*. It was a group of doctors who volunteered to work several weeks a year for free for the poor in developing countries. It was started in 1971 in France; but the non-profit, non-governmental, totally volunteer movement spread rapidly across globe. There were now chapters in almost every developed country. In the U.S., the group was known by its English name, of course: "Doctors Without Borders". The internationally accepted acronym for the organization, however, was "MSF". If you needed to be more specific, you could say: "MSF USA" or "MSF UK", etc.

Stacey wanted to know more about MSF, but she could see that Caroline was swamped between the demands of her job and her studies. So, Stacey made Caroline an offer.

"Look, Caroline, I know you have to miss a lot of classes because of your work. And, I'd really like to find out more about MSF. So, let me suggest something. I'll tutor you in French for the days when you miss class, and you can tell me all about MSF, afterwards?"

"You don't have to do that, you know? I'll be glad to tell you about MSF anyway. But on the other hand.....I could use help with the French.....and since you *did* offer..... Ok, deal!"

Caroline had begun her involvement with MSF in her freshman year of medical school at the University of Maryland. She had heard about it as an undergraduate at Dickenson College and it was one of the major reasons she wanted to be a doctor.

As soon as she entered medical school, she started trying to sign on to one of the MSF teams in the U.S. that was mounting a summer mission to South Asia or Southeast Asia or to sub-Saharan Africa. The MSF organizers wanted someone with more medical training. They told Caroline to come back her second year. So, when sophomore year came, she applied again. This time she got accepted. She was on a team headed for Rwanda. It was 1994.

That was the year of the most ferocious genocide in Rwanda. The MSF teams found themselves treating victims of ethnic slaughters rather than doing public health work among the villagers. Worse, one of the nurses on Caroline's team – a woman with a husband and two young children at home – was raped and murdered by one of the warring factions while working in a remote village. So horrific was the killing and maiming that MSF – for the first and only time in its history – called for military intervention to halt the bloodshed. It was a baptism of blood that Caroline Gorn could never forget.

As frightening a trip as Caroline had to Rwanda in 1994, it did not deter her from signing on to what proved to be a much calmer trip to Bangladesh the following year where she treated mostly children for cholera, typhoid, and dysentery and spent the rest of her time teaching the basic personal sanitation skills that would prevent the children from getting re-infected.

Caroline had stayed active and made other trips with MSF throughout her young career in medicine. She now wanted to work more closely with the MSF leadership in Paris, all of whom spoke French. That's why she was learning the language.

But it was the story of the Rwanda trip that gripped Stacey. She kept coming back to it with Caroline. The MSF folks had been caught in the crossfire of a murderous ethnic war. Several had been killed. More were injured. Caroline had seen it. She had been lucky to get out unhurt.

What appalled Stacey was that neither side in the hideous Rwandan civil war seemed to respect the foreign caregivers! Didn't they have any sense that they too would be able to get medical treatment if injured – as long as the foreign medical personnel were alive and well enough to give it to them? What could they be thinking?

Furthermore, for that matter, did any of the goddamn governments of the so-called civilized world give a rat's ass, either? None of them had done anything to protect the MSF teams!

And what was the worst – Stacey thought - were the apparent attitudes of the MSF volunteers themselves! After closely but gently quizzing Caroline, Stacey could not detect any thoughts or sentiments among the MSF's leaders or volunteers that the in-country teams needed to be protected. Unbelievable! Ask people to give their time and effort to help the poor…..and then let them put themselves in harm's way – without anyone's giving it a second thought. *Incredible!* Stacey just kept thinking to herself. *Totally incredible!*

So, she decided to do something about it.

Stacey decided that each of the MSF teams should be protected. They needed someone to check out the security side of each MSF mission before the team went in country. Then they either needed a security person to accompany each team, or they needed a whole security team to be on high alert to possibly go in and rescue the team if they were in trouble. Stacey knew just who to talk to about her idea.

The next few evenings Stacey hung out in the bar at the Officers' Club at Pearl Harbor. She quizzed the bartenders about the whereabouts of Brendan O'Curley. "Oh, Curls, you mean?" Simon the head barman said. "He'll be around. He's sure to stop in soon." The third night he showed up.

Brendan was a lieutenant in the Navy. He was a SEAL. He was Academy. And, he was clearly a very good and decent guy, Stacey had concluded from seeing him interact with people in the Club. She had met him once, but was certain he wouldn't remember.

"Brendan? Hi, I'm Stacey Coleman. We met a few weeks ago when my old ship, the *Higgins*, was in port."

"Of course, I remember. How could anyone forget meeting a girl like you?"

*Yet another Irish bullshitter!* Stacey thought not-unkindly, laughing all the while.

"Can I get you a drink?" Brendan asked.

"A Heineken would be great. But I need to talk to you, too."

"Great. Beer first. Then talk."

"So." Brendan said when the beers arrived. "What can you do for me?"

Stacey laughed again and then said. "I want you to help me put together a security team to protect volunteer doctors and nurses who go to all kinds of desperate countries to treat the sick and the poor."

"Is that all? You mean you're not even going to invite me to the ballgame?"

"What ballgame?" Stacey said flustered.

"Just kidding." Brendan said. "You mind explaining?"

So, Stacey explained. She explained about MSF, how they started, and what they do. Then she told Caroline's story about Rwanda and how – apparently – no one gave a good goddamn whether any of these MSF volunteers were ever killed or injured when they were in foreign countries helping the poor.

"You mean these doctors and nurses – with kids and family back home – out of the goodness of their hearts - go to these nothing countries out in the middle of nowhere? And there's no one keeping an eye on them?"

"That's the story."

Brendan just stood up without saying anything and walked over to the window and looked down on the ships at anchor nearby in the harbor. Stacey knew he had taken in what she said and that he was thinking about it now. So, she let him be.

After a couple minutes, he came back to their table.

"You said Paris, didn't you? That's where the MSF headquarters is, right?" Brendan asked.

"One of them – the oldest and the biggest – is there."

"Well, Ms Coleman, I think you have come to the right sailor."

"Really?" Stacey said brightening completely!

"You're not going to believe this. What an incredible coincidence? Paris, of all places!" Brendan went on.

He then told Stacey a story about how he met a group of men in the same profession one time in Paris. He had gone there on leave and was meeting up with a fellow SEAL named Tom Falkner. Tom was now an ex-SEAL. He was out of the Navy. Tom introduced him to another ex-SEAL and to a Brit who was ex-SAS. Tom also introduced him to a guy named Sergei, who was ex-Russian Special Forces, and to two other guys, Sacha and Renaud, who were both ex-French Foreign Legion.

"Curls, we want you to join our team." Falkner had said to Brendan.

Tom then went on to explain that when he left the Navy, he had been approached by a former Naval officer who was now a senior executive at a major international insurance company. It seems that this guy's company wrote a lot of anti-kidnapping insurance policies on the lives of a lot of the hundreds of wealthy oligarchs who were a plague on most of Central and South American countries. They also wrote a lot of the same policies on oligarchs' kids in Africa and Asia – places where the children of the wealthy were targets for criminals.

Now whenever there was a kidnapping – and Tom said there were many more than were reported in the press – the company usually paid a ransom and the oligarchs got their kids back. Sometimes, they paid the ransom and the kidnappers murdered the abducted children. And, sometimes – for whatever reason - they just couldn't pay the ransom. In these cases, what they really needed was a crack team to go in and get the kids back. There was where these ex-SEALs and other ex-Special Forces guys came in. The insurance guy figured that a crack team of ex-military heavies would pay for themselves many times over. Not just in freeing captive kids, but in selling the insurance policies in the first place. He could just see the approving smiles of the oligarchs as they looked over the pictures and resumes of the insurance company's "Freedom Squad". They would definitely put the oligarchs in the mood to write large checks.

Brendan told Falkner that he wasn't ready to give up the Navy just yet; but that when he did, Tom's offer looked pretty good to him. And that's the way they left it.

"Sounds a lot like the team you need, doesn't it Stacey?

"How do you mean?" She said.

"Well." Brendan went on. "Since that time, I've been back to Paris a couple times. Each time, I've made a point to spend as much time as I could with these guys. See if I'd be comfortable working with them, you know? And that's where you come in.

"Stacey, if I may say so, this is one boss group of guys. To a man, they are honorable. To a man, they have integrity. And, to a man, I see no fear in any of them. I also don't think they're in it solely for the money. I think they want to save those kids – even if the kids belong to worthless parents.

"Stacey, I think the so-called Freedom Squad is the team you need to protect your MSF volunteers. I'd be happy to put you together with them."

So, Stacey started spending the time needed between Caroline and her connections to MSF and with Brendan with his connections to the Freedom Squad.

* * * * *

Jeremy Mahikane, brilliant and respected scientist that he was, knew there was more to life than volcanoes and geology. When he looked at the City of Honolulu, he didn't like what he saw in terms of leadership. So, he ran for Mayor in the Democratic primary. He won the primary – much to the chagrin of what was left of Senator Daniel Inouye's organization - and went on to win the general election and become Mayor. Six years later he ran for Governor – and despite attempted sandbagging by the old Democratic guard, who didn't take to this outsider/upstart – and won.

Stacey Coleman had been one of Jeremy's favorite students. They stayed in touch.

As Stacey was beginning to organize her security team for MSF, she had occasion to have lunch at Duke's on Waikiki Beach with Jeremy. Duke's was fine with Jeremy. Lots of tourists who didn't know him; few fawning businessmen that did.

As Stacey was outlining how her security team would work, Jeremy asked some questions.

"You say that one of your guys will go out on the original scouting trip with the representative of MSF? Wealthy doctors can afford trips like that. Who's going to pay for your guy's trip? I can't imagine the insurance company would pay. I can imagine that the insurance company will probably not be pleased with your plan. You'll be using assets that they think belong to them.

"Not that this should ever stop you, mind you!" Jeremy added.

Jeremy asked a few more questions mostly about money. Most importantly, who would pay for the equipment and special transport that they would need?

Sure, the ex-SEALs et al., might be able to pay for a flight to Borneo. But what about renting a helicopter or a few jeeps, or whatnot, when they were in Borneo? Who was going to pay for that?

Jeremy finally answered his own questions about money.

"Stacey, while campaigning for Governor, I have come to meet probably all of the wealthiest people on these islands. Most, as you might expect, are selfish assholes. But some are real princes….ur…..or princesses, if you will." They both laughed. "I'd like you to meet one of them. His name is Jerry Diaz. He has more money than God. He has a heart of gold. And, I'll just bet he'd love to be involved and be the rich uncle in your operation."

The next week Jeremy invited both Stacey and Jerry Diaz to the Governor's Mansion for dinner. Stacey and Jerry and hit it off. Jerry was, indeed, interested in joining the team and bankrolling it. Stacey saw immediately that Jerry brought more to the table than just money. He brought much common sense and more than 40 years of business experience – which no one on the rest of the team had even a year's worth of.

A month later, Stacey, Caroline, Brendan and Jerry were on the plane for Paris. There they would not only meet with the Freedom Squad but also with the leadership of the MSF. Just as Brendan had promised, the guys in the Freedom Squad said they were in. Just as Caroline had promised, the leadership of MSF said they were delighted to have such an amazing security team. And, just as Jerry promised, everyone was more than satisfied with the financial arrangements he proposed.

A week after she got back to Hawaii, Stacey was back on the beach at Duke's reporting in to Governor Mahikane.

"What should we call the group, Jeremy? We gotta have a good name. I'm thinking: 'Safe Away'." Stacey said

"Isn't that a supermarket chain?" Jeremy teased.

"Noooo." Stacey said with fake annoyance in her voice. "It's a take off on 'Safe Home'. You know. It's what you say when someone's leaving for home. 'Safe Away' is what our team assures the MSF volunteers – that they'll be safe while they are away."

"Ok, I can buy that." The Governor said.

"But what about the French. We need a French name for the group as well. What do you think about *Sûr Au Loin* or *Sauf Au Loin*?"

"I can't say. My French isn't that good."

"Neither is mine." Stacey said. "But then neither is anyone else's. Every time I ask a native speaker of French, I get a different answer. My guess is that they just don't use this expression. After all, we don't really say "Safe Away" ourselves, either."

"So." Jeremy said, paying the check. "You can certainly coin a phrase in English. Why not in French, too? I'd say go with '*Sûr Au Loin*' and make 'SAL' your international acronym."

"Good advice as always. Thank you, Governor Mahikane. And, thanks for lunch, too."

* * * * *

Two and a half months later Brendan and Stacey both got calls from Tom Falkner in Paris. Sacha had gone on a scouting trip with a doctor from Rennes to Cambodia. The government there had just been overthrown by a five-man junta. The country was in turmoil. Most of the Army opposed the junta. But the discord had not yet broken out into civil war. Sacha recommended against sending the mission of three female nurses and five physicians, one female and four males. The doctor had apparently ignored Sacha and the group went anyway.

The group went to Krong Battambang just west of Lake Tonle and not far from the Thai border. There they had been captured by troops loyal to the junta and were being held for ransom. When MSF got the word, they called Tom Falkner and his extraction team (Nobody liked Jeremy's acronym "SAL".) for help. The guys in Paris were now calling Stacey and Brendan to meet in Bangkok to plan the extraction of the eight hostages.

* * * * *

Two days later Governor Mahikane picked up the morning paper to see a picture of Stacey in camouflage gear carrying a body bag. The paper reported that an MSF extraction team had rescued all eight volunteer health workers and had killed two of the junta members who happened to be in the same village inspecting the hostages. In the body bag that Stacey was carrying were the remains of one of the junta.

The paper went on to report that the Cambodian Army had arrested the other three junta members and proclaimed one of their generals as head of state.

The Governor picked up the phone and called Jerry Diaz. He asked Jerry to contact the extraction team and invite them to Honolulu.

* * * * *

The bold rescue took the world's breath away. No more so anywhere than in Honolulu, the home to one of two women on the 9-person rescue team – and the one captured on film carrying the remains of a Cambodian rebel in a body bag. A graduate student in her 20s at the University! And then there was the young SEAL too from the base out at Pearl. Hawaii was ecstatic!

The locals really flipped out when the Governor leaked it that local businessman, Jerry Diaz played a major role in the rescue and was a vital member of the rescue team. Yes, indeed, Honolulu had much to be proud of.

And so, the Governor ordered a parade to celebrate. Afterwards a luncheon at the Mansion for the team and Hawaii's elite where Jerry Diaz was master of ceremonies. And them finally into the Governor's private study with just Jerry and the rescue team.

After some truly touching and heartfelt comments and thank-you's, Governor Mahikane lightened up a bit.

"I understand that you have rejected the brilliant French name I thought up for your team and the equally brilliant French acronym. Well, as they say, if first you don't succeed, etc., etc. So, I have come up with a new.....uh.....not exactly a name; but certainly something to call your team. Let me show you."

Governor Mahikane held up a piece of paper with two signal flags on it, one over the other.

"Ladies and gentlemen, I give you the letter 'A' and the letter 'I'. 'Alpha' and 'India', as the sailors call them. Note the order here. It is essential. This set of flags is called 'Alpha over India'. This, I suggest, should be both the name your team goes by and the acronym it uses. Let me tell you why."

The Governor went on to tell the little group about the encounter of the *S.S. President Roosevelt* with the British freighter *Antinoe* in a gale in the North Atlantic in January, 1926.

*At 4:40am on Sunday, January 24th, the Roosevelt picked up a weak distress call from the Antinoe. The Antinoe said it was foundering. It could not give a good position because it hadn't seen sun nor stars in four days. With the help of other ships the Roosevelt triangulated the Antinoe's signal, located her and steamed to her position. The captain of the Antinoe said she was sinking and asked that the Roosevelt take her crew aboard. The waves were so high that many times the two ships lost sight of each other. So, the captain of the Roosevelt raised two signal flags that the crew of the Antinoe would be able to see. They were Alpha over India.*

*Now the Roosevelt was bound for Bremerhaven with 200 passengers aboard. Yet, for the next two and a half days, the Roosevelt kept circling the Antinoe trying to rescue the Antinoe's crew. During these 85 hours – when the Roosevelt's passengers must have been near panic – two of the Roosevelt's crewmen were killed and six of its lifeboats were destroyed by the pounding sea in vain attempts to reach the Antinoe's crew. Finally, four days after the ordeal had begun, the storm weakened to where the Roosevelt was able to get a line to the Antinoe and rescue all of her crew including her captain.*

*When the Antinoe's crew reached the Roosevelt, they said that each one of the 85 hours they thought would be their last. But throughout the gale they could always see the two flags – Alpha over India – flying from the Roosevelt's mast – even when they couldn't see the ship itself. That was the only hope they had.*

"You see." Governor Mahikane concluded. "The flags Alpha over India have a specific and very special meaning. They mean: 'I will not abandon you.'"

After a long pause during which there was audible sniffling and face wiping, Jeremy said: "That, my friends is what you are saying – each day - to the wonderful men and women who volunteer for *Médecins Sans Frontières*. You are saying to them 'I will not abandon you.' No matter where you are. No matter what trouble you are in. 'I will not abandon you.'

So, that is how these people should think of you. You are their Alpha over India."

* * * * *

Later that evening, when they were by themselves, the team voted to call themselves: A/I – Alpha over India. And that is how A/I came to be: the protectors and guardians of the volunteers of *Médecins Sans Frontières.*

* * * * *

The following day, Stacey got the Governor's secretary to tell her that she expected him to be getting back to the Mansion that night about 7pm. She and Brendan were waiting for him outside. They called to him when his car pulled up.

"What's up, you two?" The Governor said jauntily, rolling down the window of his car.

"Get out. We've got something to show you."

"Come on in. No sense standing out here."

"No. We need to show you right here." Stacey said.

"Oooo-Kaaaaay." The Governor said getting out of the car. "What do I have to see so badly?"

With that Brendan rolled up the sleeve of his polo shirt revealing a tattoo of the two A/I signal flags. Stacey skootched down her right sock to reveal the same tattoo on her inside right ankle.

"Well, I guess my little story made some impression on you two." Jeremy said, more than a little flustered.

"It did. It really did. We voted to name our team A/I, just as you suggested. And this morning, before everybody got out of town. We all went to 'tattoo alley' out near Pearl and we all got these." Brendan said referring to his and Stacey's tattoos.

"And now, you've got to get one too." Stacey said.

"What? Are you both nuts?"

"No way. I told the team all the things you told me. I told them how you brought Jerry Diaz in. You are just as much a part of this team as any of us."

"Yeah." Brendan said. "As Stacey told us, if it weren't for you, there would be no rescue team. There would be no A/I. And those poor volunteers that we pulled out of Cambodia would still be there. Or they'd most likely be dead. You are very definitely part of the A/I team."

Jeremy was definitely tearing up. "Ok." He said with as much resolution as he could muster.

"Get in." Brendan said opening the door to his car. "Tattoo alley is open till 10."

"My body guards will shit a brick." Jeremy said laughing as he got into Brendan's car.

# CHAPTER 25 - JAKE

When Michael left the White House, he didn't go straight back to his office, he went to Field Intelligence Group office the floor below and asked for Gerry Martinez. His assistant said that Gerry had gone to California to supervise the FIGs at the western end of I-40. The assistant asked if Gerry's deputy, John Jekielek, could help.

A few minutes later a tall, muscular, early-40-something guy with very short blond hair walked into the room holding out his hand. He was wearing a white linen suit with a teal blue collarless shirt underneath. Definitely not the uniform-of-the-day at FBI headquarters. "You must be Agent Cornell." The man said.

"Yes, and you're Agent Jekeliek?"

"Right. Come with me."

"I've heard good things about you." Jekieliek said as they walked down the hall to his office. "And, by the way, I go by 'Jake'. What do they call you, 'Mike' or 'Michael'?"

"Take your pick. I like them both." Michael could tell he was going to get along well with this guy "Jake".

"But the good things didn't come from my boss."

"Oh?"

"After you left, he got this call from Jim Slevin telling him to put all 75 fusion centers on, quote, 'full alert'. He figured it must have been your doing since you work directly for Slevin."

"And he's pissed at me?"

"Something like that. But, he'll get over it. Well, he didn't do what I think Slevin wanted, anyway." Jake said.

"He didn't?" Michael asked now stopping in his tracks and clearly getting agitated.

"Apparently, Slevin didn't specify Level 1 alert. He just said alert. So, the fusion centers along the I-40 corridor were already on Level 1 alert. Not a problem. So, Gerry, put the fusion centers along the I-80 corridor on Level 2 alert. And he put the other centers around the country on Level 3 alert.

"What does all that mean, Jake?"

"Don't worry about it. I figured out what Slevin wanted. Then I persuaded Gerry that they needed him out west to supervise the fusion centers along I-40. Then I called Slevin's office and confirmed that he wanted the whole country on Level 1 alert. Then, when Gerry left, I put the whole country on Level 1 alert."

"Very smooth. Very, very smooth." Michael said with a big grin.

"I thought you'd appreciate it." Jake said, with an equally big grin.

"So, has anything come up?"

"Well, they're still getting their Level 1 acts together out there, pretty much, I think. But we did get this strange little report. Not much. That's for sure. Not from anywhere near I-80. But from about 150 miles north of 80 on I-90. It actually happened in La Crosse, Wisconsin."

"I-90?"

"Yeah. I-90 is the longest road in the country. It runs from right near Logan Airport in Boston all the way out to Spokane, Washington. That about 3,900 miles.

"At Madison Wisconsin I-90 and I-94 come together as one road and proceed northwest to the little town of Tomah, where they split. I-94 goes on north to Eau Claire and then on to Minneapolis-St. Paul. I-90 turns almost due west at Tomah, on to La Crosse, and then across the southern tier of Minnesota then on into South Dakota. The only major city I-90 comes near in Minnesota is Rochester. And beyond, Rochester: nada. No other town of any size or significance all the way to the Pacific Ocean."

"Here's the report we got." Jake said handing a print-out to Michael.

*Wisconsin State Trooper Vincent J. Marino filed the following report with the Wisconsin Statewide Intelligence Center, one of two fusion centers in Wisconsin:*

*While stopping for dinner about 7:30pm on Monday, 8 September, at the Denny's at the Valley View Mall just off I-90 in La Crosse, Wisconsin, State Trooper Vincent J. Marino observed an RV with a small silver trailer behind it parked at the edge of the parking lot. The trailer caught his attention because he observed a large red and white sticker saying "Road Worn", which is a slogan of Fender guitars and basses. On approaching the trailer, he noticed there were several other stickers on it advertising different brands of musical instruments. Trooper Marino is an amateur musician.*

*Although it was a Monday night, Denny's wasn't crowded. In the restaurant, Trooper Marino observed two military-aged white males eating by themselves in a booth. Because the RV had sleeping accommodations, Trooper Marino surmised that the two men were the road crew for a band, transporting their instruments and equipment to a performance venue. The men could make better time and reduce costs if they took turns sleeping and driving.*

*Trooper Marino was aware of the fact that many road crews in the music industry used drugs. He engaged the two men in conversation. They identified themselves with Italian-American names. Both spoke with accents. Both of Trooper Marino's grandparents came from Italy and spoke with heavy accents. Trooper Marino did not recognize the accents as Italian.*

*The men said that the name of their band was "Calliope" and that it was out of Indianapolis. They said they were taking the band's equipment to a performance venue in Rochester, Minnesota. They didn't know the name of the venue. They said that they would receive instructions about where to take the equipment by phone from the band's manager, once they got to Rochester.*

*Trooper Marino also plays in a band in La Crosse. His band is called "Speed Trap". All of the musicians in the band are State Patrolmen. His band frequently plays in Rochester.*

*Trooper Marino told the men that he was an amateur musician and had never seen a road van. He asked if they'd show it to him. They agreed but expressed a nervous apprehension that Trooper Marino thought might be because there were drugs or drug paraphernalia in open view on the RV.*

*The men gave Trooper Marino a tour of the RV. No contraband or drug paraphernalia were observed. He asked to see the band's equipment. The men reported that all of their instruments and equipment were locked in the silver trailer and that the band's manager was the only one who had a key. Although the band was from Indianapolis, both the RV and the trailer bore New York license plates.*

*Trooper Marino observed that both men had speaker buds in their ears. Before and during the tour of the RV he sensed that they were receiving communications through these devices.*

*Trooper Marino thought that the men's behavior and their general circumstances were very odd. But having observed nothing criminal, he let the men go on their way.*

*This encounter aroused Trooper Marino's suspicion, however. First, he checked on the license plate and found that it was registered to a company called Calliope Music, LLC in New York. Subsequently, he telephoned contacts in the music industry in Rochester. They reported that no band named "Calliope" was scheduled to play at any local venue. He then contacted colleagues in the music industry in Indianapolis who reported never hearing of a band called "Calliope". He then filed this report.*

"Well, I'll be damned. It *is* a strange little report isn't it?"

"Seriously." Jake said.

*Ok, a small silver trailer with no key. And our old friend, Calliope – another Greek nymph.* Michael thought. *What the hell?*

"Jake, is there any way I could talk to this Officer Vincent J. Marino?"

"Well……yeah…….I'm sure we can find some way for you to talk to him. We'd have to get him to a SCIF. That's probably not in La Crosse. Probably in Madison, where the fusion center is. That's about 150 miles away. And, I'm sure the only way his office will let him be grilled by an FBI agent is if his captain or supervisor is in the room with him when you talk."

"No, Jake, no SCIF. I'm not going to mention anything about any bomb to this guy. I just want to ask him some simple questions about his report. And no Wisconsin brass. Just Marino on the call. I'm not going to *grill* him. I just want to have a friendly chat with the man. Ask him some more details about his report.

"Mike, I don't think your idea of a friendly chat will sell with the Wisconsin State Patrol. They're all probably going to stand at attention and salute when you call.

"But let me try. Let me see what I can do. Give me an hour to work my way through the locals and their chain of command. You going to be in your office?"

"Yeah. I'll wait for your call."

"Can you do the call here in our conference room?"

"Sure thing."

"Mind if I sit in on the call?"

"Absolutely not. Please do. Another head and another set of ears are always welcome."

"Ok, I'll let you know what happens."

* * * * *

Jake was waiting for Michael as he walked back into the FIG office to make the call to Wisconsin.

"Thanks again for letting me sit in on this call. My job mostly involves moving paper reports around from A to B then back to A, etc. It's nice to see a human dimension to this job once in a while."

"Glad to have you in on it. Absolutely!"

"So, here's the deal." Jake said. "Marino is going to pull his cruiser over and be ready to take your call at the top of the hour. He's going to take it on his cell phone."

"Jake, that is very cool. How did you pull that off?"

"I told Marino's commander that you were a new guy here and you just wanted to get familiar with how these types of reports were generated. I told him the type of personal details that Marino put in the report – about his music and his band, and so forth – was just the type of content that we were looking for in reports like these. So, as the new guy on the block, I told them you just wanted to talk to someone who wrote one of these reports."

"Jake, with bullshit skills like that, you could be Irish!"

“Actually, my mother’s Irish.” They both laughed. “Might-a-known.” Michael said.

* * * * *

“Is this Trooper Vincent Marino?”

“Yes, Trooper Marino here.”

“Trooper Marino, I am Agent Michael Cornell of the Federal Bureau of Investigation in Washington. My friends call me Mike. What do your friends call you?” Michael said winking across the conference table at Jake.

“Uh.” Marino stuttered, clearly caught off guard. “Vinny. Everyone calls me Vinny.”

“How did you come up with the name of your band? ‘Speed Trap’ is definitely cool. Couple layers of meaning there.”

“Yeah, that’s what we thought.” Marino said laughing. “We *were* going to call it ‘Stop and Frisk’. Michael and Jake laughed.

“So, tell me about these dudes you talked to, Vinny. I got the feeling from your report that you didn’t think these guys were who they said they were.”

“That’s exactly right, Mike. You just said the words I was fishing for. They weren’t who they said they were.”

“Tell me more.” Michael said. And as he said that, the door to the conference room opened and one of the staff put a printout in front of Jake for him to read.

“Well. You’re talking to a guy named Vinny Marino. You might guess that I’m Italian.” Michael and Jake laughed again.

"To be specific, I am 100% Italian. My grandparents came over on the boat, so to speak. I grew up in an Italian neighborhood in Chicago. All my friends growing up were Italian. My grandparents lived with us. We spoke Italian at home. My folks still do.

"So, I know Italian. These two *jabonees* weren't Italian. One of the guys said his name was Angelino. I said, 'Geez, with a name like that your must have taken a lot of shit as a kid.' The guy looked at his partner, like WTF! He had no clue what I was talking about.

"Mike, Angelino in Italian means 'little angel'. Every Italian grandmother – Nona we call them – has her 'angelinos', her little angels, her grandchildren. So, if your actual name is 'little angel' you are definitely going to take a lot of shit in the schoolyard, if you know what I mean?"

"Exactly." Michael said.

"Well." Marino went on. "These guys had no clue what I was talking about. They didn't know what an angelino was. Definitely not Italian.

"And another thing – that stupid name for their band: Calliope! Who the fuck would name a band after a funky organ that plays merry-go-round music at State Fairs. I mean 'Grateful Dead', Rolling Stones', even 'Speed Trap' – yes. But 'Calliope' – no, definitely not. No one in their right mind would name a band 'Calliope.'

"You know, Vinny, I had forgotten that's what a calliope is. Of course, the merry-go-round organ!" Michael said.

"And one final thing." Vinny said. "I couldn't bust those guys for not having the key to their trailer. And I couldn't exactly bust the lock either. No probable cause. But not having the key was very strange. I mean, I know, if these two guys were so low down on the food chain that they couldn't be trusted with a key to the trailer, then they wouldn't be there. They wouldn't be working for the band at all.

"I mean, if the band thought they might steal something they wouldn't let them near their equipment. Ya know, what does it take – a crowbar – to get that lock off? If they were going to steal, they don't need a key!"

"Sure." Michael said. "Absolutely."

"So, Mike, I can't tell you these guys are a threat to our country. But I *can* tell you they weren't who they said they were. They weren't Italian. They weren't roadies. And I'm pretty damned sure there was more than musical instruments in that trailer."

* * * * *

After they signed off on the call with Vinny Marino, Jake passed the printout he had been handed across to Michael. It said:

At 1:12pm on Wednesday, 9 September, the 911 Operator in Rapid City, South Dakota, received a call from an unknown subject, speaking with an accent, declaring that a bomb would be set off in the Rushmore Mall at 1:30 that afternoon. It was determined that the call was made from a cell phone right on the Mall property itself.

The 911 Operator immediately notified the dispatcher for the South Dakota Highway Patrol. The dispatcher notified all units within a 50-mile radius as well as the Rapid City Police Department. State Troopers Jonas Nkumba and Silas Fordyce were on the Mall premises at the time of the call interviewing two male suspects in an RV in the parking lot. They were immediately ordered to evacuate the Mall.

At 1:29pm a radio transmission was detected coming from the Mall. A voice was yelling "Anyone in here?" And then about 5 seconds later "All clear." The Highway Patrol dispatcher also heard this transmission – on the highway patrol radio. It was the voice of Trooper Nkumba checking if anyone was in the men's restroom at the south end of the Mall. There was apparently a microphone in the men's room that was transmitting remotely.

Fifteen seconds after the transmission, a bomb was detonated in the men's restroom at the south end of the Mall. The bomb destroyed two stalls in the men's room and seriously damaged a third. Relatively speaking, very little real damage was done to the Mall structure. The building was, however, filled with acrid black smoke, which made damage assessment very difficult for some time.

After several hours, the two Troopers were able to resume their routine duties. Not surprisingly, the two suspects that they had been interviewing had disappeared.

A subsequent review of radio communications in the Mall area prior to the bomb threat revealed suspicious transmissions. The first transmissions are the voices of Troopers Nkumba and Fordyce talking to the two suspects they were interrogating prior to the bomb threat. There were also accented voices, which the Troopers identified as those of the two suspects. Finally, there was another transmission: "I hear what's going on. Go along with them. I'll take care of it. I'll get rid of them." That was at 1:10pm. The bomb call came in 2 minutes later. We believe that it was the same voice.

The Troopers had observed that the RV had a New York State license number: N975B. A subsequent check with New York authorities revealed that the licenses were issued to the Calliope Music Company LLC in New York. No other information was available about the license holder. However, the New York Motor Vehicle Department related that another inquiry had come in regarding that license number 2 days previously from the Wisconsin State Patrol.

The following morning an RV and a silver trailer were found abandoned in the parking lot of the Ramada Summerset about 15 miles north. Neither vehicle had license plates. Troopers Nkumba and Fordyce identified the RV and trailer as those belonging to the two suspects they had interrogated before the bombing at the Rushmore Mall.

“Well, I’ll be damned.” Michael said.

“My sentiments exactly. It’s the same two guys that Vinny Marino talked to. I’d bet money on it.” Jake said.

“Where is Rapid City vis-à-vis La Crosse, Wisconsin?” Michael asked.

“Several hundred miles west. I’ll check.” Jake said. “But they’re both on I-90.”

“I-90? Why would anyone take I-90 to get to California? It doesn’t go anywhere near California.” Michael was getting the same sick feeling in his stomach as he had when he and Admiral McNamara’s people were chasing the *Valhalla* across the Atlantic Ocean.

“Jake, can you work your magic one more time and get us to talk to these two troopers?”

“Let me see what I can do. I’ll call you.”

* * * * *

About two hours later, Michael and Jake were back in the same small conference room in the FIG office at FBI headquarters.

“Same drill as before.” Jake said. “We call on Trooper Nkumba’s cell phone this time at the bottom of the hour.” They both looked at the clock on the wall. They were about two minutes away.

“How did you pull this one off?” Michael asked. “Same bullshit?”

“You don’t want to know.” Jake said smiling broadly.

“This is Trooper Jonas Nkumba.” The booming voice on the other end of the phone said.

"This is Agent Michael Cornell here at the Field Intelligence Group headquarters offices here at the FBI in Washington. I have Agent John Jekielek here with me. Is Trooper Fordyce there as well?"

"Yes, sir." A smaller voice said.

"Guys, I prefer to be called 'Mike'. And, unless you object, I'd like to call you Jonas and Silas, if I may.

"Guys, let me get right to the point. Another suspicious incident happened with two guys in an RV yesterday a few hundred miles east on I-90. Probably the same two that you talked to. That said, let me take a guess at why you filed this report. Do you believe that the two guys you were interrogating had something to do with the bomb?" There was a long silence at the other end of the phone as Nkumba and Fordyce stated at each other. Finally Nkumba said:

"That's exactly right, uh, Mike. We couldn't prove anything, of course. But that's what we thought. We got the strong feeling when we were talking to them, that they were, maybe, wired. That they were wearing some kind of microphones and that somebody was listening in to our conversation and then talking to them at the same time. Both of these guys had speakers in their ears. I think they figured we were going to search their vehicles - that they had something in there to hide. And, that is exactly what we were going to do. Then the bomb scare was called in. Then the bomb went off. No one was hurt of course. Then we found out about all this radio traffic right there on the Mall with our voices. Then we knew that the two suspects *had been wired* and that someone nearby – an accomplice of theirs – was monitoring our whole conversation with them.

"We can't prove that the accomplice set off the bomb – or – for that matter – that there even was an accomplice. But, when things calmed down and we had the chance to look back on what happened, both Silas and I had the gut feeling that there was an accomplice and that he had set off the bomb to divert us from proceeding with the search their vehicle.

"I know that it sounds pretty lame to say that someone set off a bomb just to prevent some search & seizure on an RV; but that's what we both think. After all, when you think of it, that bomb wasn't designed to kill anyone. It was there just to cause chaos – confusion – to disrupt what was going on – like searching that RV.

"Jonas, that is exactly what I thought when I read your report. Someone sure didn't want you searching that RV.

"Thank you guys very much. You have really been a great help."

"You think these might be the guys you are looking for?" Nkumba asked.

"They could easily be." Michael said before disconnecting.

"What do *you* think?" Jake asked.

"I have no fucking clue." Michael said standing up and walking over to a wall map of the United States with a pin at every fusion center location.

"I-90 goes nowhere near California. What are these bastards doing so far north? What are they doing on a highway that goes absolutely nowhere worth going to." Michael said running his finger along the route of I-90. "Jake, I just don't know.

# CHAPTER 26 - THE VICE PRESIDENT

Late that evening, Slevin got another call from the National Security Advisor.

"Slev, I got bad news for you. Get your guy Cornell into your office and call this number on a secure line: 202-867-5309. That's the Vice President's private line."

"The Vice President?"

"Jim, the Vice President's day job used to be geology. He was a professor in Hawaii. The first thing the boss said was to bring in the VP, so I did. Anyway, get Cornell and call us. I'll be there in his office. He's got something incredible you've got to hear."

Five minutes later Michael and Slevin were on the phone with Gill and Vice President Jeremy Mahikane. His name was pronounced ma-hee-ka-nay in Hawaii. People who didn't know him often shortened it to two syllables, like ma-cane, or McCain. Gary Gill, and most Washington types, took the middle ground, calling him ma-cah-nee.

"Jim, Agent Cornell, I'm here with Vice President Mahikane."

"Mr. Vice President." Said Slevin. "Evening, sir." Said Michael.

"Gentlemen." The Vice President began. "I'm not sure I agree with the Geological Survey." Slevin looked at Michael and rolled his eyes. He silently mouthed the words: "arm-chair quarterback."

"I don't think it's the San Andreas fault or San Francisco. They would kill millions of people, maybe tens of millions. But certainly not hundreds of millions. Gentlemen, I think the target is Yellowstone Park."

"Yellowstone Park - in Wyoming - in September - would kill more people than an atomic bomb and earthquake in San Francisco?" Said Slevin incredulously.

"Mr. Slevin, there is a volcano under Yellowstone Park, which is the largest volcano on this planet. If it were set off with a nuclear device it would kill hundreds of millions of people – perhaps 2/3rds of all the people in the United States and hundreds of millions more – maybe billions more – around the planet."

Michael and Slevin looked at each other in disbelief and shock.

"Do you know how big the bomb is?" The Vice President asked.

"Sixteen kilotons, sir." Answered Michael.

"No, Agent Cornell, I meant the diameter."

"Uh, let me see." Michael said riffling through his notes.

"The Russians said it was 70cm."

"That's about 28 inches. I was afraid of that."

"Come again, sir?" Slevin said.

"Mr. Slevin. Blowing up a bomb over the Yellowstone volcano wouldn't do much at all. You've got to get it into the volcano – into the magma chamber, which is several miles below the surface. You need a borehole. Unfortunately, the University of Utah has drilled a 30-inch borehole to accommodate a new robotic probe that's 30 inches in diameter. Gentlemen, terrorists could easily stuff a 16 kiloton bomb down that borehole."

"Mr. Vice President, are you sure about this?"

"Unfortunately yes. One of my all time best students is out there at the Yellowstone Volcanic Observatory working on this project with the Utah people. She told me all about it. With volcanoes, it's critical to get real time measurements. With the usual little 4-6 inch boreholes you can only test one factor at a time – temperature, pressure, gas make up, gas concentration, et cetera. But with this new robot, they get all of it – all at once – in real time.

"Another thing you ought to know. The development of this robot and the drilling of the big borehole – at about $100,000 an inch – was paid for by some obscure German foundation that nobody's ever heard of."

"Did you get the name, sir?" Slevin asked.

"My student said something like 'erdlust' - something or other."

"Any chance it was *Stiftung Erdlust*?"

"That's it. You know them?"

"Oh, my God! Those bastards! Yes. They're a front for terrorists."

Michael had pulled up a map of the I-90 route on his laptop. "Holy shit!" He blurted out. "Ho-leee shit!" He said again and then. "Well, I'll be goddamned!"

Slevin turned to him with a stunned look. Then the Vice President said: "Is that you, Agent Cornell? Is there something wrong?"

"Yes, sir, sorry for the French. We have been looking all over the country for the bastards transporting the bomb. We have focused on the I-40 and I-80 corridors that go to California. So far we're found zippo on those routes. But 150 miles north, on Interstate 90, we're had two suspicious incidents in the last three days. The problem is that once it crosses the Mississippi, I-90 doesn't go anywhere near any major city. But it does go right by Yellowstone!

"Mike, are you sure about this?" Slevin interjected.

“Absolutely, I’ve talked to the state troopers in both Wisconsin and South Dakotas who were involved in these two incidents. We know exactly who we’re looking for!”

“Well, Mr. Slevin, I guess you’d better get your people out to Yellowstone. Oh, and Mr. Slevin, tell them to look up my former student. Her name is Stacey Coleman. She knows the territory out there.

“I have one more piece of bad news. I actually understated the power of the Yellowstone volcano a few minutes ago. It is powerful enough to lift a dust cloud that would cover the earth for years. It could lower surface temperature to below 32 degrees. We, and everything else on this planet would freeze to death. It would be the ultimate act of terrorism – the final extinction.”

“Get your ass out to Yellowstone.” Said Slevin turning to Michael when he hung up.

# CHAPTER 27 - KYLIE WRIGHT

An hour after the call with the Vice President, the National Security Advisor called Slevin again. "The President said that all of the assets in the country are at your disposal. All of the military. All police agencies. And if you get a state involved, he will call the Governor personally. He said 'good luck' too.

"And one more thing from the Vice President. He said there's a young woman in town, named Kylie Wright, who is some super-student from Vanderbilt. The VP says she's an expert on super-volcanos. She worked with the VP's friend, Dr. Coleman, this Summer at Yellowstone. He suggests that Agent Cornell take her with him tomorrow and get an education about the Yellowstone volcano on the flight out there."

"Did the VP say where to find her?"

"No, but she came to see him today, so the Secret Service probably know."

Slevin made two calls. The first to his duty officer to track down Miss Wright. The second to Michael to give him a heads-up.

"Jim?" Michael said. "When the guys find her, let me talk to her. Having a team of FBI agents swoop down on this young woman might just overwhelm her. I'd rather handle it myself."

"Understood. I'll have them call you."

With information from the Secret Service, the agents traced Kylie Wright to the Marriott Courtyard at Dupont Circle. Twenty minutes later Michael walked up to the counter showed his ID and asked to speak to the manager on duty. He showed the manager the picture of Kylie from her driver's license that the Secret Service had taken when she entered the White House.

"This young woman is a guest of yours. Her name is Kylie Wright. I need to find her immediately. But first let me assure you that there is no trouble – no problem – with Miss Wright. She is a scientist and we think she can help us with an important case."

The manager showed Kylie's picture to her staff the woman at the front desk recognized her. Two hours earlier, Kylie had asked the best way to get to the "9:30 Club."

"Whadja tell her?"

"At night, a cab. For sure."

"Ok, thanks. By the way, where is the 9:30 Club?"

"On V Street between 8$^{th}$ and 9$^{th}$."

When Michael's car pulled onto V Street, there was a sea of humanity between him and the Club. Will Shriver and "The 'Adam E.' Project" were playing. They were the most popular band in the DC area, and their popularity was rapidly moving up the east coast.

Michael jostled his way as gently as he could to the front of the line where the security guys were. He showed them his ID and asked to see the head of security. He was ushered in and brought to a disarmingly beautiful young woman.

"Hi, I'm Julie Chamberlain, head of security. Who are you?"

"Michael Cornell" he said, showing her his ID. Seeing a look of concern capture her face, he quickly added: "There's no problem here. I just need to talk to one of your patrons. And I think I really need your help.

"There's a young woman scientist inside whose help we urgently need on a major case. If I go in there looking for her, it will spook your customers and probably scare the hell out of this young woman. Would you do it? Here's her picture."

Ten minutes later Julie emerged from the hall with a beautiful girl in tow with long curly blond hair.

Michael smiled at her and said: "Your good friend and ardent admirer, the Vice President of the United States, told me to come and talk to you." It worked. She laughed.

"Julie, can Miss Wright and I talk in private?"

"Sure. You can use my office. This way."

"Miss Wright, what I have to tell you is absolutely top secret and involves the safety of the entire United States. I don't have time to deal with security clearances; but I need your word that you will never tell another living soul what I am about to tell you."

"Uh...........ok."

Michael told her everything she needed to know. He asked her to come with him to Yellowstone the following morning at 5:30. She looked at her watch. It was almost 1am.

"Well, if we're going at 5:30, I guess I'd better get some sleep."

"C'mon. We'll drop you back at your hotel."

"As she got out of Michael's car, he said: "Our car will pick you up at 5 to take you to the airport." He looked at her for a long minute. "Miss Wright, I can't thank you enough."

"No thanks necessary. Glad to help. And call me Kylie."

# CHAPTER 28 - THE RANGER

Mustafa al-Khalid's office overlooked the sparkling sapphire waters of the Bosporus. A constant stream of ships plowed the water, and slender white minarets rose from the green hills on the other side. But he wasn't enjoying the view. He was staring at the personnel files of employees at Yellowstone National Park spread across his desk.

"There is one in particular I think you should study," said the man across from him. Samir el-Masri was a director of one the Muslim Brotherhood's front companies, the Goldman Foundation. Genial, smiling and 65 years old, Samir looked to be the exact opposite of what he was, a cold-blooded terrorist.

The Foundation kept a large and growing database of Americans who hated their country or were desperate for money—preferably, both—and possessed key skills or access the Foundation might one day need.

Mustafa opened the file of Robert Abboud, a fourth-generation Lebanese-American. His grandfather had made his career in the U.S. Navy, retiring as the captain of a battleship after World War II. His father had been a career naval officer, too; he had been wounded in action twice, received the Navy Cross twice, and was then passed over for Admiral because of the Navy's post-9/11 fear of those with Middle Eastern surnames. It had broken his father's heart and his health. His medical bills had emptied the family's bank account.

The Ranger wanted to follow his father's footsteps in the Navy, but he was denied admission to the Naval Academy. Then he was denied enlistment because of punctured eardrums, something the doctors had done to save his life as a child from spinal meningitis. The National Park Service was the best he could do with his desire to serve his country.

Robert's younger sister, Leah was everything Robert's father wanted him to be, but wasn't. She was admitted to the Academy and accepted early for the naval aviation program. When she came home after her summer cruise between junior and senior years, she complained of headaches she had been having for the last several months. Her company officer, himself a pilot, had told her never to tell a flight surgeon anything. No flier wants to be grounded by a doctor. So she hadn't gone on sick call at the Academy. But back home the pain became unbearable, and her father sent her off to Johns Hopkins Hospital to check it out.

The diagnosis was a very rare form of glioblastoma: brain cancer. It was terminal.

They told her she had six months to live, max, as there was no standard protocol for treating so rare a form of the disease. There was, however, a promising treatment that was just being developed at Duke University. The Navy, however, doesn't pay for experimental procedures, and the Duke treatment was considered experimental. It also had an experimental price tag: more than $100,000. There was nothing left in the family bank accounts to pay for this.

"You are right, Samir. This is the man we want," Mustafa said, the smile beneath his thick black moustache revealing sharp white teeth. "Perfect. Make contact immediately."

* * * * *

Robert's family were Lebanese Christians. The men who approached Robert were Lebanese, but were Muslims. They were a small group. They called themselves "Ada'ala," justice. They said that they resented the United States because it had humiliated so many millions of Muslims. They wanted some small measure of revenge, some small justice. They wanted to humiliate the U.S. government by blowing up Old Faithful and the other geysers in what was the largest and most popular of all the national parks - one that hosted 3 million visitors a year. Destroying the major tourist attractions in this great crown jewel of the national park system would mortify the U. S. government.

The men said they could destroy the geyser field by putting dynamite down a research borehole that scientists at the University of Utah's Department of Volcanology had drilled to study the volcano.

The terrorists needed the Ranger to get information for them about the borehole and keep the scientific team under surveillance. They needed him to take them to the borehole when the scientists were away and get them into the YVO building, which had sophisticated security systems. Most of the scientists were going back to the university after Labor Day. They would be away the week of September 11th.

The men told the Ranger that if he would help them humiliate the U.S. government, they would give him the $100,000 needed for his sister's cancer treatment. They also promised him a new identity in Dubai and more money than he would ever need to live. He agreed.

# CHAPTER 29 - STACEY & ROBERT

Winter in Montana was not what Stacey had in mind, but she was thrilled to get the grant to work with the University of Utah's team at the Yellowstone Volcanic Observatory (YVO), and she thought it better to begin work in January. Bad weather, for sure, but no tourists.

The YVO wasn't a major building, just a couple Quonset huts and a few large tents. The center of attention at the YVO was "Siegfried", which was what the geologists named the multifunction robotic probe that had been paid for by an obscure German foundation.

The year before the YVO had looked like a small city with four shifts of workers going round the clock to bore the 30-inch hole down over 3 miles. This hole was where Siegfried worked, going up and down every day measuring temperature, pressure, gas concentrations, ground vibrations and more. Stacey thought it was amazing to be able to get all of that data – all at the same time – and in real time. It was the first time anything like this had been done, ever.

So, Stacey spent most of her time fixed to her console in one of the Quonsets, where it was, at least, warm. When she wasn't there she just hung out at the usual places that most of the Park's permanent staff haunted. She got a small apartment in Gardiner, Montana. It was about 45 minutes from the YVO, but it was home to a few bars and restaurants that were favored by the staff who either lived nearby or actually had quarters in the Park. One of those bars, "The Geyser", is where she met Park Ranger Robert Abboud. They began dating. Stacey realized that Robert wasn't the sharpest knife in the drawer, but he was kind and he loved the outdoors.

"When both he and Stacey were off, Robert took Stacey on long treks through the wildest parts of the Park that none of the tourists ever saw. Stacey had never before seen a bison, or an elk or a wolf or a mountain lion or many of the other animals that she and Robert saw regularly on their hikes. They spent a lot of time together. When the Park officials wanted Robert to move to new quarters about an hour south of his current place, Stacey realized that he would have to drive almost two hours to see her in Gardiner. So, she asked him to move in with her instead.

* * * * *

Although all the Rangers knew that the Park sat on an active volcano and they talked about it all the time to the tourists; it didn't affect their job; so they didn't pay it much mind. Stacey's Ranger, Robert, was the same when they first met. But in the last few weeks all he could talk about were the geysers and the volcano. He went to the YVO several times to meet Stacey and had himself programmed into their security systems, so – he said - that he could keep an eye on the place when the scientists were back at the University.

He had asked if a few sticks of dynamite could set off the volcano. No, definitely not. Could a couple of sticks of dynamite shut down the geyser field? Maybe, depends on where they were placed. Where would they need to be placed? The answer was about 25 miles from the university's borehole. But why did he want to know? Why did that answer make him so upset? Why did he want to know so much about the borehole and the university team's operations there?

In the week after Labor Day, he had gone out the YVO site every day after his shift. He was asking more questions and was constantly nervous and upset.

# CHAPTER 30 - FLIGHT TO DENVER

At 5:30am on the morning of September $11^{th}$, Michael Cornell's car pulled onto the tarmac at the Fixed Base Operation at Reagan National Airport. The car with Kylie Wright showed up just behind them. Michael and Kylie climbed the steps of the FBI jet waiting for them. Hearing someone in the galley Michael said, "Laura?"

"No, I'm Jennifer." A young brunette smiled back.

"Jim Slevin told me Laura Doughty would be on this flight."

"Well, I don't know who Jim Slevin is, but I'm not Laura. We work for the same contractor, but this is my first flight for the FBI. I don't know the cast of characters there."

"Really. Well, nice to meet you Jennifer. I'm Michael Cornell. This is Kylie Wright."

"You're much too young and pretty to be an FBI agent, Kylie." Jennifer said.

"I'm just along for the ride." Kylie laughed.

"Hi, Tom, Trish. Great to see you both again." Michael said as he stuck his head into the cockpit. Tom Young, the pilot, had done many tours with the Air Force in Afghanistan winning several medals. He now worked for the contractor that provided experienced flight crews for large corporations and some government agencies. The Bureau always asked for Tom to fly their plane. They felt lucky to get him. Trish Apple was also an experienced pilot – a very attractive blonde experienced pilot – who, when she wasn't flying planes, was a very genteel horsewoman from the low country in South Carolina.

"Well I'm glad to see you guys are here, but I was told Laura'd be here too."

"Yeah, I don't know what happened to Laura. She's Jim's favorite. Always thought there was more than professional interest on his part." Tom said laughing.

"Yes. And just enough younger than Jim to be interesting to him." Trish added. They all laughed again.

"Well that *is* Jim's reputation with pretty women." Michael said. "And speaking of pretty women, I'm not even going to tell him about Jennifer. She has very seriously pretty face. And a nice rest-of-her, too. Slevin might just give himself a permanent transfer to this plane."

"You men!" Trish moaned with a broad smile. "Aren't you supposed to be on business, Agent Cornell? Or are you just here to ogle the crew? You know 'leering with intent to gawk' is a federal offense. You might just have to arrest yourself, Agent Cornell." They all laughed at that.

"New flight attendant and a new caterer too. Let's see if their breakfast and coffee are up to our usual high standards." Tom smiled.

"And we have a young scientist with us, Kylie Wright. If you get a chance to come back, I'll introduce you."

Kylie was buckling in as Michael walked up the aisle.

"Want something to drink?" He asked.

"Sure. Coffee with a little cream and sugar?"

"Right away."

Michael found Jennifer in the galley.

"Jennifer, can Kylie and I have some coffee? One black with lots of sugar? The other with a little of both cream and sugar?"

"Sure, Agent Cornell."

"I prefer Michael."

"Come again?"

"I prefer being called Michael. By the way, what do they call you? Jennifer? Jenn? Or Jenny, maybe?"

"I like Jenn."

"What's your last name?"

"Schimpf. Jennifer Schimpf. S-c-h-i-m-p-f. It's German."

"I know. Know what it means?"

"Scold."

"Well, I would have said "complain" or "crab" but now that I think of it, you're right: "scold" would have been a much better translation, the times I've seen the word."

"I hope you don't live up to your name."

"I try to live it down every day." She laughed.

"Now, let me ask you a question, Agent Michael?" Jenn said with a false serious look. "Do all FBI agents get to fly around the country with pretty young girls?"

"I'll have you know, Miss Schimpf, that Kylie is an expert on super-volcanoes, like the one we'll be investigating in Yellowstone Park after we land at Cody. As a matter of fact, she was introduced to us by none other than the Vice President of the United States, who, I recently learned, was a geology professor in Hawaii and, himself, an expert on volcanoes."

"That's a *very* good story, Agent Michael. I recommend you stick with it."

"Actually, I was lying about the volcanoes and the Vice President. Kylie is just part of my personal entourage." At which Jenn burst out laughing. Finally getting her composure back, she said: "I'd go back to the Vice President story, if I were you. It's much more credible."

A few minutes after takeoff, the pilot got a call from his company. "Are you catered?" They asked.

"Of course." Tom replied."

"The caterers called. Apparently their people haven't called in. They wanted to know if they had taken care of you."

"Yep, we're good." Tom said. "The two guys who showed up, I'd never seen before. They must be new. They probably just didn't know the routine."

"Yeah, that must be it. I'll tell them you're all taken care of."

For the next two hours, the flight went uneventfully as everyone had breakfast and lots of coffee. Michael got an education from Kylie on super-volcanos. She was clearly into her subject. She made sketches and drawings. What she said astonished Michael.

*Sleeping quietly beneath the geysers and the stunning landscape of Yellowstone Park lies the largest explosive device on the planet Earth. On May 18, 1980, the Mt. St. Helen's volcano erupted with a force equal to the largest nuclear explosion in history. The Soviet Union detonated the Tsar Bomba on October 30, 1961 on Novaya Zemlya. It exploded with a force of 58,000,000 tons of TNT. Scientists at the U.S. Geological Survey's Yellowstone Volcanic Observatory (YVO) say that Yellowstone's largest eruption blew with a force 6,000 times that of Mt. St. Helen's and the Tsar Bomba.*

*The Yellowstone volcano is so enormous that visitors can't tell they are walking on the ceiling of its caldera. The volcano is 50 miles long by 35 miles wide, - over 1,700 square miles. It is significantly larger than the State of Rhode Island. The volcano makes up almost half of the entire 3,800 square mile park. Five kilometers beneath the tourists' feet lies the magma chamber. If the volcano erupts, it could hurl over 850 cubic miles of dirt into the air: over 1.2 trillion tons. On a good day, it would only kill two thirds of the people in the United States; on a bad day it would extinguish all life on earth.*

Almost two hours later as the plane was approaching the Mississippi River, the flight service office called again. "We may have a problem. There were no new caterers, Tom. The guys they sent were the regular catering crew for Reagan. Their people can't raise them on the radio.

"Oh, shit." Said Tom.

"Yeah, because the FBI is the client, we called them and told them." The dispatcher at his company said. "They flipped out. They're sending a team over to the airport right now. I suspect they'll want to talk to all three of you.

As Tom was having this conversation with his home base, Mike's phone rang. It was Slevin.

"Holy shit!" Mike said when Slevin told him the news.

"Michael, I want you to put on your best interrogation skills and quiz Laura, Tom and Trish. Laura must have seen these birds. I want a second-by-second report on what they did and what they said."

"Jim, Laura's not here. The flight attendant's name is Jennifer. She told me Laura had to go to the office today for something to do with her security clearance."

"Her security clearance? That's bullshit! I would have known about it." A long pause. "Michael, I think something may be seriously wrong here. Do what I said about interrogating the crew – very thoroughly."

Just then Tom opened the cabin door and told Michael that an FBI counterterrorism team was on the way to the airport. Michael relayed the news to Slevin.

"I was afraid of that." Slevin said. "Those are Nick Davis' men. Michael, my boy, I didn't want to burden you with this but – you remember that message with the list of dud bombs that Nick was waving around Gary Gill's office?"

"Yeah."

"It didn't come from Russia. It came from Munich. From some very nasty people who work for terrorists."

"Oh shit! Does Davis know this?"

"I think he does, but I am going to find out right now." Slevin hung up.

His next call was to the communications center.

"Do you have a counterrorism team headed to the airport?"

"Yeah, we do, Jim. They should just about be there by now."

"Then put me through to them immediately."

"Right. CT Red Team, this is base. Come in immediately."

"CT Red Team, over."

"Red Team, this is Director James Slevin speaking. I want you to stand down and return to base immediately."

"Director, we can't. We are under direct personal orders from Director Davis."

"I am Davis' superior officer at this bureau and I am ordering you to stand down and return to base immediately. This is my direct order to you. Do you copy?" Slevin shouted into the phone.

“Yes sir. We copy. We are returning to base right this minute.” Said a clearly shaken voice on the other end.

“Gentlemen, please report to me as soon as you get here. I need to talk to you both.” Slevin signed off trying to calm their nerves.

“Will do, sir.”

Slevin hung up and called communications again.

“Listen, there must have been some airport LEOs involved in this mess. Will you get in touch with airport security, find them, and put me through to them?”

A few minutes later. “Jim, I have Officer Dunn of airport security on the phone. I told him who he'd be talking to”

“Officer Dunn what can you tell me about the AeroServe situation?

“Not good, Director. Your people called us after they got the call from AeroServe. We did a sweep of the airport. We found their truck in a commercial lot. No one around the van. But there were bloodstains – fresh bloodstains - all over the back.”

“Damn. This is getting worse and worse. Officer Dunn, will you secure the van till my people get there.”

“It's already done, sir.”

“That's great. Thank you very much. I'm sending a forensic team right now.”

“We'll be here, sir.”

“Great. Thanks again. One more thing, Officer Dunn, you monitor all the voice traffic in and around the airport, don't you?”

“I believe we do, sir, but that sort of thing is way above my pay grade.”

"Understood. But will you call your commanding officer and ask him to have those people doing the listening call me as soon as possible?"

"Yes, sir. Right away."

"Thanks again, Officer Dunn. You guys are doing a great job."

"Thank *you*, sir."

As soon as Slevin hung up with the forensic team, his assistant stuck her head in the door and said: "I have communication security at Reagan holding for you, Jim."

"Communication security" at Reagan was a part of a team from the National Security Agency that monitored all communications in and around all major airports across the country.

The next call Slevin took was from Michael Cornell.

"Jim, Tom didn't see the caterers. But Trish did. Not much to go on. Black hair. One with a mustache. Both medium height and build. She just said they just took care of the galley. They said they stowed the stuff you asked for in the baggage compartment, and then they took off."

"What stuff I asked for? I didn't ask for any stuff!"

"Trish said they said field gear - like - for in the park. Binoculors, bottled water, some food, a backpack."

"Did she see the stuff? Does she know for sure what it it?"

"Hang on....... Trish?.......... No, Jim, she didn't see anything. That's just what they said."

"Damn. Mike can you get Trish to take over and get Tom with you and put me on speaker?"

"Sure thing. Hang on............ Jim, Tom's here."

"Hi, Jim what's up?"

"Tom, I didn't tell anyone to put anything in your baggage compartment."

"Oh, shit!"

"That's what I say!"

"Tom and Michael, there's more. Airport security picked up some voicecom in German. Listen to this. Two voices. Voice #1 " is the device is set for 5100. Voice #2 said yes. Then the voice #1 asked "is the back up in place." The voice #2 said yes again. What the hell? Does that mean anything to you two?"

Tom looked at Michael for a long second. "Yes, Jim, it does. 5100 feet is the altitude setting for landing at the Cody, Wyoming, airport. That's the airport for Yellowstone." Another long second. "Those bastards put a bomb on this plane set to go off when we touch down at Cody."

"Can you be sure of that?"

"It looks like I'm going to have to bet my life on it. And everyone else's here too. Jim, the way these things work is that as the plane ascends through 5100 feet, the bomb arms. And when it descends back to that altitude, it detonates. Jim, I gotta get back to the cockpit and try and figure something."

"Tom, wait! What do you make of that "back-up" statement?"

"That I don't know, Jim." Tom said heading back to the cockpit.

"Jesus H. Christ! Mike let me know if Tom comes up with anything. I gotta go too."

Michael had tried not to notice the look of utter shock on Kylie Wright's face. She had been listening to the conversations. But now her eyes were full of tears.

He looked out the window for a very long second. "I am so sorry, so very sorry," was all he could say.

* * * * *

Just as Slevin hung up, Counterterrorism Director Nick Davis stormed through his office door.

"Slevin, what in the hell is the meaning of countermanding my direct orders to my own men. Who the hell do you think you are? Who gave you the right to stand them down against my orders?"

"I am your superior officer in this bureau and I have the right to tell any of your men to stand down. And, furthermore, I have the right to relieve you of duty, you son-of-a-bitch, which I am doing right now.

"Barbara, Slevin bellowed to his assistant. Get me Davis' #2 on the phone."

"You're doing what?"

"I am relieving you of duty right this minute. Both the President and the Director of the Bureau are aware of what I am doing," Slevin lied. "And they approve."

"You've lost what little mind you have." Said a clearly flustered Davis.

"I don't think so. You know your little message from Moscow about the dud bombs?" Said Slevin without waiting for a reply. "It came from Munich. Munich, not Moscow! Not St. Petersburg. It came from those bastards at the *Stiftung Erdlust* in Munich. And you – you worthless sack of shit – you had to have known that. What's more there's a goddamn bomb on our plane to Yellowstone. And my bet is that you know about that too!"

"So, you are relieved of duty as of this moment. Clean out your goddamn desk and report to the Director immediately with your ID and your sidearm. Now get the hell out of here – you miserable excuse for a human being - before I have your own men arrest you."

After Davis staggered out of the office, Slevin told his assistant to contact the Director's office and tell them to be sure to have the director talk to him before he said a word to Davis.

Next, Slevin got on to the National Security Advisor and asked him to inform the President as soon as possible. Seconds after that call, his phone rang again and the smooth voice of David Springer, the Director of the Federal Bureau of Investigation came on the line.

"Jim, what's this problem you have with Davis?"

Just then the unmistakable sound of a pistol shot rang through the halls.

There was a long pause. "Director, did you hear that?"

"Yes. Sounded like a gunshot right here on our floor."

"Mr. Director," Slevin said. "I think the problem with Davis is over."

* * * * *

In the middle of his explanation to Springer, Slevin's cell phone rang with Michael Cornell's caller ID.

"Jim, I have Forensics and Michael Cornell holding." His assistant, Barbara, said.

"Sir, I've got to get back to you." Slevin said to Springer. "I have an incoming from the aircraft right now."

"Forensics says it's urgent."

"Ok, put them on."

"Oh God. How awful. Thanks." That was all Slevin said to Forensics.

"Michael, what's up?" Slevin said taking his next call.

"I just came from the cockpit with Tom. I think he may be saving our asses. He's flying us to Denver. Denver airport is over 5400 feet. If there is a goddamn bomb, and if it is set to go off when we descend to 5100 feet; then were safe because we won't have to descend that far." As he said this, he noticed Jennifer was staring at him like a zombie and that she was flushed. *Poor kid.* He thought. *She's terrified too, just like Kylie.*

"Oh God. I sure hope Tom's right.

"Michael, I have more bad news. Forensics found human bloodstains in the back of the caterers' van. Some of that blood was Laura Doughty's.

"Thanks, Jim." Michael said quietly, staring at Jennifer, who was staring back at him now with dead, lead-shot eyes. She shook her head and turned abruptly toward the galley. *She's not terrified like Kiley... not like Kiley at all.*

With one fluid motion Michael pulled his phone cord out of the charger, leapt to his feet and with two quick strides tackled Jennifer from behind. On the floor, he put the cord around her neck, crossed his hands with it, and yanked as hard as he could. He heard Jennifer's larynx collapse and her backbone snap as the wire cut into her throat and she died.

As Michael got up off the floor, he saw that Kylie was crying and trembling violently. He went to her and took her hands in his. "Listen to me," He said. "Jenn was a terrorist. Jenn was the 'back-up.'

"Look at me, Kylie. We're going to be all right now. We're going to be ok. I need your help. Please look in the crew compartment and gather everything you can find that might have belonged to Jenn. Will you do that for me?"

Kylie nodded and stood up. *Need to keep this girl distracted,* Michael thought kindly *so she doesn't fall apart.*

"Hang on, Kylie." Michael said, walking by her toward the cabin baggage compartment. He opened his bag and rummaged through it.

"Here, you'd better put these on." Michael said as he handed her a pair of rubber surgical gloves. "Everything Jennifer owned will become evidence; so it's better to have as few foreign finger prints as possible. What we are looking for is a detonator. It will be a small metal or plastic device. It could be disguised as something like a lipstick. So, be careful and be gentle with whatever you find. And don't worry about repacking; we'll have a forensic team take care of that."

As Kylie began looking for Jennifer's things, Michael walked back into the main cabin. As he went past Jennifer's body with the blood stain still spreading around her neck, he knelt down and felt under her for her apron pocket. There he felt her cellphone. Her cellphone was the detonator, he was certain. *Why have another device? All she had to do was open the right app, enter the code, and press "send."*

*Dear God.* Michael thought as he got back to his seat. *Ten more seconds she would have been in the galley and detonated the bomb. Ten seconds from being dead.*

"What just happened?" Slevin said calling back.

"I found out what the terrorists' 'back-up' was, Jim. It was Jennifer, the flight attendant."

"*What*? What are you talking about, man?"

"When we land, forensics can clean her cellphone. If they don't find a detonator app, they'll have to arrest me for murder."

"You killed Jennifer?"

"Yeah. I realized what was going down the minute that you said Laura's blood was in the van. Don't you see? To pull this off, they had to kill Laura too. And they had to replace her with one of their own. Someone they could trust to detonate the bomb if the air pressure didn't trigger it. The two fake caterers were terrorists, and so was Jennifer. Jennifer was the 'back-up.'"

"Jennifer was watching me as I told you Tom's plan about landing in Denver to avoid the air pressure trigger. I could see it in her face. She turned and went toward the galley to detonate the bomb. I tackled her before she got there. She was going to take out her cell phone, punch in the code, and blow us all to hell. So I used my phone cord. That's what happened. That part of the terror is over. Now all we have to worry about is the barometric trigger."

"Jesus! Jennifer! 'Al-yad.'

"What did you just say? 'Al-yad, the hand?'" Michael asked.

"'Yeah. I think it's 'Al-yad al-yosra lay-la.' It means 'the Left Hand of God.' It's what terrorists call the little infidel kids they train as suicide bombers. Not very nice. The right hand is sacred to them. They eat with their right hands and *salaam* with it. The left hand is unclean. They wipe themselves with it. So, they call their infidel lackeys that they brainwash 'the Left Hand of God'.

"Wow, Jennifer, the flight attendant, was their back-up! Ok. Makes sense. I'll have a bomb squad and a forensic team waiting in Denver. I sure hope Tom's right about Denver. What's your ETA?"

"Tom said about a hour from now to Denver. And about hoping that Tom is right? We're all with you on that one."

Thirty seconds later Slevin was back on the line. "Michael, I think you should know that our friend Davis just committed suicide."

"Dear God! That bastard! This bomb stuff is all Davis, isn't it?"

"I'm sure of it." Slevin said.

"Why? What for? What could he possibly have gotten out of it?"

"Mike, I don't know. Somehow they got to him and turned him. I dunno. Maybe they were blackmailing him for something. Maybe they offered him a fortune and a new identity. I just don't know what in the name of God would make a man do something like this."

"I'm going back to practice law."

"No you're not. You're going to Denver." Slevin said regaining his usual crusty composure. "God speed."

* * * * *

An hour later, the plane landed unscathed at Denver to the grateful applause of two relieved crew and two passengers. Michael saw the tears in Kylie's eyes again. Then he felt his own eyes burning. Trish came back from the cockpit. Everyone dissolved into a mass of hugs.

The plane was met on the tarmac by an ordinance disposal team from the local Bureau office, as well as a forensic team.

Slevin had also asked the Denver office to organize a charter for Michael and Kylie to Cody, Wyoming. They were in the air again in a matter of minutes. The Denver office put an agent on board to take Kylie's and Michael's statements on the way to Cody.

"This time, no bomb." Michael said meekly as he and Kylie boarded the plane. They both forced weak little laughs.

# CHAPTER 31 - STACEY, KYLIE, ROBERT, & MICHAEL

Kylie and Michael pulled up across the Street from 44 Jardine Road in Gardiner, Montana. About ten minutes later a white pick-up with Utah plates and a University of Utah crest on each door pulled into the driveway across the street. Out of the truck came a pretty, young blond woman with a bag of groceries.

"Stacey!" Kylie yelled jumping out of the car.

"Kylie?" Stacey said squinting and craning her neck. "What are you doing here? You're supposed to be back east."

"I'm here with this guy who needs to see you." Kylie said jogging across the road.

"This guy?"

"Yeah, he's actually an FBI agent."

"An FBI agent wants to see me. Why doesn't he just kick the door in?"

"Stacey, it's not like that. He's very nice. There's no trouble or anything. He just wants to talk to you about your work in the Park."

"My work in the Park?"

"Yeah, with the volcano."

"Let me get this straight. This FBI guy brings you all the way back to Montana just to talk to me about the volcano? FBI? Volcanos? Hello?"

"It's true. That's him in the car over there."

"Oh, well, no point standing out here with these groceries in my arms. Bring him in."

"Lieutenant Coleman, how nice to meet you?" Michael said stepping through the door behind Kylie.

"Uh-oh, lieutenant? Is this some Navy thing?"

"No. Just showing respect. I'm Michael Cornell." He said showing Stacey his FBI credentials.

"Wait a second, you bring supergirl here, 2000 miles from DC just to talk to Stacey Coleman about the volcano I am working on?" Stacey said nodding toward Kylie.

For the next 45 minutes he quizzed her about the Yellowstone volcano. She told him everything he asked. She liked him. He was probably mid-forties and not bad looking. He had a nice way about him. Made her feel at ease.

As Michael and Kylie left she walked them to his car. When Michael got in, he looked up at her and found a smile on her face.

"Did I say something funny?" He brightened.

"No… it's just that, with all these questions about the volcano, you sound like my boyfriend."

"Who's your boyfriend?" He clouded over.

"Oh, he's just one of the Rangers here."

As they wound back down Jardine Road toward Route 89, Michael said: "Do you know if there's any place to pull over around here? I need to make a call."

"It's a long way back to Cody. Why don't you let me drive? You can make your call in the car."

"No can do, Kylie. Unfortunately, it's something you can't hear."

"Oh….. Turn right when you get down to the highway. About a half mile on your left is the Gardiner Market. Can you get out there and make a call from their parking lot?"

"Yep. That'll work."

Michael got out of the car and started walking towards the back of the parking lot. Then he went back to the car and stuck his head in the window.

"Kylie, do you know Stacey's boyfriend's name?

"Yeah, it's Robert. Robert, not Bob."

"Last name?"

"Sorry. Dunno."

Michael walked away and placed a direct call to Jim Slevin. He asked Jim to have his people get the Yellowstone Park Rangers' files from the National Park Service database, check out each one – especially any one named Robert - and turn the results over to the Bureau's profilers.

A few hours later, Stacey and Robert were eating dinner late at her house after his return from the YVO site. He was more overwrought than ever. In the middle of dinner, his phone rang. He looked at the caller ID as he always did but instead of ignoring it, as he usually did, he took the call. He didn't just take the call at the dinner table, he ran outside to take the call as if there were something he didn't want her to hear. It was the leader of Mustafa's men. When Robert came back, he was a mass of raw nerve cells. He stuttered out that he had to go back into the Park to work for a friend who had taken sick on the job. It was at the other side of the Park at Mallard Lake Dome, not far from Old Faithful. He'd be away a few hours. She shouldn't wait up. Then he was gone.

Now she was worried. Worried about him. She'd never seen him so distraught. She had thought over the last few days that Robert was overwrought because of his sister, Leah. But that couldn't be causing this, she thought. As she wandered aimlessly from room to room, she saw he'd left his pistol and gunbelt on her sofa near the front door. He'd left without them. He would never do such a thing!

She picked up her phone and called the Ranger station. Where exactly was he meeting the sick friend? What sick friend? They didn't know of any sick Ranger. But they GPS-ed her boyfriend's car and saw that he was in the park. Where was he heading? To Sour Creek Dome – where the YVO was. Why? And, why was that FBI man so interested in the YVO too?

She didn't like this at all. What could she do? As she was staring down at the floor she saw the tattoo on her ankle. A/I, it said: "I will not abandon you." She picked up her purse, checked for her car keys and headed out to her car. Just before she got in she turned around and went back inside. She picked up her boyfriend's gunbelt. She took the gun out of the holster and checked to see if it was still loaded. It was. She put it in her purse and took off in her car. In her distraction, she didn't see her cell phone sitting on the table by the door.

* * * * *

Michael had organized rooms for Kylie and himself at the Holiday Inn at Buffalo Bill Village in Cody, Wyoming. He was amused by the name. The locals went out of their way to call the great mangy beasts "bison," definitely not "buffalo." But then there was Buffalo Bill Cody, who must not have gotten the memo. He definitely wasn't Bison Bill Cody.

After checking in, they walked down Sheridan Avenue to the Proud Cut Saloon for dinner. It never failed but that, in the middle of dinner in a crowded restaurant, a call would come from the office – one that he couldn't risk anyone overhearing. "I'll call you right back," he hushed into the phone. He shrugged at Kylie and signaled the waiter what he was doing, ran out the front door, and called Washington back.

"Oh, dear God!" Not only had the profilers turned up a ranger named Robert Abboud that had serious problems with his country, but a check with NSA revealed that they had detected a strong interest in Abboud from the profilers at the Goldman Foundation as well.

The terrorists at the Goldman Foundation. A resentful park ranger. The missing Russian bomb. The Utah borehole. It all came together. He told Washington and told them to call in an air strike… if there were only time.

It was a longshot. The 388$^{th}$ Fighter Wing flew out of Hill Air Force Base in Ogden, Utah. But that was 250 miles away. A unit so far inland had probably never scrambled in history other than on 9/11. Threats seldom come from within. Furthermore, Yellowstone Park covered more than 3,800 square miles. Their onboard radar would never find 28-inch hole in the ground, even at stall-speed.

"Oh shit!" Michael said running back outside.

Michael called Stacey to warn her. Her cell phone on the hall table kept ringing.

Then he called the Yellowstone Park Rangers' barracks. Where was Abboud? He got the same story Stacey got. Only the dispatcher added that Stacey had called worried about him and that Robert wasn't going where he told her. So, where was he going? To the YVO borehole!

Cornell asked to speak to the officer in charge. When he came on the line, Cornell told him he had reason to believe that there was major trouble at the YVO site. He told the officer to get as many men as possible out there immediately. He said he was coming out in a helicopter. He asked for the precise coordinates of the YVO station. He called them in to Washington with instructions to pass them on to the 388th Fighter Wing.

He hung up and called the local tourist helicopter office. He had taken the precaution of going there and identifying himself in case he needed them. He needed them now.

# CHAPTER 32 - ENDGAME

Robert met the three terrorists at the gate to the YVO where he had directed them.

"Do you have the money for my sister?" They said yes. They were ready to transfer it to her bank account. Robert gave them the routing number and account number for his sister's account at the Bank of America in Baltimore where his family lived.

A few moments later they confirmed that the transfer had been made. Robert took out his cellphone. He dialed the Bank's 24-hour number and entered the codes for his sister's account. The balance was $100,247.58. The transfer *had* been made.

Robert then put his hand on the fingerprint scanner and looked into the retina scanner. A green light flashed on at the gate and it unlocked. The terrorists drove their van in and left the gate open.

He took them into the outdoor site of the borehole. They examined the borehole, thanked him, and shot him at point blank range.

Stacey had driven out to the YVO. She saw the gate was open and unattended, which it never should be. She walked softly toward the borehole where she saw lights and heard voices. Just before she reached there she heard a gunshot. A van loaded with equipment stood between her and the scene before her. She moved closer when she noticed the unmistakable international markings for radioactive material. They she saw the writing in Cyrillic letters. No mistaking what she was looking at. This was why Cornell was in Yellowstone. This is what the FBI was looking for.

Then she looked up and saw her boyfriend on the ground. She saw the three men standing around the borehole. She reached in her purse for

Robert's gun. One of the men turned and headed toward her and the van. Before he could react to her, she fired a bullet into the man's chest. The other two turned toward her clearly startled and fumbling for the guns in their pockets. Stacey raised her pistol. The men's eyes widened in shock. Before they could get their weapons out, Stacey shot the one on the left in the face, blowing the back of his head off. The other man looked first at his accomplice and then back at Stacey. The last thing he saw was her smile as she squeezed the trigger and put a bullet right between the man's eyes. She went to the men lying on the ground, kicked their firearms away, picked them up, and threw them into the woods. The three men seemed dead.

Stacey went to Robert. He was still alive, but barely. She could see he was bleeding to death from the gunshot wound. He recognized her. "Why?" her eyes asked him. "They said they were just going to dynamite the geysers. They promised me the hundred thousand for my sister. They put the money in her account. Please go to her and make sure she gets the treatment."

He lost consciousness. She stood up. She heard a moan from one of the three men on the ground. She walked over to him. He was on his back and looked up into her eyes. She pointed her boyfriend's revolver at the man's forehead, and fired twice.

She called the Ranger station. She reported a Ranger down and asked for backup. It was already on the way inbound. Be there any minute.

She walked over to the van and looked again at the Russian nuclear device. *Dear God*, she thought. *It would have been more than enough to set off the entire volcano! It would have killed billions of people all over the world!*

She noticed that there were several sticks of dynamite in the van as well. She took them and a blasting cap and walked over to the borehole. The university team's work was finished there. They wouldn't need the borehole any more. Better that no one else should ever try this again. And with that she loaded the blasting cap, dropped the dynamite down the hole, and quickly ducked from the explosive plume that shot up. The borehole was gone. No one would use it again.

It was then that she heard the helicopter and saw the lights of the Rangers' wagons.

When Mike saw the small flame shoot from the borehole he realized it was over. He called Washington to call off the air strike.

* * * * *

Istanbul is 9 hours ahead of Yellowstone. So just when the action was going down at the YVO, Mustafa al-Khalid was rising and making his way to the Blue Mosque for prayer. Uncharacteristically, he carried his cell phone with him into this holy place. He was expecting a call from Munich. The call never came. At noon, he got back into his limo with bitter gall in his mouth. As he crossed the Bosporus Bridge, he swore to himself that there would be another day.

# CHAPTER 33 - THE PRINCE

Agent Michael Cornell sat on the balcony of his condo on 142$^{nd}$ Street in Ocean City, Maryland, looking northeast over the Atlantic Ocean. He had bought the place after the sub-prime mortgage crisis when there were places that could be had for pennies on the dollar. He didn't need three bedrooms and the down payment took a big chunk of his savings. But, his tennis-playing real estate buddies told him that he could use it two weeks a year, rent it out the balance of the time, and that it would pay for itself. They were right. It more than paid for itself. He was paying the mortgage off faster than he originally planned *and* putting a few dollars back into his savings account.

But this morning Michael wasn't gloating over his triumph in beach realty. He was troubled and was deep in thought.

"Are you actually going to drink that coffee or are you just going to hold the cup up to your face while you watch the ocean?" Admiral Molly McNamara asked sitting across from him.

"Sorry, just distracted." He said.

"You didn't even notice this tiny little robe I bought just for you."

"You bought it for *me*? Well, it wouldn't even fit me. And it looks so much nicer on you. Especially when you aren't wearing anything under my new, tiny little robe."

"How….. how did you know that?"

"I'm a detective." He said, smiling finally – his eyes beginning to light up. "Detectives must be excellent observers." He said with solemn pseudo-seriousness.

“Detective! Rubbish! You must have been watching me get out of the shower. Not so much a detective as a peeping Tom.” Molly said.

“Well, voyeurism *was* my best subject at Georgetown.” He said pursing his lips and squinting his eyes at her. They both laughed.

“Why so serious, Michael?” Molly asked. “Still worrying about what could have happened at Yellowstone?”

“Yes, that and your friend, the President’s, new quest to find the group responsible.”

“Well, he’s been very gracious to me; but I’d hardly call him a friend.”

“Molly, I’m sorry I’m such rotten company this morning, especially on our first date.” Michael said sheepishly looking down the front of Molly’s robe.

Molly laughed and said: “It’s just crazy that you can talk terrorism and look down the front of my robe at the same time.”

“Well, I know men are not good at multi-tasking; but I’ve been practicing.” Michael came back.

“You know, I just think this quiet little witch hunt the President’s going to take everybody on is a real wild goose chase and couldn’t come at a worse time.

“But, Michael, what’s he supposed to do? Forget about it till next time when we might not be able to stop it?”

“Molly, the President’s all-agency team of inquisitors is only going to drag out al-Qaeda, ISIS, al-Shabaab, and all the other usual suspects. There are some 70 ‘groups’ whom we classify as ‘Foreign Terrorist Organizations.’ We are going to spend thousands of hours and God-knows how much money screwing around with these people – and for nothing. All the while, odds are that the real bad guys will try again. Yellowstone wasn't any of these groups."

"How can you be so sure?"

"Molly, you know your 'Principle of Singularity'?" Michael said nervously running both hands through his light-brown hair.

"Yeah. How do you know about that? It's classified."

"I actually found a copy of your article that the Navy didn't burn. Anyway, terrorist groups exhibit their own singularity. The each have a distinct *modus operandi*, or m/o as they say at the Bureau. Each behaves in its own peculiar way.

"Now, I am not familiar with the intimate details of each of these 70 groups' m/o's but I do know that none of them uses ships or anything else with names like, Calypso, Deceiver of the Gods, Valhalla or Elysian Fields. Out of the 70 groups on the President's list, I doubt if more than one or two even know who Calypso is or what Valhalla or Elysium are. How many terrorist groups are into Tolkien or Viking death metal bands? Can you just see them sitting around in a circle planning terrorist attacks while listening to Viking metal bands or, after deciding to murder a few thousand innocent people, they have a group reading from the *Lord of the Rings*?"

"Michael, are you still on this gods-and-afterlife shtick that you entertained CMDR Hall's people with?" She was giving him such a soft look that it muted the apparent harshness of her words.

"Molly, the trigger mechanism for the bomb was unloaded in St. Catherines, Ontario. The freight forwarder had two bridges to choose from to drive his truck across the Niagara River to the U.S. The close one is the Lewiston-Queenston Bridge. The other bridge was 30 miles away near Buffalo – where there is a lot more security and a lot more scrutiny of bridge traffic. Guess which bridge the truckers used?"

"The farther one?"

"Yep. Know what its name is? The Peace Bridge. They went out of their way to use the Peace Bridge. You know why? Those were their instructions."

"Michael, you don't think some of this could be coincidence?" Molly said softly.

"Molly, the truckers said that they were told to use the Peace Bridge and promised a bonus for doing so. When they dropped the mechanism off near Buffalo, they were given a large bonus when they showed the terrorists their receipt from the Peace Bridge customs office."

"That does sound very strange.....very strange." Molly said beginning to show real sympathy for the first time.

"And now for my last piece of evidence, your Honor." Michael said beginning to lighten up.

"The terrorists were looking for a small coastal freighter from one of our Atlantic ports to meet the *Deceiver of the Gods* and deliver the goods to Canada. I checked our ports from Portland to Miami. On the day I checked, there were 47 such ships for hire – 47. And the terrorists chose one called the *Elysian Fields*. But that's not all. There is a ship out of Baltimore that is a coastal freighter and its name is *Persephone*."

"Wait. Persephone's a Greek goddess, yes?"

"Close enough. She was a nymph whom Hades, the god of the underworld, kidnapped and dragged into Hell to be his queen."

"And.... so what about the *Persephone*?" Molly asked definitely warming to the direction the conversation was going.

"Molly, I talked to the managing partner of the Heffner Shipping Company in Baltimore. It's a family company and Katherine Mary Heffner is the boss. Heffner Shipping owns the *Persephone*. Ms Heffner goes by

Katie. She said she was contacted several weeks ago by a German firm who wanted her to meet a ship off Labrador, and take on a shipment for delivery to Ontario. Katie declined. They offered her double the going rate. She was tempted, but she said that the *Persephone* was already booked for the days in question; and the booking was from a very reputable machinery firm that Heffner Shipping had done a lot of very lucrative business with and whom Katie didn't want to piss off by cancelling a shipment.

"Two days later she said the Germans called again. This time they offered her *five times the going rate*. This time Katie was really intrigued. She asked for details of the shipment. She was told she would take several rubber barrels of marine fuel north to just off the southeast coast of Labrador where she would rendezvous with a fast passenger boat that was bringing the machinery from Europe. The passenger boat would be almost out of fuel, so the *Persephone* would transfer the fuel in the rubber containers to the other ship. Then her crew was supposed fill the rubber barrels with water and deep six them. The passenger vessel would transfer the machinery to the *Persephone* and leave. The Heffner's ship would proceed on to two ports in Ontario.

"Katie told me that the more she listened the more she forgot about the big money being offered and the more she smelled a rat. First and foremost, filling the fuel barrels with water and sinking them was illegal ocean dumping. Could mean a big fine or even a license suspension. The point is that no reputable firm would ever ask a shipper to do such a thing

"So, she started asking the Germans some questions. Why didn't the *Deceiver of the Gods* just fuel up in Labrador and take the machinery into Canada herself? Why was the machinery on such a fast boat? Why did machinery need to be in Canada in such a hurry? What kind of machinery was it? Who were the owners of the machinery? Who were they shipping it to?

"Katie said the Germans sounded taken aback by her questions. They claimed they didn't know the answers. They said they were just brokers. But they told her that they would get the answers to her questions and get back to her. They never called her back. Two days later, they booked the *Elysian Fields*."

"OMG, they offered the woman *five times* more money than usual? Just to get a ship named after the King of Hell's wife?" Molly said. Then after a pause. "Michael, I'm sorry I've doubted you. There are just too many coincidences here, aren't there?"

"That's what I think. For sure."

"Well, frankly," She said regaining a coquettish smile. "I was going to entice you back into the bedroom. But I can see that you're not in the mood. And, now that I think about it, neither am I. So, what do you say? Back to the real world?"

"I sure don't want to. But we'd better. You've got a Navy to run. And I've got to find a way to track down a group we've never seen nor heard from before that have unlimited funds behind them and horrendous plans for us and the rest of the human race."

Snapping to, Michael said: "You go ahead and get dressed, Molly. I'll get these dishes."

"You don't want to watch me get dressed?" She said cocking her head?

"Raincheck?"

"Of course, raincheck." She said kissing him softly on the lips.

* * * * *

"Michael?" Molly said surprised. "What's the matter now? You haven't budged in 20 minutes. What about he dishes?" She said gesturing to the dirty cups and plates on the balcony table.

"Molly, I've been thinking something. *We're not looking for a terrorist group*."

"We're not?"

"Remember when I was teasing you a few minutes ago about terrorist groups sitting around reading the *Lord of the Rings* or listening to Viking metal bands?"

"Yeah.......?"

"Well, by the same token, can you imagine a terrorist *group* sitting around trying to decide whether to charter a ship named after a mythical heaven, or one named after a Greek goddess? Do you think there's a bunch of these bloodthirsty bastards somewhere sitting around discussing classical literature?"

"Of course not." She snorted very gently.

"Neither do I.

"Molly, we aren't dealing with a group here. Groups don't exhibit such idiosyncratic behavior. People do. Individuals do

"Molly, we're not looking for a group." Michael said again, squinting up at her. "We are looking for one man. Only one. Very rich. Very powerful. The absolute incarnation of evil. The one who would have destroyed the entire world at Yellowstone. *We are looking for the Prince of Darkness.*"

# CHAPTER 34 - RUCK'S

Robert's funeral was at the church of Our Lady of Lebanon across the district line in Northwest DC. The viewing had been at the Ruck Funeral Home on York Road north of Towson, Maryland, where Robert and his family lived. Michael Ruck wanted everything to be perfect for the Abboud family whose only son had died in the line of duty; so he made it so.

The funeral cortege had to travel 47 miles to the Maronite Church. Robert's family weren't particularly religious, but they made the trek to Our Lady of Lebanon four or five times a year, on the major religious holidays and, of course, for the church's Lebanese Festival. But the family wanted the viewing close to home so their friends could get there.

Robert was buried with the full honors of a federal law enforcement officer killed in the line of duty. Nobody wanted the real story to get out.

The story on the street was that he was killed by three intruders stealing valuable equipment from the University of Utah's on-site science lab. The story was that he got all three of them before he died of his wounds. The ballistics' report, of course, confirmed that all three intruders had been killed with the Ranger's gun.

"Michael, I want to tell you something about Robert." Stacey said quietly to Michael as they stood just outside the viewing room. "I know you must think he was a traitor; and he was. But there was more to it than that. Robert's sister, Leah, the pretty dark-haired girl over there in the Naval uniform," Stacey motioned unobtrusively. "She has Stage 4 brain cancer. There's an experimental treatment at Duke. Apparently the only one in the world. Uncle Sam doesn't pay for experimental treatments. It costs $100,000. Robert's family doesn't have that kind of money. The terrorists said they'd give Robert $100,000."

"Well, that's a very compelling story, Stacey. Still it doesn't excuse treason."

"No. It doesn't. The terrorists told Robert they would put the money in Leah's bank account. Robert had her account information and confirmed that the transfer was made. Then they shot him. When I got to him he told me all this. He begged me to go to Leah and make sure she got the treatment. So, when I got here I told Leah. We checked her account. No money. Those dirty bastards somehow double-crossed Robert. Then they murdered him."

Michael had slipped Stacey his card and quietly asked if they could talk soon.

"Yes. Where."

"The back of the card."

It said "Tark's 7:30."

"Where is this place"?

"About a mile from here. It's my favorite."

# CHAPTER 35 - DINNER AT TARK'S

Stacey was staying downtown on the Baltimore harbor at the Marriott Courtyard on a street with the charming name of Aliceanna. It had been named many, many years ago after the two granddaughters of a waterfront developer. The hotel was a block from the Chesapeake Bay in an area called HarborEast. Stacey was from Hawaii, after all, and there was no ocean in Wyoming. She missed it.

Tark's was about a half hour away. Michael lived in DC. How was a restaurant north of Baltimore his favorite?

When she arrived he was standing at the bar talking to a rugged looking man with a shock of grey/white hair and a deep tan. Michael introduced him as Tark.

"Are you *the* Tark, the namesake, owner, or both, of this place"?

"That I am Miss. And you are?"

"Tark, let me introduce Dr. Stacey Coleman." Michael interjected.

"And what are you a doctor of, Stacey, if I may call you that"?

"Of course you can. Volcanology."

"Volcanology? Well, you know, that's exactly what we need around here." Tark grinned. "There are so damn many volcanos in Maryland, it's getting difficult to get around with them all going off all the time."

"That's why I'm here. I'll have the situation under control in no time." She smiled back and they all laughed.

"You know, Dr. Coleman, you're much too pretty to be a scientist."

"And you, Mr. Tark, have much too good a tan to be a restauranteur. Sure you're not a surfer or a skier?"

"Hmmm, shall we sit down, Stacey?" Michael said. "Tark's sitting us at a special booth tonight."

"In your honor, I might add, Stacey. Aren't you, at least, going to buy the lady a drink?" Tark asked Michael.

"Have you quit serving alcohol at tables?" Michael came back.

"You are a drinking girl, aren't you, Stacey? Ah….. I mean, a drinking volcanologist?" Tark asked.

"As a matter of fact, I am."

Then Tark leaned over and in a conspiratorial tone said: "The other night we had a reception here and I was standing with a gentleman I didn't know. A server came over with a tray of drinks and offered us each one. The gentleman and I each took one, but then he asked if there were alcohol in the drink. The server said yes. He put the drink back and said 'I would rather commit adultery that drink alcohol.' I put mine back too and said to the server: 'Sorry, I didn't know there was a choice.'"

"What shall I have for dinner?" Stacey asked Tark when they all stopped laughing.

"The Hanger Steak and the Chicken Pot Pie are our house specialties, Stacey. But since, I assume, you're not from Maryland, I'd recommend the Crabcakes. Maryland crabcakes are the best in the world. And mine are the best in the State."

"What's with the tan"? She asked as she and Michael headed for Booth 301.

"Tark isn't his real name. It's actually Terry Arenson. That's where the T-A in Tark comes from. And the other two letters, R-K, come from "Ray

King", a nickname he got because of the great tan he always had as a lifeguard in Ocean City while he was at the University of Maryland."

"And that tan just never seemed to fade in the Winter?"

"You got it."

"This is a little far from D.C. to be your local hang-out. How do you know Tark so well"?

"First of all, it's one of the coolest restaurant I've ever been too. The food is fabulous and Tark runs this place like the legendary Toots Shor ran his place in New York. My parents used to go there every time they went to the City. They said Toots knew everyone in New York. My folks would go there once, maybe twice, a year. Toots would greet them by name the minute he saw them. Tark's just like that.

"When the Redskins are away and the Ravens are home, I come to the game and then come here."

"Is this a big football hang-out"?

"Yes and no. It certainly isn't a sports bar, as you can see. But it has a lot of sports connections. The Ravens' front office, their coach and some of their players hang out here. Same with the Orioles. Same with the University of Maryland coaches. Even some of the Washington sports figures wander in occasionally. The place actually has some pretty neat sports history.

"In 2008, the Ravens' quarterback, Joe Flacco, was a senior at the University of Delaware when Ravens' head coach, John Harbaugh, invited him over to talk. They had dinner right here at Tark's in the booth we are sitting in. During that dinner, Harbaugh liked what he saw. So, he told Flacco he would pick him in the first round of the NFL draft in April. So, the Ravens drafted Flacco and four years later he won them the Superbowl and was the MVP of the game."

“That’s quite a story.”

“I take it you’re not a football fan”?

“Well, I know that the ball they use isn’t traditionally round as it is in most other ball games. Actually, in Hawaii no one knows how to spell NFL. I think games come on TV about 7am on Sunday.

“Ok, now Special Agent Cornell, you didn’t bring me here to just to regale me with football stories, did you?”

“No, I actually have ulterior motives.”

“Good, so do I. Can we start with mine first? How did you know to come to the Park that night? The FBI doesn’t do volcanos. How did you get involved? Why Yellowstone? What were you really doing”?

“Whoa! We’ll get to all that. But first we need to get you a drink. What would you like”?

“Should I really have the crabcakes”?

“Absolutely.”

“Then I’ll have a Pinot Grigio.”

“Jackie”? Michael beckoned to a server. When she came over, Jackie and Michael hugged and exchanged “how-have-you-beens.”

“Jackie, this is Stacey. Stacey, Jackie.”

“Nice to meet you.” From both.

“Sweetie, could you get Stacey a pinot grigio”?

“Sure. Are you ok with your martini”?

“Yes, and that’s all I’m having. No ride tonight. I’m driving. So, how about an iced tea”?

"Sure thing, hon."

"Sweetie?" "Hon?" Said Stacey arching her eyebrow. "If you called a server "sweetie" in Honolulu, she would pull out her machete and cut your head off.

"Dr. Coleman, I'll have you know that the proper form of address for a male customer to a female server in Maryland is either "sweetie," "hon," or the more formal "sweetheart." And, the proper form of address for a female server to a male customer is "sweetie," "hon," or "sweetheart." I should add that "hon" is a special Baltimore word." They both laughed.

"Okay. Enough sports. Enough local linguistics. Now, to business."

"Not quite yet. One more sports story. Jackie works in the publicity department for the Baltimore Orioles."

"The baseball team?"

"You are, indeed, a helluva sports fan"!

"Is this an Orioles hangout too"?

Yeah. Sort of. Cal Ripken comes in here a good bit."

"Cal Ripken?"

"Oh, dear. He's only one of the most famous baseball players in history."

"Sorry about that." She said tilting her head with a big toothy grin.

"Ok, business. You fired a blizzard of questions at me a minute ago. What do you want to know first?"

"I don't really know where to begin. How did you find out what was going on? How did you find me?"

"Well, as they sometimes say, let me begin at the beginning. It all started with a message from Russian counterintelligence in Moscow…"

Michael told Stacey as much of the story as he could.

"And that is how I wound up – quite literally - on your doorstep.

"So, we knew there was a bomb. We believed it was headed for the Utah team's site at the YVO. Then you mentioned Robert with his sudden unexplainable interest in the volcano. Robert came up on our radar. We also saw that he had come up on a hostile radar site that profiles enemies of our country. I'm sure Robert told you about his father.

"That he didn't make admiral."

"That he didn't make admiral because he had a Middle Eastern surname in the days right after 9/11 when everyone was paranoid about terrorist moles."

"He didn't say anything about that."

"Did he say anything about the Naval Academy?"

"Yeah, he told me all about Leah."

"No. Not about Leah. About him. About Robert."

"What?"

"He was rejected for admission to the Academy."

"He was?"

"Yep. And after he was rejected, he wrote a letter to the Academy saying they should let him in because the Navy had screwed his father. Crazy to do something like that. But, what the hell, he was only 18 – and a very angry 18! What's more – when he went to enlist in the Navy, they wouldn't even let him join. Something about a childhood medical treatment that left him with punctured eardrums. So, that's how Robert Abboud showed up on our profile , *and*, more importantly, on the profile of a German terrorist organization, which, by the way paid for your professor's volcano robot and all of those extra inches in the diameter of the borehole."

"Oh, my God!" They paid for the robot and the borehole? And they were Germans? I thought they were Arab terrorists."

"The Germans were working for some Muslims. How did your professor decide on Yellowstone?"

"I don't really know. He just contacted the YVO and said he wanted to test his robot at Yellowstone. When they told him how much it would cost to expand the diameter from 6 inches to 30 inches, he said he had the money.

"Well, he got the money from a German Foundation that fronts a lot of terrorist operations. But the Germans were just go-betweens. The money came from a Muslim terrorist?"

"What terrorists? Do you know who they are?"

"No. Not yet. The trail, as they say, went dead in Munich. I wish we could find a way for our Russian friends to interrogate the Germans. They're not talking.

"But that brings me to *my* ulterior motive.

"This terrorist – whoever he is – and his German accomplices. We think they will try again. They clearly think big. And they clearly know that creating some ecological disaster will kill more infidels than crashing a plane into an office building.

"So, the Bureau thinks it's time to set up an environmental counterterrorism unit. They want me to run it. And I want you to come and work with me. After all, right now, you and I are the two most experienced people on earth on environmental terrorism."

"Oh, dear..." was all Stacey could say staring blankly straight ahead.

"Dr. Coleman, is this man bothering you?" Said Tark suddenly appearing. "Hasn't he gotten you anything to eat? Is he trying to ply you with liquor? We have laws about abusing beautiful young women here in Maryland." They all laughed.

"You saved me." Stacey said.

"From what?" Said Tark. "From this beast?" He said, pointing at Michael.

"From embarrassing myself...."

"Oh!" Said Tark, suddenly - and rarely - taken aback. "Looks like I wandered into TMI territory. I think I'd better go count my crab cakes."

"Gosh, I didn't mean to embarrass you." Michael said to Stacey as Tark walked off.

"Oh, no." Stacey said. "It's just that I didn't know what to say when you asked me to work with you." Stacey flushed. So did Michael.

"Michael, I have to think about it. I just don't think I can do it right now. I have some important unfinished business to take care of. I need money. I am sure the FBI pays more than the University, but I need a lot of money, like $100,000."

"This is for Leah Abboud, isn't it?"

"Yes. I was thinking of telling my story to a book publisher. Some of my colleagues at the University know people in the book world. Publishers sometime give large cash advances. I could get that money to Leah. Time is running out for her.

"Well you could write a book. Although the Abboud family and the U.S. Government would probably not want you to tell the full story. Wouldn't be good for Robert's memory and would probably scare 3 million visitors away from Yellowstone each year. But it is a free country. You have freedom of speech….. Still, I think there may be an easier way of getting the money for Leah."

When the terrorists had transferred the money into Leah's account, they attached a "time bomb". If a specific code was not entered into the account within three hours of the deposit, the transaction was reversed and the money would disappear back into the depositor's account.

As soon as the FBI had focused on Robert they checked out everything about him and his family. They saw the $100,000 deposit hit Leah's account and they detected the time bomb and altered it. So, at the end of the three hours, the $100,000 vanished from Leah's account but it didn't go back to the terrorist's bank. Instead, it went into an imprest account at the United States Department of Justice.

At the funeral home Stacey had told Michael what the $100,000 was really for. The FBI had just thought it was a bribe to Robert that he was hiding in his sister's account. Michael confirmed Leah's medical condition with the Academy. Then he talked to Jim Slevin about getting the money for Leah. Slevin was a good friend of Dyan Brasington, the Deputy Attorney General, who, in turn, was a good friend of Chief Judge Frederick Smalkin of the U.S. District Court for Maryland. The wheels of justice turned – quickly for a change – and Judge Smalkin agreed to sign an order transferring the money back to Leah's account. It would take a day or two for the paperwork to catch up with the telephone calls: but it would happen, for sure. When General Brasington heard the story about Leah, she was only too happy to help. Turns out they were both alumnae of the Bryn Mawr School.

Stacey, of course, didn't know any of this.

So, Michael just said: "Stacey, I have the $100,000 that the terrorists gave to Robert."

"You *do*?" Stacey said with total astonishment.

Michael explained all he thought was prudent and then said: "The money will be back in Leah's account by early next week. She can start on her treatment as soon as possible."

"Oh, my God, Michael, that's unbelievable, really?"

"Yes. So, now that Leah will get her treatment, why don't you come and work with me?" He said quickly, pressing his case.

"One more question. You've used the word 'terrorist' instead of '*terrorists*' twice. What haven't you told me about the people behind Yellowstone."

"Stacey, I haven't convinced the Bureau of this yet – and definitely not the White House yet – but we aren't looking for a group of terrorists or a *group* of anything. We are looking for one man."

"Oh my God!"

"Yes. One very rich, very powerful man. A man that doesn't just want to strike out against the U.S. No, this man wants to end the world. He wants to destroy this planet. He is the goddamn Prince of Darkness! And he's going to try again for sure!"

"Oh, my God." Stacey said again. "Well, that certainly makes my decision a lot easier, doesn't it." Said Stacey solemnly, more to herself than to Michael.

"Yes.....yes, I *will* join your team." Stacey said very seriously and looking Michael straight in the eye. Then tilted her head abruptly and smiled.

"You shouldn't smile like that at this man, Stacey." Said Tark appearing with two full dinner plates. "You'll just egg him on. And speaking of eggs – as an ingredient, of course - here are the best crab cakes in the world!"

- THE END -